the

POPPY FIELD

DEBORAH CARR

A division of HarperCollins*Publishers*
www.harpercollins.co.uk

First published in Great Britain in ebook format by
HarperCollins*Publishers* 2018

A catalogue record for this book
is available from the British Library

ISBN: 978-0-00-830101-9

Typeset in Birka by Palimpsest Book Production Ltd,
Falkirk, Stirlingshire

Printed and bound in Great Britain by
CPI (UK Ltd), Croydon CR0 4YY

the POPPY FIELD

Deborah Carr lives on the island of Jersey in the Channel Islands with her husband, two children and three rescue dogs. She became interested in books set in WW1 when researching her great-grandfather's time as a cavalryman in the 17th 21st Lancers.

She is part of 'The Blonde Plotters' writing group and was Deputy Editor on the online review site, Novelicious.com. Her debut historical romance, Broken Faces, is set in WW1 and was runner-up in the 2012 Good Housekeeping Novel Writing Competition and given a 'special commendation' in the Harry Bowling Prize that year. The Poppy Field is her second historical novel.

𝕏 @DebsCarr
f www.facebook.com/DeborahCarrAuthor
www.deborahcarr.org

To Rob, James and Saskia, with love

Chapter 1

Gemma

2018 February – Northern France

"Merci, Monsieur," Gemma said, as the taxi driver placed her two suitcases at her feet. She rummaged in her shoulder bag handing him several notes, waving away the change in lieu of a tip. He gave her a gap-toothed smile, looking cheerful for the first time since collecting her from the station.

It was already dark and beginning to rain, and Gemma's body ached after the rough and longer-than-expected crossing on the ferry from Jersey. She picked up her bags and hurried up the front path of the house where she would be staying. She'd have to wait until daylight to see what she had let herself in for by coming here. It was probably a good thing, she thought, aware that even in the dark the place looked almost derelict and she was too tired and emotional to deal with it yet.

Spots of rain dampened her face and Gemma grabbed

1

the handles on her cases and pulled them to the door. Pulling out a large, iron key, she pushed away a strand of ivy, hoping her hand didn't meet any hidden spiders. She inserted the key into the rusty lock and attempted to turn it.

It wouldn't budge. Gemma groaned. "Come on," she pleaded through clenched teeth as she tried once more. Nothing. "Balls." She didn't fancy spending the night outside in this weather. She took a deep breath. "Right," she said, determined. "You can do this, Gemma."

Wiping her clammy palms on her jeans, she gave it another shot, relieved when the key finally turned. Bolstered by her success, Gemma turned the door handle and when the door wouldn't budge, kicked it as hard as she could in frustration. The wooden door creaked in defiance before flying open, launching her forward onto the dusty flagstone floor where she landed heavily.

Furious with her clumsiness and miserable situation, she stood up and brushed most of the dust from her jeans. She blew on her hands, rubbing them gently to ease the stinging sensation. For the first time, she noticed how quiet it was here. Raindrops tapped on the roof and several trees and branches creaked noisily outside, but unlike her flat in Brighton, there was no traffic sound and no people talking nearby.

She peered through the open door back out onto the road outside. Was this entire place deserted? She hadn't seen many homes on the way here from the station, which had surprised her. She thought back to when she'd looked the area up on the Internet and she'd realised that she really was on the very outskirts of Doullens. Distracted by the sound of the rain coming down heavily outside, she remembered her luggage and ran out to rescue her things.

"Okay," she said, bumping the door closed with her bottom. "Let's see where I'm going to be living for the foreseeable future." She immediately loved the impressive inglenook fireplace with two arm chairs set on either side, although one was considerably more worn than the other. She assumed the chair with stained arm rests must have been where her father's cousin had preferred to sit when he still lived here. She doubted there was any other form of heating, so it was a relief to note there was at least some way of keeping warm. A roaring fire would also cheer the place up, she decided.

Next, she went to check the kitchen, which was basic, and she worried that if this was the standard of the kitchen, maybe she would have to use an outside bathroom, too. The idea didn't appeal to her and Gemma shivered. This place was eerie, and she didn't fancy investigating going upstairs until daylight. Deciding that the cleanest of the two chairs would have to do as her bed for the night, she unpacked a fleece blanket out of her smaller case.

Sitting down, she pulled the blanket over her legs and chest and tried to get comfy. This was a little too far out of her comfort zone, but she was here now and determined to make the most of it. This was her first experience of being spontaneous, and she worried that she had failed already. Perhaps she should have ignored her father and returned to Brighton. Recovering from her failed relationship in comfort there would surely have been easier than coming here to do it.

After a cold, uncomfortable and mostly sleepless night, Gemma's resolve had completely vanished. Her regret at coming to this foul place was almost overpowering and she was contemplating booking an immediate return ticket on the ferry. So what if her mother would sneer at her lack of mettle? She'd never expected Gemma to succeed at anything anyway. Just then, a loud banging on the front door interrupted her troubled thoughts.

Gemma recalled her father mentioning that he had booked a contractor to come and help with the renovations during her stay. Hoping work would begin immediately, Gemma pushed her fingers through her curly blonde hair and hurried to the door.

She pulled it open with a bit of effort. "Good, um, I mean, bonjour," she said, her breath making clouds in front of her mouth as she spoke. She smiled at the elderly man standing next to a young teenage boy, whom she assumed had been the one to knock. The old man pointed at the roof and to the back of the building before firing a barrage of words at her.

Frowning, Gemma shook her head. "Sorry, um, pardon. Je ne parlé pas le francais," she said, embarrassed at her basic schoolgirl French.

The man jabbed the boy in the shoulder with a gnarled finger, shouting something she could not understand. The boy nodded, staring at Gemma.

"'e say, 'e do not the work for you."

"What? Why not?" If this was the builder, then she wasn't sure if him letting her down was such a terrible thing. He seemed far too frail to work on the roof. Gemma doubted that the boy was out of school yet, so couldn't imagine him being able to work here either.

"Tres, difficile," the boy added, giving her an elaborate shrug of his skinny shoulders.

Gemma contemplated what she should do next. She needed to make sure the roof was weatherproof as soon as possible. It was late February, and although she hoped they didn't have much snow in the Picardy area, she didn't fancy rain coming through while she was living here. If she stayed.

She tried to come up with a useful sentence. If they weren't going to do the work, then she needed someone who would.

"D'autres, er," she mimed hammering a nail into the front door, much to the amusement of her visitors. "Dans le village?"

The boy's face contorted in concentration. His eyes widened in understanding and then he turned to the old man. "Grand-père?" He waited patiently while his grandfather chattered away.

Gemma tried unsuccessfully to fathom what was being said. Forcing a smile on her face, she willed them to hurry up and answer her question. It was freezing standing on the doorstep, despite the watery sunshine. She waited, but they didn't seem to be making any headway.

The boy gave her a pensive look. "Non, pas du tout."

"What? No one?" She glared at them. They had come here to let her down without any suggestion of who else might do the work? She closed her eyes briefly, determined not to cry with frustration.

"Non."

"Merci," she said eventually. "Thanks for telling me."

"Au revoir." The boy looked relieved as he followed his grandfather down the path to the road. She watched them leave, trying not to panic, as they both got into an ancient blue car and drove away.

Unsure what to do next, Gemma took a moment to gather her wits. Well, she decided, she still needed to know the extent of the renovation work. She retrieved her puffy jacket from her suitcase and pulled it on over her hoodie that was now creased from being slept in.

The air outside was so cold it took her breath away. Zipping up her jacket, Gemma walked carefully along the uneven pathway and out to the yard. At the back of the house to her right, she found a small u-shaped courtyard. It was made up of the house, attached to which were two small outbuildings at a right-angle and what looked like a three-sided barn, or car port. She wasn't certain what any of them could have been used for but assumed she would find out soon enough. To her left was a sloping muddy pathway between two rows of hedging leading to a wooden five-barred gate. She stepped over several smashed tiles, groaning inwardly when it dawned on her they had come from the roof.

"At least it's sunny," she said, trying to be positive.

Having worked in a trauma unit for two and a half years, Gemma knew that there were times when all seemed impossible, only for near miracles to happen. She didn't expect any to happen here, but it helped to attempt a semblance of cheerfulness.

She didn't need experience at renovations to know she wouldn't be able to do this alone. This place was a wreck, but despite her earlier panic, she was going to give it a go. Gemma knew her mother expected her to fail, but she wasn't ready to quit and give her the satisfaction of being right. Not yet, anyway.

Checking her watch, she saw that it was almost eight o'clock. Time to venture into the village and see if she could find someone to do the work for her. And maybe, she thought, buy a few things to make her stay here a little more comfortable.

She was relieved to discover that the centre of the village was only a five-minute walk away. The birdsong cheered her up, as she made her way along the peaceful road, as did the bunches of mistletoe she spotted growing in a poplar tree. She couldn't remember the last time she'd seen it growing anywhere, she thought, pushing her gloved hands deep into her jacket pockets.

Gemma wished she had a friend she could invite over to come and help with the work on the house. She didn't mind being alone most of the time, but the mammoth task ahead of her was a little daunting. Her mood lifted slightly as she arrived at the main street and saw the belfry standing high over the town. It was exactly as she had pictured a typical French town to look, with the imposing Town Hall and the architecture so different from home. She would have time for sight-seeing another day. What she needed now was to find a builder. She spotted what looked to be a hardware store and decided it was the best place to start.

She entered the dark shop and a bell jangled announcing her arrival as she stepped inside. It looked to her as if it hadn't been updated for decades. She wasn't sure how much of her shopping list she would find in here, but it was a useful exercise to look through the stock to see what was here for future reference.

Two men turned to look at her, and by the expressions on their faces, they were surprised to see her. Maybe it was because she was new to the area? The younger man, who Gemma assumed to be in his early thirties, gave her a brief smile before turning and continuing his conversation with the shopkeeper.

Gemma took her time studying the shelves along the short aisles, wishing she wasn't the only customer there. The wooden floorboards creaked with each step - the shop-keeper didn't need alarms to tell him when someone was walking in his shop, Gemma thought amused. Spotting a few of the items she needed, she picked up a wire basket and placed cleaning products, sponges and a scourer into it.

She took her items to the counter and placed the basket onto the worn wooden surface.

"Bonjour," she said, forcing a smile first at the shopkeeper and then at the other customer who stood back to let her in front of him.

"Anglais?" the shopkeeper asked.

Gemma nodded. What was it with her accent that showed her roots so obviously? "You speak English?"

He shook his head, scowling.

She didn't blame him. It must be irritating when people came to live in another country and expected the locals to speak English to accommodate them. "Pardon," she said apologising. "Je, um, je achete un…" She cleared her throat and mimed lifting a kettle, pouring water and drinking a cup of tea. "Kettle?"

"The word you're looking for is, bouilloire."

Gemma spun round, her mouth opened in surprise. "You're English?" she asked the man who only moments earlier had spoken fluent French to the shopkeeper. At least she thought it was fluent, it certainly sounded impressive.

He had broad shoulders and was handsome, in a scruffy sort of way. His muddy brown hair needed a brush, but his navy-blue eyes twinkled with amusement. Gemma tried to look more confident than she felt. This would soon be over and then she could return to the farmhouse.

"Marcel should have one somewhere." He spoke quickly to Marcel, who cheered up instantly. Gemma assumed it must be the thought of selling more than the items she had already chosen.

"I'm Tom, by the way," he called over his shoulder as he walked to the first aisle. "Tom Holloway."

She watched him as he rummaged around through the

contents of an already untidy shelf at the far end of the shop. He was gorgeous, and even in his faded jeans and thick sweater, she could see that he was muscular.

"Here you go," he said eventually, giving her a triumphant smile. "I knew Marcel would have one of these somewhere."

"That's wonderful, thank you," she said, trying not to let her attraction to him show. "At least I can make endless cups of tea now."

He held up a battered box as he passed her. Placing it on the counter, Tom opened the box and lifted out a cream kettle that looked as if it came from the seventies. "It's not the latest model, by any means," he smiled. "But if it doesn't work, let me know and I'll find a replacement for you."

"You work here?" Gemma was surprised.

"No, I'm a contractor." He packed the kettle back into its box and said something to Marcel, indicating Gemma by nodding his head.

Excitement made Gemma's heart pound rapidly. "Could you, um repair a roof?"

"Yes." He frowned slightly. "Why?"

"How about renovating a farmhouse and outbuildings?" She asked, willing him to agree.

Tom stopped what he was doing and narrowed his eyes. "That depends. I've got quite a bit of work on. I'd have to come and see what needs doing before I could give you a definite date for carrying out any work."

It didn't sound quite so positive. Gemma's smile slipped.

"How bad is it?" Tom asked.

"There are tiles in the yard. They looked to me as if

they've been there a while." She chewed the inside of her cheek, trying not to sound too desperate. "I'm renovating the place for my dad," she explained, not wishing Tom to think she was completely disorganised. "He arranged for a builder to come and do the work, but he came this morning to tell me he couldn't do it, after all. Then he left."

Tom frowned thoughtfully. "Was he an older man, with a young lad?"

"Yes. Look, I don't want to be annoying," she said, not wishing to begin her stay in the area by getting on the wrong side of him. "If you can't do it, maybe you could recommend someone else who can."

Tom gave it some thought. "There really isn't anyone else in the area." He looked at the clock on the wall above Marcel's head. "Is it far from here?"

"Only five minutes by foot."

"Tell you what, I've got to be somewhere in just under an hour, but I can give you a lift back to your place. That way you won't have to carry these things back and I can have a quick look to see what can be done," he shrugged. "If I can't do all the work, I'll figure out when I can make temporary repairs to keep it watertight for you."

Gemma didn't care that her relief showed on her face. "That's very kind. Thank you," she said, grabbing his right hand and shaking it.

Marcel cleared his throat and pointed to the ancient till.

"Sorry," Gemma said letting Tom's hand go to retrieve her purse from her bag and pay for her shopping. She spotted a mop and bucket to the side of the till. "If you're giving me a lift, then I may as well buy these while I'm here."

They carried everything out to his blue pick-up. Tom loaded everything while Gemma quickly popped into a shop for a couple of essentials. Minutes later they arrived at the farmhouse.

"Ahh," he said, stopping halfway along the pathway to the front door. He looked up and stared at the missing tiles. "I recognise this place," he said. "I don't think I've ever seen anyone living here though, not for the past ten years or so, anyway."

"Twelve, more like," she said, hoping he wasn't going to be put off by seeing how neglected the place was.

He raked a hand through his hair. "Not good," he murmured. Spotting Gemma staring at him in horror, he added. "But don't worry. Right, let's get this lot inside." He followed her into the house, carrying most of her shopping into the kitchen

They put the bags on the kitchen table. "Not much going on in here, I'm afraid," she said surveying the basic kitchen with its chipped butler sink, larder cupboard, fridge and electric cooker.

"I doubt this room has been updated since the fifties," Tom said.

"It's quaint, in a strange, grimy way," she joked, unused to being so relaxed with someone she barely knew.

Tom strode over to the window and looked outside. "There's a decent yard out there. You know, I think you could do a lot with this place."

12

Bolstered by his reassurances, Gemma asked. "Shall we take a look upstairs?"

"May as well," he said, smiling and waiting for her to lead the way. "What's it like up there?"

"I haven't dared look yet," she admitted. "I hope it won't seem so bad if I'm not alone."

She walked up the stairs carefully. She wasn't sure how rotten the wood was in this place and didn't want to take any chances.

Reaching the landing, she pushed the door on her left open, wincing when an acrid smell of mould hit her nostrils. "Ooh, that doesn't bode well."

"Be brave," he said. "We may as well go in. At least we'll know what we're dealing with then."

She liked the thought that she wasn't alone with this project any more. "Come on then." She stepped into the room, covering her nose with the top of her hoodie. "There's damp everywhere," Gemma cringed.

Tom was right behind her. "They," he said, pointing at the huge group of mushrooms growing in one corner of the room. "Must be directly under those missing roof tiles. Right, I've seen enough here. Next room."

Gemma moved on to the next room, as Tom closed the bedroom door behind them. She was grateful she wouldn't be needing the spare room any time soon. "I hope this is better than the first one," she said. "I don't fancy living in a house that's a health hazard."

"This bathroom isn't so bad," she said unable to hide her relief. "I'll soon clean this up with some scouring and

13

bleach." Reaching the final door on the landing, she took a breath and opened the door. Sighing with relief, she stepped aside to let Tom join her.

"This isn't too bad at all," he said, pressing the weight of his foot on various floorboards. Some creaked in defiance, others seemed much stronger to Gemma. "All this needs is a good clean and some decoration."

"A new bed mattress, too," she said looking at the striped ticking mattress that had been rolled up and tied with twine. They turned to leave the room at the same time, bumping into each other. Gemma gasped.

"Sorry, did I hurt you?" he asked, grabbing her arms and looking her up and down.

Gemma was too embarrassed to admit that it was the unexpected physical contact with him that had caused her reaction. "No, I'm fine," she said, hurriedly scanning the room for something to use as an excuse. Noticing a tiny fireplace, she pointed. "I just spotted that. It's going to be useful without any heating up here."

"It certainly is, but I can't help thinking—" He hesitated.

"Is something wrong?" Had her erratic behaviour frightened him off? She hoped not; the last thing she needed was for him to change his mind about doing the work.

"Are you sure you want to live here while this work is being done?"

She didn't like to admit that right now she would prefer to be staying in her sparsely furnished, but warm modern flat in Brighton. "I'm doing this project for my dad," she said. It wasn't the entire truth, but she didn't know Tom well enough to confide in him just yet. "I'm happy being here by myself."

She didn't add that she needed time living alone to work through the grief brought about by her ex's unexpected death and the discovery of his deceit. "I think we've finished up here now. Do you want to take a proper look outside, while I test out that retro kettle?"

"Sounds good to me," he said as they went back downstairs. "I could do with warming up a bit. Coffee, little milk, no sugar."

She watched him go and then unpacked her shopping. Tom seemed pleasant enough, but then again, she had thought that about her ex. Filling the kettle to the three-quarter mark, she plugged it into the old-fashioned socket.

By the time Tom returned to the farmhouse, Gemma had managed to get the fire going as well as having two steaming mugs of coffee waiting for them both. "There you go," she said pointing to the freshly wiped table in the living room. She indicated for him to sit on the cleaner of the two chairs. "Tell me what you think."

He rubbed his unshaven chin. "The most important thing is that temporary repairs are done to the roof as soon as possible," he said. "The forecast is dire for the next few days. I'll come back later, if I have time. If not, I'll make the temporary repairs first thing tomorrow."

"That's very kind," she said grateful to him for this thoughtfulness. "And the rest?"

Tom looked concerned. "Couldn't you stay at the B&B in the village for a few weeks? At least until the main bedroom is cleaned thoroughly and the bathroom sorted out?"

"No, I'll be fine here," she insisted, wishing he'd drop the matter. She had spent her life deciding what was best for herself. Even as a child with her absent mother focusing on her legal career while her father excelled in finance, Gemma had been left to her own devices. Bored nannies and housekeepers were happy to let the timid child in their care lock herself away with her books and daydreams. "I'll clean the bedroom and bathroom today and I can always get a takeaway if the cooker doesn't work."

He looked as if he was trying not to argue with her. "It's February, though, and freezing."

"Seriously, I'll be fine." She forced a smile and took a sip of her coffee. The heat of the liquid warmed her throat. "I'm tougher than I look," she insisted. "And certainly, more capable. Anyway, if I'm not staying here then I can't get on with the renovations as well as I could if I was on site."

He smiled. "Fair point." He put his cup down on the table and pulling out a small notepad from his jacket pocket made a few extra notes. "This place has been empty for a long time," he said. "It's isn't surprising that it has a damp issue. You'll need to keep the fire going as much as you can to dry it out slightly."

They stared at the fire in silence for a moment.

"How come you've taken over this place then?"

Gemma studied the musty room. "It belonged to my dad's elderly cousin," she explained. "He was ninety-eight when he had to go to a care home. Dad said he'd lived here his entire life, so it must have been heart breaking for him to go."

Tom frowned thoughtfully. "Poor guy. I'll have to ask my mum if she remembers him. She doesn't live too far from here. Do you know his name?"

Gemma tried to recall if her father had ever mentioned it. "Sorry, I can't remember. I'll ask Dad the next time I speak to him."

Tom drank the rest of his coffee. "Right. I've got to get going."

"Thanks for stepping in like this," she said, relieved to feel like she was getting somewhere. "I'm very grateful."

Gemma watched him leave, and the place seemed very empty without someone else in the room. To keep from feeling sorry for herself, she decided the best thing to do would be to get on with the cleaning.

She was half aware of the wind picking up. Stopping half way through wiping down the furniture in the main bedroom, Gemma listened at a loud creaking. She walked over to the window to try and find out what was causing the noise and saw a large branch swing back and forth in the gale. It looked as if it was about to come away from the trunk. Telling herself she was worrying unnecessarily, she continued cleaning a large chest of drawers.

A few moments later, a larger gust of wind howled through the house followed by a loud crack. Gemma rushed over to the window in time to see the branch coming towards her. Crouching instinctively, she covered her head with her hands waiting for the smash of the window pane.

The house shuddered on impact and she squeezed her eyes closed. Tiles shattered under the weight of the branch as it fell from the tree, smashing on the ground outside, as the glass from the window pane exploded inwards.

Holding her breath, Gemma waited for everything to become still. Her breath came in short bursts as she opened her eyes. Several sharp-edged twigs were suspended inches from her face. Even in her shock, she could tell she'd been extremely lucky not to have been caught by any debris. She needed to get out of the room though. Gathering her composure, she grabbed hold of one of the larger twigs attached to the branch and climbed carefully over it, pushing her way through the pine needles to the other side.

"Damn," she groaned, breathing in the scent of pine and sap filling the room. She had thought the room was in a bad way before, but it really needed some work now. The gale didn't appear to be quietening, so she decided that the safest place to be was downstairs. She reached the bottom step, just as Tom shouted from the front door, banging loudly to be let in.

Shocked to hear him, but relieved that he was at the farm, she ran over to let him in. "What are you doing here?"

"I was on my way here to check if you were okay," he said, pushing the door closed behind him. "I've seen the damage to the side of the house." He squinted and pulled several pine needles from her hair. "Have you been upstairs inspecting the damage?" he asked. "Because if you have," he added without waiting for a reply. "It was a bloody dangerous thing to do."

"I was already up there, if you must know," she snapped, irritated by his outburst. Who did he think he was talking to?

Tom's mouth dropped open for a second. "Hell, are you alright?" He narrowed his eyes and leant forward to check her face.

Gemma stepped back frowning. She wasn't used to such close inspection from anyone.

"Sorry, I didn't mean to make you uncomfortable," he said, turning away from her. "You stay here, I'll go and check upstairs."

Relieved to have some time alone, Gemma walked over to the fireplace and added a couple of logs. She was used to being the one to check people for damage, not the other way around. It had taken her by surprise, that's all, she reasoned, still disconcerted by what had happened. She could hear his footsteps upstairs and some banging. What is he doing up there, she wondered, relieved to have time to untangle her emotions. Maybe if she'd had siblings or demonstrative parents growing up, she might have learnt to be tactile and would not have reacted so embarrassingly.

She could hear him coming down the stairs again and pretended to be adding another log to the fire.

"I think you've probably already got too many on there," he said entering the room.

They stood in awkward silence.

"Look," Tom said. "I'm sorry. I'm used to being hands on."

"It's fine, forget it. Thanks for coming to see if I was

alright. Is the damage going to put the renovation work back much?"

He shrugged. "Not really. It's only the end of the branch. The window frame is fine, and the panes of glass can soon be replaced."

"I really do appreciate your help," she said, wishing to make amends for acting so oddly.

He smiled, his beautiful navy-blue eyes crinkling sexily, causing her stomach to contract. "It's no problem. I've got to help a fellow Brit, haven't I?"

She smiled, enjoying his casual friendliness. She could get used to having him around in no time. "I'm not from the mainland," she explained. "I'm from Jersey, in the Channel Islands."

He folded his arms across his chest. "I went there once. In the summer holidays with my mum. Nice place." A large gust of wind rattled the window upstairs and they both looked up at the ceiling. "I remember being amazed when I spotted the coast of France from the guest house where we were staying," he said.

Gemma suspected he was trying to distract her from the gale going on outside. "I can see the lights in France from my old bedroom at my parents' place," she said, recalling how comforted she had been to be back there for the past few months, even if her mother had tired of her presence quicker than she would have liked.

"Do you still live in Jersey, then?"

"No, I left five years ago," she explained thinking back to how excited she had been to leave the small island for a fresh start on the English mainland. "I live in Brighton now, or at least I did."

"Is this your first renovation project, or something you do for a living?"

Gemma laughed. "I'm a nurse," she said, amused at the thought of how different the next few months were going to be compared to what she was used to. "I work in a trauma centre, near Brighton."

All amusement vanished from his face. "Oh, I see," he said.

Confused by his reaction, Gemma thought it best to change the subject. "How come you speak fluent French?" she asked, intrigued.

His shoulders relaxed a little. "My mum's French," he explained. "She's from Amiens, about twenty miles from here."

Gemma recognised the name from reading books about the First World War at school. "I suppose we're near the Somme battlefields here, then."

"We are," he said. "There's a lot of history around this place for you to discover."

"Have you been here long?" she asked nervous not to say the wrong thing again.

"A couple of years full time. I spent most of my summer holidays growing up coming here to stay with my grandparents. My parents ran a small restaurant in Devon before they divorced. It was useful for them to send me here when they were at their busiest."

They chatted for a while longer. Gemma rarely had

company at her flat and usually preferred being alone, but it was a relief to have Tom here. She didn't mind being in this strange house, but the gale and damage to her room had unsettled her.

It seems to be dying down now," he said standing up. "I'd better get going, or my mum will be wondering where I am. I don't want her worrying. I'll be back first thing tomorrow to cover the exposed area on the roof and sort out that window."

"Thanks for stepping in to help me, Tom," Gemma said, extending her hand. He smiled and shook it. "I really appreciate your thoughtfulness."

She showed him to the door and wished she had the same relaxed way about her as Tom did. There was something haunted about him though, she mused. He hid it well, but she couldn't help wondering what was behind the sadness he tried to keep hidden.

Chapter 2

Gemma

February 2018

"That's the window done," Tom announced the following morning, as he descended the ladder and joined her on the front path. "The tarpaulin should keep the roof watertight, at least until I can replace the missing tiles."

He withdrew a piece of paper from his jeans back pocket and handed it to her. "I jotted down a list of what needs doing and how much it'll cost. I'll get it typed up for you. I thought you might like to have a heads-up before you receive my quote."

Gemma unfolded the paper and read his list and the total. "Yes, this amount looks similar to the one my dad was sent from the other chap," she said, noticing it was marginally cheaper. "How soon can you start work?"

He lowered the ladder and carried it to his pick-up. "I've postponed another job for a few weeks," he said as Gemma followed him. She watched him attach it to the roof. "They weren't in any rush."

"Are you sure your other client won't mind?" she asked, wishing she didn't feel the need to ask.

"It's fine. It's their second home," he said, turning to her. "They won't be back in the area until April, at the earliest."

Gemma couldn't believe her luck. It occurred to her that he might be putting himself out to help her. She wasn't used to getting favours from anyone and didn't know how to accept one now. "You're not doing yourself out of any work, are you? Not on my account, anyway. I'm sure I can wait a few weeks," she fibbed.

He laughed. "We both know that's not true. You need the most urgent work doing straight away, especially if you're determined to stay here. Anyway, I'm happy to do it. I'll start tomorrow."

"Thanks, Tom. I'm really grateful," she said.

A week later, Gemma couldn't help being excited that Tom had already replaced the roof tiles smashed during the storm, as well as the broken window. He had also replaced a cracked pane of glass in the small living room window near the front door. She had removed ivy from the front of the house that had covered the original window and the difference it made to the light in the room was staggering.

"Right," he said, letting his metal tape measure retract. "I've fixed the loose floorboards over there and will go and buy more to cover the rotten ones I pulled up this morning. I'll see you in a bit."

"Thanks, Tom," she said to his retreating figure as he walked out into the hallway. Her stomach growled loudly.

Tom stepped back into the room. "Shall I buy something for you to eat, while I'm out?" he asked, grinning.

"Please," she blushed, as he left for a second time. She was getting used to being around Tom. He was hardworking and thoughtful, as well as being extremely good looking. She wondered if he had a girlfriend. Of course, he did. A guy like Tom wouldn't be single.

Determined to stop thinking about him, Gemma stepped over one of the gaps in the floor to leave the room, when something shiny caught her eye.

She crouched carefully over the hole. Reaching down into the space, her hand met an irregular shaped object. She couldn't make out what it could be and lifting the dusty item out she discovered it was a brooch in the shape of a poppy. Intrigued, she rubbed it against her sleeve to remove the excess dust, blowing the remainder away. Its red enamelling was still bright, she noticed. Who could have owned such a beautiful object?

She turned it over and peered at the back, surprised to see it was gold. Saddened to think that someone had lost such a thing of beauty, she wondered again who could have owned it. Poppies had long been a representation of remembrance, she knew that much. Maybe someone had come here from one of the casualty clearing stations close by. Or even during the Second World War?

Tom returned and came up to her bedroom. "I've left you a cheese and tomato baguette on the living room table," he said, entering the room carrying the new floorboards. "What's that?"

Gemma showed him what she had found.

He put the floorboards onto the floor. "It doesn't look very old," he said, turning it over in his hands. "Not that I know anything about jewellery."

"It was incredibly dusty," she told him, returning the brooch to the bedside drawer, as soon as he had finished looking at it.

"Maybe the previous owner lost it, or his wife?"

"I don't think he ever married," Gemma said thoughtfully. "I suppose it could have been a friend, or relative who came to stay here at some point."

Tom stared at her thoughtfully.

Gemma wasn't sure if he wanted to say something, so waited for him to speak. "Right," he said handing back the brooch. "I'd better get on."

Feeling slightly awkward, Gemma remembered that he was going to help her remove the old mattress from the bedroom. "Shall we take this old thing outside?"

"Good idea. Then you can get on with your bits, and I'll replace these bits of flooring."

They dragged the old mattresses from both bedrooms up the muddy path to the meadow. Gemma brought him old magazines, and anything else she didn't want from the farmhouse, while Tom set up the bonfire. They watched everything take light, standing with their hands outstretched towards the flames.

"Is it feeling a little more like home now?" he asked

eventually. He picked up a small branch lying under a tree and prodding the magazines pushing them further into the fire.

"Slightly," she pushed her hands into her pockets, glad he'd begun talking again. "It's much nicer having someone else to chat to, in between jobs."

"Good. I'm glad." He turned and gazed at the farmhouse. "It's an appealing building. Once all the work has been done, I think it's going to be somewhere you'll be very happy."

"I'm not staying here," she said. "Just doing it up, so my father can sell it on."

She was taken aback by his surprise. "I didn't realise you weren't wanting to keep this for yourself. So, you're returning to the UK then?"

Was that disappointment she saw in his face? Don't be ridiculous, Gemma, she thought. Why would he care whether you lived here, or not? "Yes, I've taken a sabbatical from nursing," she said, not adding that it hadn't been a planned event.

"Good for you. Don't you miss it?"

Gemma thought back to the last day at work and the meltdown she'd had. "I thought I might, but no, not yet."

He stared at her briefly. "Did you always want to be a nurse then?"

She nodded. "Ever since I can remember. You?"

He pulled a face. "What be a nurse?"

Gemma nudged him and giggled. "No, silly, a builder."

27

He gazed into the flames, not answering for a several seconds. "No."

Unsure if she was being too nosy, Gemma asked, "What did you want to be when you were younger then?"

Tom smiled at her, and Gemma's heart did a somersault as his perfect lips drew back revealing his straight, white teeth. He really did have movie star looks, she thought. She realised he was saying something.

"Sorry, I missed that."

"It doesn't matter," he said, throwing the stick into the fire. "We should be getting back to work. This lot can take care of itself."

Disappointed that she'd missed what he'd said, she was tempted to ask again. When she glanced out of the corner of her eyes at him, he was deep in thought striding along the muddy pathway back to the house.

"I've enjoyed cleaning this place more than I expected I would," she admitted, catching up with him. "You've been a wonderful help, stepping in like you did."

"I'm glad you're happy." Tom said, his smile not reaching his eyes. "I'd better get on."

That afternoon, Gemma's new mattress was delivered. Tom helped her carry it up to her bedroom.

"Now you've finished the floor in here, it's almost habitable," she said.

"It'll be much better than sleeping in the living room," he said looking out the window at the bonfire. "I'd better get back and check on the fire."

She had already washed down the bed frame, walls,

skirting boards and floor, so all she needed to do was make up her bed. Gemma tried to fathom what she'd said to alter Tom's mood. But unable to work it out, she focused on rehanging the faded floral curtains she had washed. She stood at the doorway and surveyed the results of their efforts, there was still an enormous amount to do, but she could see a big difference in here at least.

She wondered if she and Tom would be able to keep in contact after he'd finished working for her. She hoped so, she thought, swallowing a lump in her throat. Maybe instead of trying to be braver and bolder, she should concentrate on just making some friends. She hadn't realised before spending time with Tom how much more enjoyable her days could be with someone to have a laugh with. She had spent her entire life believing that she was too dull to befriend. Her first boyfriend had tried to persuade her to emigrate with him to Australia to start a new life, but she had been too timid to go with him and now, seeing how she was coping here doing something new, it occurred to her that she had an awful lot to learn about herself.

Her chest constricted with emotion. She was over-tired and being ridiculous. All she needed, Gemma mused, was a decent night's sleep in her new bed. She could worry about how things were going in the morning.

Gemma woke after her first night sleeping on her new mattress and stretched. It had been like sleeping on a cloud. For the first time since arriving at the farmhouse, she hadn't woken up with a backache. She must have been in a very deep sleep, she thought, feeling a little groggy. She rubbed her eyes to try and wake up properly.

Slipping her feet into her cold trainers, she winced. It was going to take some time before she got used to not having central heading, she thought shivering. She had always enjoyed watching programmes on television where people bought a rundown property and did them up but was quickly discovering that the reality was not nearly as comfortable as it looked. She rubbed her arms to keep them warm while she decided what to wear. It was too cold to care about appearances, so she grabbed her nearest sweater and pulled it on.

She opened the curtains and let sunshine flood in to the room. The warmth of the sunny spring day on her face cheered her. For the first time she thought that maybe her father had a point suggesting she come here. Looking after the renovation work, instead of rushing back to her job at the trauma unit was definitely helping her come to terms with what had happened. Her mood dipped as the image of her ex, dying from his injuries in a car crash swooped into her mind. How could she hate someone who had died so tragically, she wondered? Then again, if she had discovered he was still married before he'd had his accident, she could have finished with him and not felt so guilty. She pushed all thoughts of him from her mind and went downstairs.

She was enjoying working with Tom. He seemed a little mysterious, but very nice. She smiled, thinking how she looked forward to the days he was here more and more.

Sundays were the only day Tom didn't come to the house and they seemed to stretch on forever.

Gemma went downstairs to the kitchen. She heard Tom singing to himself through the open window, as he crossed the courtyard to the three-sided barn. Watching him carrying tools into one of the smaller outhouses, she noticed his t-shirt was filthy from the grime of the disused rooms. For a second, she wondered what he looked like without it on.

Shocked by her reaction to him, she tore herself away from the window and went back to the living room, forcing her attention on the walls, now washed with sugar soap. Finally, they were clean and ready for her to paint. She looked at the wooden floor deciding if it needed a large colourful rug, but it was no good, she couldn't focus, she had to go outside and see him.

"What are you doing?" she asked, finding him with a crowbar trying to force open a fitted cupboard at the back of the barn that she hadn't noticed before.

"I found this door. There was sacking nailed over it, but it was rotten and practically disintegrated when I went to lift it." Tom put down the crowbar. "I can't imagine why anyone would cover it up."

She was intrigued. "What do you think's in there?" she asked, wondering why someone would hide a door?

"I'm concerned there might be old gas canisters, or something else that needs to be removed. It's been painted over many times. Probably because the previous owner couldn't be bothered to open it."

"I can see why," Gemma laughed. "If it's too much bother, just leave it. I doubt something that's been closed off for years will bother me, or any other potential owners. It's a bit of a strange feature, but it gives the inside of the barn a little character, don't you think?"

"Maybe." He didn't sound convinced. He turned to look at her. "How was your new mattress? Get a better night's sleep than on your ancient armchair?"

"It was bliss," she said. "I slept soundly all night."

"I'm not surprised after sleeping on that chair for so long."

She smiled at him. "I certainly feel more refreshed today, than I have been doing."

"That figures." He turned his attention back to the cupboard.

Not wishing to hover over him while he worked, she decided to go and get out of his way. "I'll go and make us a bite to eat," she said. "I bought a fresh baguette last night. It should still be okay this morning. I've also got some perfectly ripe Camembert."

"Sounds great," Tom said, his voice straining as he pushed against the end of the crowbar. "Just give me a shout when you want me."

Gemma had to resist answering with a joke and left him to it. She was cutting chunks of the bread, placing them on two plates, when Tom bellowed for her. Terrified he had injured himself, she dropped the knife onto the table and ran outside.

"What's the matter?" she shouted, hoping he wasn't too badly hurt.

"Look in there," he said, standing back and indicating for her to peek inside the now open cupboard. "Shall I take it out for you to have a proper look?"

Relieved he was fine, she peered into the cupboard at a large black tin box. "It's a small trunk," she said, unsure why anyone would go to such great lengths to hide it. "What do you think is in it?"

"As long as it's nothing gruesome, I don't mind," he teased.

She took hold of a handle at one end and tugged. "It's not too heavy," she said pulling the box again. It moved forward and was just about to fall off the cupboard shelf when Tom caught it.

"Going by the layers of paint over the door, it must have been in this cupboard for decades," he said.

She tried and failed to undo the clip on the front of the tin. "Shall we take it inside to have a proper look?" she asked, hoping there wasn't anything too disgusting inside.

"I think I should try and open it here first, just to be sure."

He was right. At least then, if it was something nasty, they could dispose of it outside, rather than in her now clean house. "Go on then."

She waited for him to fetch a pair of cutters from his truck. He cut through the lock from the box. "You can open it, if you like?" he said. "It's your box. You should do the honours."

Excitement coursed through her. She forgot her initial concerns about the contents and giggled. "This is fun," she said, slowly lifting the lid, hoping that whatever was inside didn't disappoint them.

"Letters?" she said, unsure what to make of them. They stared at the vast number of letters stacked neatly in the tin. "There are two batches," she said, unnecessarily. "Both tied with a ribbon."

"I wonder who they belonged to?" Tom said, staring at one as Gemma slid it carefully from the front of one of the bundles.

"It's addressed to someone called Alice Le Breton," she said thoughtfully. "I know of some Le Bretons in Jersey. I wonder if they're related to her?"

"I think we need to get this box inside," Tom said. "It's very damp out here and you don't want them damaged. I'll carry them in. We can eat lunch and see who they're from."

Inside the living room, Gemma draped a tea towel on the table before Tom placed the box onto it.

"Would you like me to make the coffee while you look at the letters?" he suggested.

Excited now, Gemma nodded. "It's easy to find everything," she joked. "There's only one place where I can store anything in that kitchen."

While Tom clattered around, filling the kettle and spooning coffee into two cups, Gemma pulled up a chair and sat down. She lifted out the first bundle of letters. The envelopes were slightly discoloured with age but seemed in excellent condition otherwise. She tugged gently at the ends of the ribbons and untied the bundle. Winding the red velvet ribbon around her hand, Gemma noticed that in the first bundle of letters Alice Le Breton was writing to a Lieutenant Peter Conway. In the second, however, the correspondence was between her and a Captain Edgar Woodhall. She must have had two sweethearts, Gemma mused.

Taking the letter at the bottom of the bundle, she studied the envelope. She noticed the stamp was on at a strange angle. She saw that other envelopes had stamps stuck on in unusual ways, too. The perfectionist side of her couldn't help being niggled by the lack of uniformity.

Curious to see what the first letter said, Gemma slid the folded paper carefully from its envelope. Unfolding the single sheet of paper, she began to read.

Chapter 3

Alice

August 1916

Casualty Clearing Station No 7,
Doullens, Northern France

"Brace yourselves nurses," one of the orderlies bellowed from outside the cramped bell tent where volunteer nurses, Alice Le Breton and her colleague, Mary Jones were deep in an exhausted sleep. "There's a convoy on its way. You're needed. You've got ten minutes, before Matron comes looking for you."

"Thank you," Alice replied, her voice croaky from sleep. It had been a long six weeks since the big push on July and still the battles were raging. "Mary, did you hear?"

There was no sound from the occupant in the other camp bed. Alice rubbed her eyes and sat up. Her feet and back ached. She looked over at Mary recalling how they had instantly become friends when sat next to each other on the train from Gare du Nord to Doullens the previous year.

If she had done as her mother had insisted, she would be waking up to breakfast in her marital home right now, instead of having to endure another day of drudgery dealing with bloodied bandages and crabby Sisters barking orders at her. This was still preferable though, Alice thought, certain she'd done the right thing. Marriage was not for her. She was going to decide what she did with her life, not her mother, or her ex-fiancé. She pushed away the guilt that seemed to shadow her everywhere.

"Come on, Mary," she said, stretching. At least this new convoy of injured men would take her mind off what she'd done.

"Stop nagging," Mary moaned, covering her mouth to stifle a yawn. "Give me a minute."

Alice smiled at her rosy-cheeked best friend, grateful they had met on the train soon after finishing their training for the Voluntary Aid Detachment.

"You have seven minutes to get there now," Alice said, throwing back her covers, grateful for the warmer mornings. "I'll wash first. Hurry."

"Are we ever going to catch up with our sleep, do you think?" Mary's sleepy voice asked.

"Probably not until this wretched war ends," Alice said, stretching. "I can't recall ever being this exhausted."

Her heart ached. They had been here long enough to know what to expect. She stood up from her camp bed and pouring water from a jug into the porcelain washbowl on a stand at the end of her bed, she quickly washed her face, hands and underarms. Then, carefully taking her pale blue uniform from the little canvas chair that was forever falling over, pulled it on over her underclothes.

Mary followed the same routine as Alice. She took her uniform from the tent pole that they had wound a leather strap around to create a make shift place to hang some of their clothes.

"This tent is leaking again," Mary said, picking up her towel and drying several spots next to the small mirror on her trunk. She brushed her hair and checked her handkerchief-style cap. "Wouldn't it be a dream if we could have a chest of drawers for our clothes, instead of keeping everything in these," she said slapping the top of her trunk.

"We wouldn't fit one inside this tent, though, would we?" Alice pinned back her hair and tied up the laces on her sensible shoes.

"When I get home," Mary said, picking up her hand mirror to check her teeth. "I'm going to find a man who can buy me a proper dressing table. I fancy one of made of walnut. What about you?"

"I haven't really thought about it," Alice said, glancing at her watch before pinning it to her uniform. "Come along, we need to get a move on if we want to avoid a reprimand from Matron."

They walked quickly along the dusty pathway that months before had been covered in grass. Alice yearned to return to her uncomfortable bed in their cramped tent. She was used to the long days and nights on shift but knew only too well that she had at least another ten hours until she could lie down and close her eyes again.

"There she is," Alice whispered, indicating Matron Bleasdale who was waiting for them, hands clasped in front of her apron as she stood at the helm of the other over-tired nurses.

"Did I tell you about the letter I received from my aunt yesterday?"

Alice shook her head. "I don't think so."

Mary straightened one of her sleeves as they walked. "She wrote to tell me that the Black Tom Island munitions plant in the States, you know, it's in Jersey City where my cousin works, well it was destroyed by an explosion."

Alice gasped, covering her hand over her mouth when a couple of the other volunteers turned to see what had shocked her. "That's horrible. Is he alright?" she asked, finding it strangely unnerving hearing the familiar name of Jersey being mentioned and relieved her friend wasn't talking about her home island.

"He was, thankfully. Absent from work with a fever of some sort, my aunt says. Apparently, German saboteurs are suspected of bombing the place. She also wrote that the Statue of Liberty was damaged by shrapnel from the explosion. Shocking, isn't it?"

Alice thought it strange that the Hun had caused damage so far away from Europe. The notion made her uneasy. "Poor people."

"I know. It shook my aunt up a fair bit, I can tell you."

Mary slowed her pace slightly. "I forget we're not the only ones dealing with injured people."

Alice did, too. "I always feel sorry for the families of these poor men," she said matching her friend's speed. "I'm relieved I don't have a sweetheart at the Front, or anywhere else," she said. It was the one thing she was certain about. "The worry of him ending up like some of our poor patients would be too dreadful."

They reached the group of nurses and other VADs at the ten-minute deadline. Both stood silently at the back of the line on the walkway behind Matron, who raised her watch, staring at its face for a few seconds before lowering it and studying the group before her, eyes narrowed. "Nurse Le Breton, your uniform is incorrect."

Embarrassed, Alice patted her head to check her cap was straight. She mentally worked through her outfit, mortified to note that she had forgotten to tie her apron. She quickly did so, smoothing down the skirt and clearing her throat. "Sorry, Matron," she said before giving Mary a sideways glance.

"You four," Matron said, pointing to Alice, Mary and two nurses next to them. "Go and ensure all necessary trolleys are readied. I want all free beds made up. Go," she shouted when they didn't move the instant her order was out of her mouth.

They had all perfected the art of hurrying without breaking into a run. Matron loathed running. As they reached the wards, two went to help make up beds, while Alice and Mary kept going to the supplies hut.

"That was your fault," Alice teased, grabbing several packets of dressings from the shelf in front of her. "Telling me things about your cousin."

Mary took several more. "I thought you'd be interested."

"I was," Alice admitted, not wishing to fall out with someone with whom she shared a small tent. "Sorry, I'm tired, that's all."

"Apology accepted," Mary smiled, throwing a pack of dressings at her.

Outside, they waited silently in the uneasy calmness. The only sound interrupting the quiet orderly grounds being the occasional burst of shell fire from the Front. Alice wondered if she would ever get used to the noise. The worst was when she felt the earth shudder beneath her feet. The closeness of those explosions never failed to give her a fright. Mary had told her countless times to try to ignore it, but how was she to do that when each explosion almost certainly meant the death or mutilation of at least one soldier, usually many.

A bugle sounded, jarring Alice out of her reverie as it signalled the arrival of the convoy.

"Let the nightmare begin," she whispered to Mary.

Mary grimaced. "I hate this bit most of all."

Alice didn't. The bit she dreaded most was nursing a soldier as he screamed in an agony she could only imagine, unable to lessen his pain. And the fear some of them showed, her heart ached at the thought. It was something she knew she would never get used to, no matter how long this damn war continued.

The sound of motor ambulances arriving over the hardened summer ground increased as they neared. Horses whinnied as they pulled ambulances to the rear of the convoy.

"There are so many," Alice said nervously, as the vehicles drew up in front of the casualty clearing station and parked long enough to unload their damaged passengers. Orderlies ran to take stretchers from the vehicles. "There must have been another big push."

Cries and agonised pleading for help rang through the early evening air. Alice braced herself for what was to come.

"Do we know how many?" One of the sisters asked as the first driver opened the back of his vehicle.

"At least seven, maybe eight ambulances," he said. "These are all from the fighting going on near Pozières. I was hoping the worst of it was over, but it just goes on and on."

"It does seem to."

"All of these are full. We'll be going back for more later. By the looks of things, you're going to have around two hundred wounded brought here over the next few hours."

Alice wondered how many more patients they could take, or how many soldiers there were still left to injure in the battles being fought in various areas across the Western Front. She waited for stretchers to be lifted from the vehicles. Matron read their tags to check injuries and the severity of damage to the new patients. Some didn't need checking, even Alice could see from where she waited for Matron's instructions, that they were horribly injured.

"Nurse Le Breton, Nurse Jones," she called waving over

Alice and Mary. There's a pile of bandages at the back of the tent there," she said pointing. "Take them to be burnt and get back here straight after."

Alice was carrying a pile of soiled dressings, trying not to get blood on her clean apron, when a smirking patient stood in front of her on the boardwalk dragging on a cigarette.

"Excuse me," she said, trying to side-step the man. When he didn't move, she stepped to the right to pass him, only for him to block her route once more. Not wishing to get into an unnecessary argument with him, she glared at him.

"What the hell are you doing?" Doctor Sullivan bellowed coming up to them. "Move aside and let the volunteer nurse pass, now."

The patient did as he was told. He doesn't look nearly as full of himself now, she realised, amused.

"Thank you, Doctor Sullivan," she said hurrying off, hearing the doctor scolding the patient. Having thrown the revolting mess into the fire, Alice washed her hands in the sluice room and returned to wait near Matron.

As she walked, she thought of the doctor and his eighteen-hour long shifts battling to save patients. Alice didn't know how he and the other surgeons carried on working, day after day. They rarely had a day off, or at least, that was how it seemed to her.

A loud uproar alerted her to a disturbance outside the ward. Without hesitating, Alice grabbed the string of a large jar containing a lit candle and ran outside to help.

More ambulances had arrived. The crying and groaning increased. Matron, the front of her beige uniform bloodied, pointed for Alice to go and assist with the ambulance next to where she was standing. Doctor Sullivan and two other surgeons ran from the direction of their huts to the theatre wards.

Three men were lifted out of the first ambulance, all of whom were conscious. Alice noticed that there was a further patient. This one was still, and she had to take his pulse to be certain he was still alive. He was. Just. "Take these men to Ward Five," she said. "Please, hurry. There are nurses in there who'll tell you which bed to put them in," she said, as the fourth man's stretcher was slowly pulled back from the vehicle.

Holding up her lantern, she narrowed her eyes and studied the patient. He was covered in dried earth and lice, but then so many of the men were. She lifted the tag attached to his uniform jacket and saw that he had received a shrapnel wound to his head and a bullet had grazed his hip.

"Bring him with me," she said, covering him up to his neck with the brown blanket. "This way."

They followed her to Ward Five. Inside, she scanned the tent for a free bed. He would need one as far away from the door as possible, she decided. He needed to be kept warm and Alice was relieved to discover a bed at the other end of the ward. Hurrying over, she carefully passed nurses stripping, cleaning and tending to wounds on the new patients.

"Here," she said. They placed him down on the bed and left her to it.

The poor man was very cold, despite the warm day. Much colder than the other soldiers she had come across that evening. Alice didn't like to think how low his body temperature must have fallen. He groaned and winced as she undid his uniform jacket.

"You're safe now," she said. "My name is Nurse Le Breton. I'm going to wash and change you. A doctor will be here to check on you as soon as he can."

When she moved his head slightly, blood covered her hand. Alice saw Mary finishing with a nearby patient and waved her over.

"Can you help me, please?" she asked and Mary hurried over. Alice held the patient up by his shoulders while Mary removed the clothes from his torso. Carefully resting him down again, they both removed his trousers and under-clothes. Keeping him covered as much as possible, they quickly washed him before cleaning and redressing his hip wound. "Fetch an extra blanket," she said quietly to a passing probationer. "Be as quick as you can."

Alice was aware that she should not move his head any more than was necessary, but his bandage was filthy and soaked with blood. "We need to change this," she said, waiting for Mary to raise his head slightly, so she would remove the dirty dressing. Cleaning the wound as best she could, Alice pressed two new dressings against it before bandaging it.

"That's better," Mary said, lowering his head gently onto

the pillow. "I'll make up his records, while you let Matron know his situation."

"Thank you," Alice said. "He's," she checked his tag again. "Captain Edgar Woodhall."

Alice spotted Nurse Haines returning to the ward and took the extra blanket from her. Lying it over the Captain, she took his temperature, once again. "We need to bring his body temperature up, slowly, but surely," she said to Mary. Alice knew her friend was as aware as she, what needed to be done for the patient, but could not help herself.

Mary gave her one of her, bugger-off-and-leave-me-to-get-on, looks. Alice took a deep breath. "Sorry, I'll go to speak to Matron."

She went to Matron's office but couldn't find her there. Alice assumed she was still frantically working with her nurses on the new patients. They all knew that the sooner the men were cleaned, settled and their records were taken, the sooner they could be given the correct treatment for their injuries and start to recover.

Alice was diverted from her ministrations by cries of pain emanating from the surgery tent. She shivered, imagining the surgeons battling to save lives. Slipping and almost falling on the wooden pathway, Alice righted herself and spotted Matron coming out of one of the furthest wards.

"What is it, Nurse Le Breton?" she said in hushed irritation. "Oughtn't you be busy elsewhere?"

Indignant at the other woman's accusatory tone, Alice had to contain herself from answering back. Her mother always criticised her for being too sure of herself.

"I was looking for you." Alice explained.

"I can see that, but why?"

Alice explained about Captain Woodhall's low body temperature. "He's not responding much and seems very cold."

Matron's expression changed from one of annoyance, to concern. "I gather he was stranded overnight in No Man's Land." She glanced in the direction of the ward. "I'm surprised he survived," she added, her voice lower, so as not to be overheard. "What with his injuries and the night being one of the coldest we've experienced for weeks."

"He's lucky he's made it this far," Alice said almost to herself.

"What was that, Nurse Le Breton?" Matron asked as they hurried to the ward.

"Only that he must be strong," Alice said, without thinking.

"And lucky," Matron said. "to be found by a casualty dog. It stayed with him until stretcher-bearers could reach him."

Alice had heard about the dogs, who were trained to take medical supplies to injured soldiers. She recalled hearing a patient say how the dogs carried first aid packs to wounded soldiers on the battlefield and that if the soldier was unconscious, the dog would snuggle up keeping him warm.

The thought of Captain Woodhall being kept alive by a little dog brought a lump to Alice's throat. There were so many cruel and unnecessary acts being performed every day. At times she wondered if she was ever going to feel real joy again. Discovering that a small dog could make the difference between life and death made her heart swell. It reminded her that every small, seemingly insignificant job she undertook helped one of these men.

"Now nurse, unless you have anything you wish to ask me, I suggest you return to the ward and keep a closer eye on Captain Woodhall. He must be observed at all times. Or, at least until his body temperature returns to within the normal parameters."

"Yes, Matron." Alice turned and hurried to the ward. It was a relief to find the captain sleeping and Mary checking his temperature.

"Don't look so concerned," Mary said, her voice barely above a whisper in the now relatively quiet tent. "He's slowly warming up. I've put two extra blankets on him and Sister has just checked his vital signs."

Alice drew up a stool and sat next to his bed. "Matron wants me to stay with him."

"Then you'd better do as she wishes," Sister Brown snapped.

Mary opened her mouth to speak, when a cry from another injured patient pierced the air. "I'll go see to him," she said and left Alice alone.

Alice watched the captain sleep. She could see his eyes moving under his closed eyelids. He must be dreaming, she thought. He looked so handsome now that the dust and caked blood had been washed from his face and his head wound freshly bandaged. She couldn't help wondering if he was going to make it. She hoped so.

She didn't think his head wound was too deep. She did, however, know from experience that it was deaths brought about through infection that came as more of a shock, especially when it had stemmed from a minor injury. Alice had been here a year and knew not to assume that those with lesser injuries would definitely survive. She had learned to expect the unexpected. It made sense not to allow herself to get too close to any of the patients, the heartache when they were discharged, or died, would be too hard to stand.

She felt the captain's forehead with the back of her hand, and he sighed as her skin came in contact with his. Alice thought of the more severely injured patients she had been surprised to see make incredible recoveries, and how floored she had been by two seemingly healthy men dying unexpectedly on her shift. This was a place of miracles and heartache.

"How is he doing?" Matron asked a couple of hours later.

"He's not very responsive. He's been asleep most of the time."

She watched Matron examine him. "We'll do our best for him," Matron said, making a note on the captain's records. "I'm not holding much hope, I'm afraid," she whispered so quietly that Alice barely heard what she said.

She studied the captain's tanned face, his lashes fanned on his scratched cheek. She willed him to survive. Surely, he must have a wife, or sweetheart waiting to hear from him back in England somewhere?

"I'll send someone to take over from you," Matron said, resting a cool hand on Alice's shoulder.

"I'm fine, Matron," she said, not ready to leave him. "I don't mind staying."

"You've been here long enough," the older woman said quietly. Her voice didn't invite argument. "We must take care not to become attached to any of the patients, Nurse Le Breton. However handsome they might be."

Alice went to argue but thought the better of it. "Yes, Matron," she said, mortified. Had her thoughts about the captain been that obvious, she wondered?

Chapter 4

Gemma

2018

Gemma finished reading the note about Captain Woodhall on the back of Alice's letter. Alice seemed to be developing a soft spot for him and Gemma couldn't help hoping he survived. Knowing what she did about his condition, she couldn't help fearing the worst for the poor Captain, especially as the nursing staff at the casualty clearing station must have been pushed to their limits. How did they find the time to focus on the more fragile patients?

It had been a bonus to discover the extra snippets on the back of most of the letters, written in Alice's rounded script. The added insight into Alice's day intrigued Gemma. They were both nurses, albeit Gemma was highly trained, and Alice had only received three months' worth of training. However, the experiences Alice endured during her time assisting on the wards was something no training could ever hope to prepare someone for, Gemma was certain of that much.

She wondered how different it must have been to deal with the constant arrival of horribly damaged men. She thought the trauma unit to be busy if there were a dozen patients arriving at once and that didn't happen too often, she thought. Gemma couldn't imagine how shocking it must have been for Alice to nurse those poor soldiers. Gemma had seen old film footage that gave her an idea of the devastation to life during and after a battle. But would Alice have known what she was letting herself in for when she'd registered for her training? Gemma doubted it.

The notes referred mostly to someone called Ed, and Gemma presumed Alice must be referring to the injured Captain, Woodhall. But why would Alice write the notes on the back of Lieutenant Peter Conway's letters?

Distracted by footsteps, Gemma wondered how long had she been engrossed in Alice's story? She noticed that the fire was lit, which she was sure it hadn't been earlier. Gemma looked up to see Tom walking into the kitchen.

"Sorry, I didn't mean to be rude," she said, aware she had been unsociable.

"It's no problem. I don't mind being ignored," he smiled. Holding up a mug, he added. "I hope you don't mind, if I made myself a coffee. I can make you one, if you like?"

She shook her head. "No, it's fine, thank you. I should be getting on with work, too," she said guiltily as she stood up.

"Why? Carry on reading your letters. I'd be interested to hear what they're about."

"I shouldn't really," she said, wondering why she found it so difficult to sit quietly in someone else's company.

"Rubbish. You read on. I've got to get back to work. I don't want to let my client down." He gave her a cheeky grin. "I don't want her sacking me before I've finished."

Amused by his gentle teasing, Gemma held out the letter for him to see. "Alice was a nurse, like me," she explained. "I was comparing how different our lives must be, despite similar work."

He took the letter and scanned it quickly. "I can't see that it would be that different. If you worked in a trauma unit, then isn't that really what she was doing?" He handed her back the letter a little abruptly.

Gemma was disappointed that he hadn't taken the time to read it properly. "I suppose so," she said. "Although I could at least get away from the day's drama. She lived on site, so there was no real relief from it."

"That's true."

Gemma told him about the notes added to the back of most of the letters. "I had a sneaky look at a few from the other bundle and most of those have notes, too. I'm not sure why yet. They seem to be like diary entries, but without the dates."

"Maybe they were parts of her story she recalled afterwards."

Gemma assumed that to be the case. "Or she might have

written on the backs of the letters because she knew the information would be hidden away."

"Possibly," he pushed up his sleeves. "It's intriguing."

Gemma agreed, even though she could see Tom was only being polite about the letters. He could be squeamish, she thought, aware that not everyone had the stomach she did for gore. Tom was a bit of an enigma to her. Always easy going, but with a haunted air about him that she hadn't worked out yet. "Still," she said. "No need for me to ignore you when I invite you inside for a coffee."

"You weren't," he shouted over his shoulder. "Don't worry about it."

She heard him washing his mug in the sink. Returning to the living room, he glanced at the open tin containing the letters. "You won't miss having a television," he said. "Not with all those to keep you busy. You can tell me more about what you've discovered so far, if you want?"

Gemma put the letter she was holding down onto the table next to her. She picked up her mug, nodding as she took a sip.

"That's probably cold by now."

It was, but she barely noticed. "It's fine, thanks," she said, not wishing to lose her chance to share her excitement with someone. "I don't know why these letters were hidden here," she looked around the room, trying to picture how is must have looked one hundred years before. "I assume Alice must have lived here at some point?" When Tom waited for her to continue, she added. "When I said she was a nurse, she really was a VAD."

Tom shook his head. "Volunteer?"

She motioned for him to take a seat. "Yes, a VAD was a voluntary nurse in the Voluntary Aid Detachment. The women who enrolled had to be at least twenty-three. So far, I've discovered that Alice was stationed at one of the casualty clearing stations near Doullens. I don't know where exactly, but I believe there must have been a lot of them around, as it's near to the Somme area."

"It is," Tom said. "She must have been a brave lady," he added staring into the flames of the fire.

"Very. They all were." Gemma took another sip of her tepid drink. "When you think of some of the horrendous injuries they came across, on a daily basis, too." She thought of some of the horrors she had been expected to cope with at the trauma unit. "I've seen some devastating injuries in my time, but I think war is another matter entirely. The injuries would have been far worse and back then there was a constant stream of injured men needing medical treatment." She shook her head thoughtfully. "It doesn't get any better either, I don't think."

"Hmm," he swallowed and stood up. "I'd better get on. I don't want it to get dark before I've had a chance to really make some headway today."

"Okay, sure," Gemma said, aware his mood had slipped, but unsure why. As she watched him go through to the back of the house, she had a feeling that the letters had disturbed Tom in some way. Was there a reason talking about the war or her work made him uneasy? She never failed to be impressed by the almost magical differences doctors made to some patients, even those in the trauma unit since she'd began working there. However, she was aware that some people, most, probably, didn't like to think of such things.

Gemma watched him go outside and close the door behind him. She finished her drink and thought back to two months ago and her last day at work. She still felt sick when she recalled her shock at discovering that the man she'd thought herself in love with had not only lied to her about being single but was in front of her on a trolley, dying. One day, she hoped to discover her lost love of nursing, but she couldn't see it happening for a long time yet. If ever.

Gemma swallowed the lump forming in her throat. All her yearning to be a nurse followed by years of training, dashed away. Maybe she just wasn't cut out to deal with traumatised people. It wasn't as if she had experience of opening up herself. She wondered if it was the loss of a life-long dream that upset her most or walking out of her job. No money coming in, no purpose.

She recalled her dad's serious expression when he'd sat her down to tell her of his idea about her coming to Doullens to renovate the farmhouse. She couldn't help wondering if her dad had wanted her to come to France for her own good, or simply to appease her mother and get her out of the house.

She had always been the cuckoo in her parent's love nest and it stung whenever anyone joked about a baby being a mistake. She assumed most won their parents around to be cherished in the end, but Gemma wasn't sure what that must feel like. She shook her head, enough wallowing. She was a strong, independent woman and renovating this place was going to prove it to herself as well as her parents. You had to reach the bottom to rise again, didn't you?

Gemma folded the two letters she had been reading back into their envelopes. She slipped them at the back of the bundle, to keep everything in order, determined to savour every one. She was determined not to miss out any of Alice's letters by getting them muddled.

Tom had been right, she thought as she washed her mug, she did have a lot to read. It would keep her mind off everything that had happened in Brighton and her parent's rejection. She felt like she had made a new friend in Alice, albeit one she would never meet. She couldn't wait to discover more about the woman's life.

Gemma tidied away her letters and washed the kitchen floor. Hearing Tom working outside, she couldn't think of a reason not to go and speak to him. When she found him, he was up the ladder checking the roof above the barn. Gemma opened her mouth to speak, when Tom reached forward to test a tile and the bottom of his trouser leg lifted revealing a prosthetic right ankle.

Gemma covered her mouth instinctively with her hand, not daring to make a sound. She didn't dare distract him, frightened he might fall. Stunned by her discovery, she stared briefly before deciding to go back into the house.

She'd only walked a couple of steps when Tom dropped a cracked tile onto the cobbles. Gemma glanced up. She noticed Tom watching her and blushed

Desperate to cover up what she'd done, she forced a smile. "I was just wondering if there was anything I could do to help," she said, aware how guilty she sounded.

He narrowed his eyes. "Is there something wrong?" he asked before carrying on with what he'd been doing.

"No, nothing. I'll be in the house," she added, retreating.

Hoping Tom would come in to speak to her, which he usually did at the end of each day, Gemma kept herself busy by cleaning. Her mother loved preaching that keeping busy was good for clearing the mind, but Gemma had never believed her until now. Putting her energies into scouring the landing floor was doing little to calm her though.

How had he lost his leg? Had he been in the Army? Gemma dropped the scourer into the grimy water as a thought dawned on her. Was that why he'd reacted as he had earlier when she'd been droning on about injuries sustained during wars? Of course, he must have spent time in a trauma unit.

"I'm such an idiot," she groaned to herself.

"And why would that be?" Tom asked, her giving her a fright.

"I didn't hear you come in," she said playing for time. She knew she had to broach the subject of his leg, just in case he had noticed her looking earlier.

"Sorry, I should have knocked."

"Not at all," she said, mortified. "Look, I hope you don't

60

mind me asking," she said, nervously. "I noticed you have a prosthetic ankle."

"Leg, actually," he said. "But only the lower half." Tom laughed. It was a sad laugh, filled with pain. Gemma could see he was trying to put on a brave face. "Sorry, I never really know how to react when people bring it up. It's fine, though Gemma, really. I don't want you to feel awkward."

"I don't," she fibbed. "I didn't know you were an amputee, that's all."

"That's all?" he looked towards the golden glow of the sun streaming through the bedroom window onto the wet floor.

Gemma cringed. What a stupid thing to say. She wondered how many times Tom must have had to deal with idiots like her who stumbled over their words. "I mean that seeing you work, well, it isn't obvious." Damn. That still wasn't right. "That is—"

Tom leant forward and placed his right hand on hers. "It's fine. I know what you mean." He shrugged. "I am a little sensitive about it sometimes," he looked down at his right leg. "I can still do everything that I did before," he said. "In civilian life, at least."

"You were in the Army then?" So, she had been right. "Is that where it happened?" She couldn't help being intrigued.

"I was," he said, his voice distant. "For seven years. And yes. I lost this, and three friends when an IUD exploded in front of our patrol in Kabul in 2013."

Gemma wished she hadn't brought the subject up

hearing such pain in his voice. She needed to put her professional head on, what there was left of it, to try and salvage the awkwardness between them. "I'm so sorry, Tom."

"Me, too." He let go of her hand. "They were good men; good friends. They didn't deserve to die."

"You didn't deserve to suffer in the way you've done either."

He walked over to the window and rested his palms on the sill. "I didn't think I was lucky initially," he confided. "The prospect of not being able to stay with my unit was unbearable at first. I missed the camaraderie, and the friends who'd been killed."

She stared at his broad shoulders, drooping as he stared out at the garden, his back still to her and her heart ached for him. "Had you always wanted to be in the Armed Forces?"

"Yes," he said thoughtfully. "My grandfather had been a soldier and I'd never considered a life on civvy street, but after this, I was left with no alternative." He looked down at his hands. "It was a lot to take in," he said quietly. "I still have a brother in the Army. I'm envious of him and worry about him in equal measures."

Listening to his experiences made her feel doubly guilty for dwelling on her own loss of purpose. "Was this why you chose to come and live in France?"

She hoped he didn't think she was over-stepping the line between them. They didn't know each other well, but she hoped to learn more about him. She was aware that it was a strange question, but it was her life taking an unexpected turn that had led her to being here, maybe Tom's reason was due to what had happened to him? Maybe, she thought, he was here because it was easier to move away from all that was familiar in England and those who only knew him as a soldier?

"Partly," he said mysteriously. He sighed heavily and gave her a tight smile. "Basically, I just needed to get away and be somewhere away from anything that reminded me of that time." He turned to face her. "Right, I'd better get going. I'll leave you to your letters," he said. "See you first thing tomorrow."

"Thanks for everything you've done today, Tom," she said. "I really appreciate it."

"No worries." He gave her a brief nod and left.

She suspected he wasn't used to sharing his feelings. Then again, she hadn't ever shared her thoughts with anyone either. Apart from maybe her first boyfriend, and he now lived on the other side of the world. Another decision she hadn't been brave enough to take. Gemma tidied away her bucket and scourer. She wondered what her life would have been like, if she'd chosen to go with him when he emigrated and not stay behind and continue with her nursing training. But it was too late to regret that decision now, she mused.

Gemma took the bucket downstairs and tipped the dirty water down a drain outside the kitchen door. She and Tom had been relaxing with each other more every day, now though, she sensed something in their relationship had shifted, and not in a good way.

A log dropped from the fire and sent a lump of charcoal onto the floor in front of her chair. Running over to grab the small shovel at the side of the fireplace, she quickly slid it under the burning ember and flicked it back into the fire. Noticing a burn mark left behind on the wooden floorboard, Gemma slumped down on her armchair and began to cry as a sadness gripped her. Sadness for her own situation, but also for Tom and the pain he had suffered.

Waking hours later, she rubbed her puffy eyes gently. The fire was low, and she was cold. She banked up the embers thinking how her mother often insisted that a good cry was a release of pent up emotions. After her faux pas earlier in the day, she was glad to be rid of the accumulation of emotion inside her since her arrival. Deciding she wasn't going to be any use in the morning if she didn't get some proper sleep, Gemma went upstairs.

She washed and changed into her pyjamas. Then, cleaning her teeth, she looked in the mirror and hoped that her eyes would look less swollen in the morning. She didn't want Tom to think she felt sorry for him. That would be the worst thing she could do. She hated what he had been through, but he had found a way to cope with a life-changing injury and she admired him for it. He was a strong man physically, that much was obvious when you looked at him, but now she knew that he was mentally strong too.

She lay in bed staring at the moonlight shining through the small gap in her curtains. Gemma thought back to the letters and couldn't help wondering how Alice had coped a hundred years earlier. The nurses at most casualty clearing stations didn't have the luxury of a building to sleep in. How brave she and other women like her friend Mary, must have been to volunteer. The horrific wounds and traumatised soldiers would have been bad enough, but Gemma found it difficult to imagine dealing with such pressure day after day, year after year. No antibiotics or penicillin to help battle infection, far more basic implements than she was used to having at her disposal. She could only imagine how exhausting it must have been.

Working in a trauma unit, she'd seen many injuries that would forever be engraved in her mind, but never in the numbers that Alice and her friend Mary would have faced. Their food, sleeping quarters and being far away from their families, only increased Gemma's admiration for them and the other medical staff.

"And I'm lying here feeling sorry for myself," she said to the moonlight. "I need to focus on this farmhouse." After all, she wasn't having to live in a tent and this work would get easier and more enjoyable as the weather warmed up.

And Tom. What about him? She pictured his navy-blue eyes, always twinkling, having to deal with the unwelcome changes in his life. There was something about him; maybe it was the cheeky look he gave her, or maybe, the way he helped her without her having to ask him first. It was as if he was in tune with her. It wasn't something she was used to and despite her resolution to stay man free, she had to admit that she quite liked him. She was glad that he had been lucky enough to have modern medicine to help him survive being blown up. Unlike so many men that Alice must have helped look after.

She plumped up her two pillows and tried to make herself more comfortable. She was desperate for sleep and for her mind to stop whirring and tormenting her. She hated it when her mood was low, especially when she acknowledged that she had very little to be miserable about. What was it about Alice's letters that had upset her, she wondered? Probably the fear that came across in them. The fear of losing loved ones, as well as the uncertainty that the war didn't seem to be coming to an end.

"When did you come here, Alice?" she whispered, aware that she would have died of fright should anyone reply. Had she just visited and hidden her letters, or had she lived here? She hoped Alice had been happy here at the farm.

Eventually, Gemma contemplated getting out of bed and going down to the living room to read more of Alice's letters. She tried to fight against getting up but, unable to sleep, threw back the covers and slipped her feet into her trainers. She pulled on her dressing gown, grabbed the blanket from her bed and carried it over her shoulder.

She was going to look like hell in the morning, she thought, tying the fleecy belt as she walked down the stairs. She made a tea, added a few sticks of wood to the fire, with a larger log on top and turned on the light. Opening the black tin box, she gazed at the two batches of letters inside.

She was tempted to go to the last one and read it, she never had much in the way of patience, but these letters were too fascinating to read them out of order.

Sitting down, she made herself comfortable and read the next letter.

Chapter 5

Alice

1916

"Nurse! Nurse, come quickly."

Alice heard the frantic tone of the patient lying in the bed next to Captain Woodhall's. She hurried over to see what was wrong.

"He was havin' a fit, Nurse," The young private said, his eyes wide with fear.

Lifting the captain's wrist, Alice took his pulse, flinching at a loud explosion she estimated to be only a couple of miles away. Taking a calming breath, Alice felt the captain's forehead. He was running a temperature and she knew it could be the reason for the convulsion, although her instinct told her he wasn't in immediate danger.

"He's fine, Private Allen," she soothed, pushing him gently back against his pillows and straightening his sheet. "Try to relax. I'll look after Captain Woodhall."

The private grimaced and waved her closer. "I would,

Nurse, but I've wet me bed," he whispered, glancing from side to side to check no one else had overheard. "I'm sorry. Those loud bangs, they frighten me silly they do."

"Leave it with me," she soothed. "We'll sort you out in no time."

She waved over one of the probationers. "I think it's near enough time for the men to have some refreshment, don't you?" She gave a pointed glance in the private's direction.

"I'll see to it right now, Nurse Le Breton," the young girl said.

Alice pulled a screen around the private's bed and helped him out. "Change out of those things and I'll bring you some clean pyjamas."

She was back a couple of minutes later with fresh clothes and bedlinen. Alice hated seeing the poor boy so embarrassed. She understood how terrifying the nearby explosions were to some of the men. Hadn't she nearly jumped out of her skin many times on hearing them? And she hadn't spent months sleeping on a fire step in a muddy trench with explosions going off all around her.

She helped him to wash quickly and change. "You do up your jacket and I'll change this bed. You'll be back in it in a jiffy." She smiled at the volunteer nurse. "It's Nurse Jenkins isn't it?"

"Yes, that's right," she said. "I arrived last week. Still haven't quite found my footing here."

"You're doing fine."

The bed changed, Alice left the young private to be settled by Nurse Jenkins and turned her attention to

Captain Woodhall. She gave him a thorough check to be sure she hadn't missed anything. Determining to try and reduce his temperature, she dipped a flannel in a bowl of cool water, rung it out and placed it over his hot forehead. His eyes flickered briefly, then opened. He took a while to focus before gazing up at her.

"Where am I?" he asked, his voice croaky from lack of use.

Alice poured a little water into a glass and raising his head gently, held the drink to his lips. He took a few sips. Looking exhausted from the effort, he closed his eyes again.

She lowered his head and sat down on the chair next to his bed, waiting for him to gather the strength to address her again.

"Is this a casualty clearing station? No," he answered without opening his eyes. "It can't be, I didn't think there were VADs at a CCS."

"We're welcome in many more places than we were a couple of years ago," she said, straightening his sheet. "You have a bit of a fever."

"How long have I been here?"

"Three days."

His eyes scanned the room. He went to sit up, wincing in pain, before collapsing back on his bed.

Alice could see the panic on his face. She was used to men reacting in this way when they recovered consciousness. Their first reaction, once discovering that they were in a medical unit, was often wanting to ascertain why they were there and what damage had been done to their bodies.

"Rest, now," she said calmly.

"What happened to me?" He went to sit up again, then must have thought the better of it and closed his eyes. "Everything hurts. Please, what are my injuries?"

Aware he would fret until he knew, Alice answered with as much reassurance as possible, "You've received a shrapnel wound to the side of your head," she said. "You were lucky, it wasn't very deep. You've also been shot in your side, near your hip. Again, you should be fine." He visibly relaxed. Alice stood up. "That's enough for now. You need to get as much rest as possible. You can ask more questions in the morning."

"Thank you, Nurse," he said, calmer. He opened his eyes. and Alice saw that they were the colour of dark chocolate. A kindness emanated from them, she liked him immediately. "What's your name?" .

"I'm Nurse Le Breton," she said, smiling at him.

"You don't sound French," he murmured.

"I'm not," she said, amused that he was so inquisitive, despite being drowsy and in pain. She was intrigued that his focus had gone from worrying about his injuries to her home. "I'm from Jersey." He opened his mouth to speak again and she shook her head. "No more questions. You need your rest. Now, sleep."

He closed his eyes again and she saw him relax slightly. But as Alice began walking away a bugle call sounded and her heart plummeted. Another convoy of broken men on their way for treatment. She looked around the tent, crammed with occupied beds. How were they supposed to fit in any more wounded?

She hurried outside to wait with the others for Matron to give her orders. Ambulance, after ambulance rolled into the dusty yard. How was it possible for these poor men to keep coming in? Soon there would be none left to fight at this rate.

"Nurse Le Breton, Nurse Fielding, you take the second ambulance over by Sister Brown."

They hurried over to it, arriving as the driver opened the door. Several orderlies appeared to help carry the injured men. Alice took Sister Brown's lantern, lifting it so she could inspect the soldier's tag attached to his uniform jacket.

"Take him to Ward Two," Sister instructed the orderlies. Lowering her voice so the semi-conscious soldier couldn't hear, she added to Alice, "He needs to be away from the door, in one of the quieter beds. I'm not sure he's going to make it."

She nodded, handed Sister Brown's lantern to Mary and followed the stretcher to the ward.

The following two soldiers weren't as close to death as the first one, but both had bloody bandages around stumps on their legs.

"These men are to be taken to the Theatre Ward, as soon as possible. "The surgeon can check them and decide what he wants to do."

The final stretcher was pulled from the back of the

dusty ambulance. Alice forced a calm smile on her face when she gazed into his dirty, panic-stricken face. The bandage covering half his face was thick with layers of dressing, but still the blood was oozing through. She read his tag, but his face was the only injured part of him mentioned.

"Ward Seven?"

Sister Brown looked at her and nodded.

Of all the wards, Ward Seven was the one that Alice found the most difficult to deal with. She wasn't sure why. After all, the men who had lost limbs were going to find it difficult to integrate into the outside world, too. Somehow though, the men with damaged faces, found it harder to cope than those who'd lost limbs. Alice supposed it was because people found it hard to look in the mirror and not recognise the person staring back.

She couldn't help hoping their loved ones would put aside any misgivings about these men's new physical situation to support them. It upset all the nursing staff when they heard of a fiancée calling off an engagement after seeing the result hot shrapnel had done to their loved one's face.

The night was long and filled with the usual cries of pain, panic and horror, but Alice didn't mind being on night duty, especially after a new influx of injured came to the station. The time flew by as she moved from bed to bed, assisting the sisters, or Matron.

Just after two in the morning, Alice was finishing redressing a leg wound. She enjoyed having established recognition from Matron Bleasdale and being allowed to carry out tasks usually only permitted to be done by qualified nurses.

"Nurse Le Breton," one of the younger volunteers shouted, breathless from running to find her. "Doctor Sullivan needs you to assist in Theatre Two immediately."

Alice stood up. Ordinarily she would never pass on work to a probationer, but this was an emergency. "This is nearly done," she said handing over the bandage carefully. "You'll need to finish it for me."

Excitement coursed through Alice. Ever since joining the VADs she had dreamt of assisting during a surgery. This, though, was the first time she had been called to do so. She arrived at the theatre tent moments later, trying not to show her nervousness.

"Wash your hands in there," Matron Bleasdale instructed, removing a blood-stained apron. "Hurry, now. The surgeon needs you to relieve the current nurse, she's unwell." She left Alice to prepare.

Alice quickly scrubbed and dried her hands. Pulling her apron straps over each shoulder she crossed them, fumbling with the material as she tied them in a bow at her back, before rushing in to the theatre.

"What kept you," the surgeon barked, his black eyebrows knitted together in a frown. "I called for you long ago."

She didn't care to argue. "Sorry, Sir," she said.

Alice had noticed how strained the surgeons seemed recently. The continuing arrival of patients increased the relentless surgeries each man had to perform. Alice was exhausted, with every muscle aching, but she could only imagine how they must be feeling. If only more tents and beds could be brought to the station, as well as more surgeons and nursing staff, she thought. Surely, they would be falling ill soon themselves, if they didn't get some relief from the endless work.

"Hand me that clamp," he said indicating the instrument he wanted. He then looked down on the operating table at the soldier, his chest opened on one side. "Blast. Another, now."

Trying not to panic, Alice did as he asked. "Call another nurse to assist. We're going to need more hands here."

Alice went to leave and do as instructed.

"Bloody shout from the door. We don't have time for you to fetch people. They'll come to you."

Alice nodded and went to the opening. Pulling back the canvas flap she called for someone to help.

Matron spun on her heels, glaring at her. "Nurse Le Breton, what is the meaning of this?"

Alice hadn't seen her. "Doctor Sullivan's, instructions," she explained. "We need assistance here, now."

Matron pointed to another nurse and waved her over. Alice didn't wait to hear what was being said, but dropping the canvas returned to the operating table. She knew Matron might be a bit of a tyrant, but she was brilliant in an emergency. Seconds later, another nurse ran into the side room.

"I'm washing my hands, I'll be there in a moment," she called.

"Wadding," the surgeon bellowed, ignoring her. "Lots of it."

Alice grabbed a handful of the wadding, handing it to him.

"Hold it there." He grabbed her hand and pressed it against the boy's open wound.

She did as she was told, wondering if there was any chance the bleeding in the boy's side could be stemmed. "It's not stopping, Doctor," she said, without thinking what she was doing.

"I can see that for myself, Nurse." He continued working on the boy, concentration etched on his perspiring brow.

The patient began to convulse on the operating table and Alice held her breath. She wasn't sure what to do and almost sighed with relief when they were joined by the other nurse.

"Where the hell have you been?" the doctor growled. "Here," he said pointing for them to place their hands over the side of the open wound. "Hold him there. I need to think."

They did as he said, not daring to look at him or each other. Alice wondered if the other nurse was shaking as much as she was right now. The soldier convulsed, once again and Alice's bloodied hands slipped away from his side.

"I said hold it," the surgeon roared, grabbing Alice's wrists and pushing her hands against the torn bloody side. "Damn, this isn't doing anything."

He took her hands away and reaching inside the man's wound, groaned. "Quick, the smallest clamp."

Scrambling around on the metal tray to find the correct implement, Alice grabbed it, handing it to him. The two nurses watched in awe as the surgeon took a deep breath, visibly calmed down and closed his eyes, his two hands lost inside the bloody mess of the soldier's side as he worked.

Finally, he withdrew his hands. "Yes, that's it. We've managed to stem the bleeding."

She wasn't sure she had managed to do anything of the sort but was delighted to be included in his congratulatory delight.

"Can he be left like this?" she asked, relieved enough to forget herself.

"What? No, of course not," the surgeon, looked shocked at her ridiculous question. "I've just bought the boy time, that's all. We must clean up this mess inside him. I need to see the damage before I can close him up."

Alice couldn't see how that was possible. However, she had witnessed many miraculous actions by Doctor Sullivan, so trusted that he'd manage it somehow. She did as he instructed, giving the handsome surgeon an occasional side glance. He glowered back in concentration and she realised he was addressing her. "Sorry, Sir?"

He exhaled sharply. "Pay bloody attention. Apply the dressing, Nurse Le Breton. See to it that he is kept sedated for at least the next twelve hours. He needs fluids and must be kept still at all times. We do not need him back in surgery to stem a haemorrhage."

"Yes, Sir." Alice did as he asked. He left the theatre and

she could hear him washing in the canvas room next door.

"You lucky bugger," Mary whispered as she and Alice crossed paths later. "I heard you assisted Doctor Sullivan today." She lowered her voice further. "I think he's sweet on you."

"Hush, Mary." Alice frowned at her cheeky friend. "Don't talk nonsense."

She marched into the ward her face red with fury and embarrassment. What did Mary think she was doing, saying such things? She could start all sorts of unnecessary rumours. Alice couldn't imagine the doctor even noticed her, beyond her skills as a nurse. She was glad of it, too.

She thought of Dr Sullivan's deep voice and how she had cringed the first time she'd heard him addressing a patient. She had been shocked when he didn't use a gentler approach. But having seen his expertise achieve almost the impossible, her feelings towards him had softened over the past year. Alice smiled; she had seen the other two surgeons deal with patients at the station, and neither had the harshness of Doctor Sullivan, nor his brilliance.

They barely had time to catch up with their ministrations when Matron announced that another convoy of injured men was on its way.

"Not again," Mary groaned. "I don't know how much more of this my poor feet will take."

"Come along," Alice said, thinking of how impressed she'd been by Doctor Sullivan's dedication. "We can do this."

"Once the beds and trolleys are ready for the new intake

79

of men, I suggest you all find yourselves something to eat and have a cup of tea," Matron took a deep breath. "I have a feeling we're going to need it."

Alice and Mary returned to their ward to help move beds even closer together as more space was needed to allow further beds to be brought into the ward. Having made up the new beds and replenished the trolleys with implements, disinfectants and dressings, they went to the dining room for lunch.

"I heard one of the orderlies talking about a village — Guillemont, I think he said was the name," Mary said quietly, as they poured strong tea into their cups. "He said a battle has been raging there for the last couple of days. I think these men could be the injured from there," she said taking a sip of her steaming drink.

"I can't imagine ever sleeping without hearing men's screams in my dreams," Alice admitted rubbing her eyes. "Sometimes I wish I could stay awake all night. Then I remember that I need my sleep to do what I must each day."

Mary put down her cup and rubbed Alice's forearm. "It is relentless, but it's got to end sometime."

They stared at each other. Both reading panic in the other's eyes that they might be wrong.

Alice closed her eyes briefly, then opening them, forced a smile. "It will. You never know, maybe it'll all end sooner than we expect."

"Yes, it just might," Mary said.

Alice knew they were fooling themselves, but if they

remained positive then they were better placed to help the patients. "I wish they didn't discharge them straight back to the trenches as soon as they were well."

Mary didn't reply immediately. She drank the remainder of her tea. "I can't help wondering at the fruitlessness of it all."

"That's enough of that," Matron snapped from behind them making them both jump and Mary spill her tea. "No feeble talk from my nurses," she said. "I want you back at your ward now. The convoy will be here shortly."

They stood up and cleared their plates and cups.

Alice waited for Matron to leave the room before exhaling. "I hate being caught out like that," she said, embarrassed.

"Don't you think she feels the same as us sometimes?"

Alice looked at Mary and shrugged. "I imagine so, but the difference between her and us is that she'd never allow her feelings to show."

And neither should she, Alice decided. She was here to do a job and bleating about it wasn't going to help anyone. She needed to buck up her ideas.

Reaching the other nurses and orderlies waiting on the wooden walkway, Alice heard the bugle announcing the arrival of the ambulances. First Matron stepped forward, followed by two nurses and two orderlies. Once they had been told which ward in which to take the initial casualty, Matron checked the next man, and so on, until it was Alice's turn.

"Ward Four," she said. Alice looked down at the conscious man who winced in pain as the orderlies lifted his stretcher from the back of the ambulance. She accompanied him across the wooden boards to the ward.

"We're in here," she said, aware she was stating the obvious, but not sure what else to say until she had discovered what his injuries were exactly.

Indicating the vacant bed next to Captain Woodhall, Alice checked the tag on the man's jacket. "Corporal William Healy?"

"Yes, Nurse, that's me," he said, in a gentle southern Irish accent. He gazed around him.

He appeared to be in his mid-thirties. He was pale, thin, and, like most of the men who came here after spending months in the discomfort of the trenches, utterly exhausted.

"You have a gunshot wound to the right foot, I see," she said, waiting while the orderlies lifted him carefully from the stretcher onto the bed.

"Yes, and stings something dreadful, it does."

"I don't doubt it." She unbuttoned his dust encased jacket. "Let me help you off with this filthy uniform," she said. "Then I can wash you and help you change into your pyjamas. You'll be more comfortable then."

"Thanks, nurse," he said, gritting his teeth as she slowly worked his trousers down past his bandaged foot. He looked to his right and nodded at the captain in the next bed.

"Welcome to The Haven," the captain said, smiling up at Alice. "Most of our nurses here are angels." He lowered his voice. "Matron can be a bit of a tyrant, but I've noticed that her heart is in the right place."

Alice was relieved to see the captain had improved

dramatically since she'd last seen him. She went to speak to him, but two more injured soldiers were carried in to the large tent, diverting her attention. One was writhing in pain and Alice noticed Mary assisting a sister as she attempted to calm him. The two men next to her stopped talking, as both stared anxiously at the weeping casualty.

Alice emptied the corporal's pockets and placed a photo, wallet and letters onto the small chair by his bed that he'd be sharing with Captain Woodhall. She dropped the trousers and jacket in a heap that a probationer would take away with a mound of other dirty uniforms.

"Poor sod," the corporal said. "He was in my battalion. I wondered what had happened to him."

"He's here now," Alice said, trying to sooth their concerns. "We'll ask Sister to give him something for his pain shortly."

"There's far worse than that arriving," Captain Woodhall said quietly.

"Thank you, Captain," she shook her head. "I need to clean Corporal Healy. You can impart your survival tips afterwards."

Alice washed and partially changed the corporal into pyjamas.

"I'm going to have to change this dressing," she explained, concerned that the heat in his damaged foot indicated an infection might have set in to the gunshot wound. "If you lie back," she said taking him gently by the shoulders and pushing against the freshly plumped pillow. "Then I can have a proper look."

Taking a pair of large tweezers, Alice held her breath, nervous at what she would find. She gently pulled back the filthy dressing, relieved it didn't stick to the wound. Dropping the once white gauze into a metal bowl, she began meticulously cleaning the area with hydrogen peroxide.

"Hell, that stings," Corporal Healy grimaced, his eyes watering from the pain.

"I know, I'm sorry," she said hating having to inflict more pain on him. "I'm afraid it's necessary."

"How is it looking Nurse?" he asked, moments later.

She suspected the pain of his wound must be intense. She moved his foot to the right, hearing him wince. "Sorry, Corporal. I think the bullet exited through your foot cleanly."

"Don't you worry Nurse," he said. "You do what you must."

Alice fixed a smile on her face. She was determined not to show how saddened she was that her suspicions were right. Infection had begun to swell the damaged area on that side. "I'm going to ask Doctor Sullivan to have a look at this," she said, trying to instil positivity in him. "We need to ensure no fragments of bone are left in there that might hinder healing."

Satisfied she had done all she could for now, Alice carefully placed clean gauze on his foot and finished dressing him.

"There you go," she said returning his smile. "Try to rest. You must be exhausted after what you've been through."

Alice smoothed down her skirt. "I'll leave you now. Tea should be here shortly."

"Thanks, Nurse—"

"She's Nurse Le Breton," Captain Woodhall said, giving Alice a shy smile.

"I'll leave you two to become acquainted," she said, hoping her face wasn't as red as she suspected it might be. Alice wished the rules about becoming too close to any of the patients wasn't so absolute. She knew the captain would be discharged at some point, but she daren't risk ruining any chance she might have of training to become a fully qualified nurse after this war ended.

She helped Mary wash and change her patient who had calmed down a little after receiving a morphine injection. These new arrivals always unsettled the patients, thought Alice. It was upsetting to witness those that had found comfort in the security of the hospital, to be reminded of what they would probably return to.

She glanced over at one patient, relieved to see one of the sisters soothing him. The recent amputation of his lower leg meant he had to be kept as still as possible. The last thing they needed was for him to haemorrhage. Alice doubted most of these men would ever come to terms with what they had experienced.

"Were you at Guillemont?" she heard the captain quietly ask Corporal Healy. "I heard it was particularly bad there."

"Yes," he hesitated. "It was a nightmare. We've been there since the third of September. That's where I got this hole in my foot. Some bloody Hun caught me in the village, just as I was running for cover behind a wall."

The captain frowned. "Many men down?"

The corporal shook his head and cleared his throat, his voice cracking as he answered. "Far too many. It was a bloodbath. Men were being mown down in their droves. I wonder if, in a hundred years, anyone will remember all the Irish blokes who lost their lives there this week?"

"I think about that often," the captain admitted. "All of us cannon fodder. I can't help thinking about all the families that will never be. Will future generations commemorate what we've done, or do their best to forget us?"

Alice wondered the same thing. She had never heard the captain speaking so frankly before, but he voiced what most of them must be thinking. It was only September and the war had been dragging on for over two years now. Unable to bear seeing the endless columns of names of the missing and fallen, Alice had stopped reading the papers months ago.

"How about you?" the corporal asked Captain Woodhall. "What brought you to this place?"

He touched the bandage on his head. "Thankfully, this is more of a graze than anything," he said. "Could have been far worse." They both looked over at two men on the other side of the ward, both with thick dressings covering one side of their faces and heads. "Also, a bullet sliced through my side, near my right hip."

"I'm hoping this is a Blighty one," Corporal Healy whispered. "My wife's struggling to cope at home with the kids."

"How many have you got?"

"Six. Five boys and a little girl," he smiled, groaning as he reached to lift up a photo from his small selection of personal items. "My daughter, Kathleen's only nineteen months old."

Hearing the corporal talk about his children chilled Alice. What if he was to lose his leg to infection? She had heard about it happening too many times to count, men with families losing the ability to obtain gainful employment after losing a limb. Her concern for how these injured men and their families would survive after the war ended, kept her awake at night.

She hoped the corporal wouldn't be one of them, not with such a large family relying on his earnings. She'd speak to the surgeon as soon as she finished helping Mary. Sister Brown would be furious if she discovered Alice had over-stepped her authority, but she couldn't take a chance that his infection might be missed. If he needed surgery as soon as possible, and she was almost certain he did, she needed to speak up. She had seen how rapidly and uncontrollably infection could spread through these weakened men's systems once it took hold.

"You got any kids?" She heard the corporal ask and glanced over at the two men again.

Captain Woodhall shook his head. "No. No kids."

"Married?"

There was a hesitation before Alice heard him answer, "No. No wife, either."

Alice looked at him then and their eyes met for a few

seconds, before he turned away to answer another of the corporal's questions. Something had happened to him, she could tell. But what? Had his fiancée called off their engagement, like she had done?

Spotting Matron standing in the entrance, Alice finished redressing a wound on another patient when a particularly loud bombardment exploded nearby. Alice's heart pounded heavily and a few of the newer patients stared at her, their eyes wide with concern.

"It probably sounds closer because of the wind direction," she said, recalling how this explanation had calmed her on her arrival. "We're perfectly safe here."

She was interrupted by shouting outside the ward. Alice walked as quickly as she could to find out the cause of the commotion. Two of the orderlies were restraining a young patient in the middle of a grand mal episode on the wooden walkway. Alice returned to the ward, grabbed a blanket and pillow and went back to help. She carefully raised the patient's head and placed the pillow underneath. She didn't want him banging his head, causing himself even more damage. His contorted body finally relaxed, but the man seemed barely conscious. She covered him with a blanket to keep him warm and glanced at the closest orderly.

"We need a stretcher. We must take this man back to his bed."

She worried how the men suffering from shell shock should be nursed. Morphine and Asprin made no difference to their wellbeing when the pain was in their minds. She wished there was more they could do to aid this man and others like him. More and more seemed to be arriving at the station recently. She accompanied the soldier back to his ward and settled him in his bed.

"I'm s—sorry, nurse," he said, as Alice straightened his pillow and went to cover his chest with his blanket.

"Nothing to be sorry for," she said, giving him a gentle smile. She hoped he wasn't one of those who would have to endure the trauma of almost constant fits. "You try to sleep, if you can."

Those men suffered terribly when explosions shook the earth. How could they recuperate properly with this ever-present reminder? she wondered. She wished there was more she could do to help them cope.

"You all right, Nurse Le Breton?" The deep voice immediately alerted her to the doctor's presence. Mortified to have been caught lost in thought at such a busy time, Alice's face reddened as he walked beside her.

"Yes, I'm fine thank you, Doctor Sullivan," she said. "Please can I ask you to check one of the patients for me? It's a Corporal Healy. I think the gunshot wound in his right foot has started to become infected. I'm not sure, but I suspect he might need surgery to ensure it's properly cleaned out."

"Do you indeed?"

Alice cringed. She hadn't meant to presume to tell the doctor how to do his job. "I'm sorry," she said. "I didn't mean to overstep my position."

He shook his head. "Not at all. I'm comforted by your dedication, nurse. Just don't let Matron know you've spoken to me about this. She likes you to go via her, or at least one of the sisters with anything." He gave her a reassuring smile. "I'll look at him as soon as this has been done."

Her step faltered. "I'm sorry, what do you mean?" Had she missed something?

He lowered his voice leant his head closer to hers. "I need you to accompany me," he said striding ahead of her, before she had time to question him.

Alice ran after him, trying to keep up and not daring to ask what he wanted her for.

"In here," he said, arriving at Matron's office and opening the door for her.

What had she done wrong? Was he going to report her for speaking out to him, after all? Her heart pounded painfully. Alice tried to think of anything she might have done that she could be reprimanded about.

The doctor waited by the open door. "In you go, quickly now," he said waiting for her to enter Matron's sparsely decorated office.

"Ahh, Nurse Le Breton," Matron said, a surprised look on her face when she saw that she was accompanied by the doctor. She went to stand, but he waved for her to remain seated. "I was going to send someone to fetch you."

"I found her on my way here," Doctor Sullivan said, without looking at Alice.

She glanced from one to the other, still unable to work out why she was standing in Matron's office waiting for them to address her.

"Nurse Le Breton," Matron said, finally. "Doctor Sullivan

will be attempting a new procedure and has requested that you assist him."

Confused, Alice nodded. Usually, one or the other told her to assist, and that was it. Why the severity of their meeting now? She waited for one of them to continue.

Matron stared at Alice. "The doctor needs someone who'll keep their head. This is a dangerous operation, and hasn't been attempted before, so the outcome is unknown."

Alice was sure that most of the operations he carried out were dangerous, but simply nodded.

"I need someone who won't faint on me," Doctor Sullivan said. "I know that most of the nurses can be relied upon to act in the most professional of ways, but this procedure is a little more delicate than the ones I'm used to carrying out."

Intrigued now, Alice asked, "May I ask what it is?"

He glanced at Matron, then back at Alice. "This time it's being performed on one of your colleagues."

Alice's mouth fell open. She had thought the bombardment was a couple of miles away. Had one of the nurses been hurt? "I don't understand."

Matron leaned forward. She looked over at the closed door before focusing her attention back to Alice. "The silly girl has found herself in a delicate situation," she said taking a deep breath before continuing. "A short while ago she was discovered in one of the residential tents, having attempted a termination." She almost mouthed the last three words. "I need you to assist the doctor. Do you have any religious beliefs that will hinder your part in the operation?"

Alice couldn't believe what she was hearing. One of her colleagues was with child? "No."

"Good," Dr Sullivan said, his usually severe tone gentle. "Naturally, this must remain between the three of us, and the nurse who discovered her. It is a reportable offence to terminate a pregnancy." He sighed. "An illegal offence, but I think the girl has suffered enough, don't you?" He waited for Alice to reply.

She nodded. "Yes, I imagine she has." She was seeing a different side to both matron and the doctor and it was one that she admired. She was reassured by the knowledge that the woman in charge of them had their best interests at heart. "I understand," she said, not sure if the doctor could go higher in her estimation than he was right now.

"There's no time to lose," he said. "We'll leave here and go straight to the theatre. The nurse who found her is with her now."

Alice followed him to the door.

"Thank you, Nurse Le Breton," Matron said. "I'll ensure your duties are covered while you're in theatre."

Alice's mind raced as she followed the doctor. Who in their right mind would attempt such a dangerous thing? Becoming pregnant was shocking enough, but to be caught trying to terminate it, well, it was too much for her to contemplate.

They arrived at the theatre and the doctor held back the canvas flap for her to enter. Alice was stunned to see Mary changing the padding being used to capture some of the woman's blood.

"It won't stop, sir," Mary said, her face ashen. "I don't know what else to do."

Alice stared at the unconscious patient. She could only imagine how desperate the young nurse must have been to attempt such a terrifying procedure on herself. "She must have been frightened out of her wits," she said, shocked by Mary and Doctor Sullivan's glances when she realised she'd said the words out loud.

"We'll take over now, Nurse Jones," the doctor said. "Take a break, but remember, this must remain between us, and Matron."

"Yes, I understand," Mary said, passing Alice.

Alice wasn't surprised to see that Mary was trembling as she left the tent.

"More padding, Nurse Le Breton," he said. "I suspect that there's no alternative but to give her a full hysterectomy."

"Yes, doctor."

He examined the unconscious nurse. "As I thought," he said shaking his head sadly. "She's damaged herself badly. It's the only way we're going to have any chance to stop the haemorrhaging. We're going to lose her if I don't hurry."

She assisted with the anaesthetic. Although Alice doubted the woman would be waking during the operation, going by the amount of blood loss she'd seen in the brief time she'd been there. Enthralled by the surgeon's skill, Alice wondered if the gentleness he used during surgeries was ever allowed to show with his patients, or anyone else. She watched as he concentrated on the task in hand. Instructing her about what instrument to pass to him, and when.

Almost two hours later, he finished closing the long incision across the girl's pale stomach. Wiping the back of his hand across his brow, he closed his eyes. Alice could see he was utterly exhausted.

He pulled off his cap. "I think we'll set her up in the recovery room next door. I want a sign on the tent flap stating, 'No unauthorised entry'. We don't want rumours spread."

"What's going to happen to her?" Alice asked, her eyes pricking with tears as she gazed at the sedated nurse. "Does she have any family to take her in?"

He shook his head. "I have no idea. Matron is planning to send her on the next available boat to Blighty." Alice opened her mouth to speak. "She'll be accompanying a couple of other nurses who were wounded in a bombing raid last week. No one need know the true cause of her surgery."

Alice was relieved.

"We'll move her to the next room ourselves. I'll need you to sit with her and I'll go and inform Matron how everything has gone."

The following lunchtime, while the nursing staff were ensuring the patients ate their lunch, Alice accompanied the nurse in the ambulance to the nearest hospital. No one else had been told of the reason for her departure, apart from Mary. Alice arrived back at the station just before midnight, exhausted and drained.

She went straight to her tent, washed and slipped into her nightie. She tried to sleep, but an hour later lay wide eyed and tearful. She blew her nose, unable to shake off the experience in the theatre.

"I thought so," Mary said, pulling back the tent flap quietly and stepping inside carrying a steaming cup of tea for Alice. "I know you well." She waited for Alice to sit up and handed her the cup. "Drink that, it'll help you sleep."

Alice hoped so. She took a mouthful, spluttering when she tasted it. "That's vile," she grimaced.

"Is that all the thanks I get for trying to help you?" Mary smiled, pointing to the cup in Alice's hand. "Good brandy that is, I had some last night and it helped me."

Alice grabbed her friend's hand. "It must have been a dreadful shock finding her like that?"

"It was, but I'm trying not to think about it," Mary said as Alice sipped her drink.

"Where did you find it?" she asked taking the last mouthful and shuddering as the burning sensation from the alcohol coursed down her throat.

"Matron."

Alice's eyes widened. "Matron?"

Mary nodded. "Yes, it was her idea." She shrugged. "Who knew Matron would have a stock of brandy in her tent?"

Alice doubted there could be much left, but giving in to the warm feeling flowing through her, she was grateful for Matron's ministrations. She handed the cup back to Mary. "Put it on my trunk, will you?"

"That's right. You get some sleep. It's been rather a tricky day, in one way or another."

She closed her eyes. "I've always respected Doctor Sullivan, Mary," she said yawning. "But today I saw a different, more passionate side to him. He really is a good man, under that severe tone of his."

Chapter 6

Gemma

2018

The knocking at the front door woke Gemma with a start. It took a moment for her to gather where she was. Standing up so quickly that she gave herself a headrush, she walked over to the front door. Irritated to have been woken so abruptly, she opened the door, scowling.

"Yes?"

"You're okay," Tom said, stating the obvious Gemma thought.

"Why wouldn't I be?"

"I'm sorry, you're usually up and about much earlier than this," he explained, his hands pushed deep into his jeans' pockets. "I worried something might be wrong."

Mollified by his concern, she waved him inside. She realised she must look a fright and surreptitiously pushed her fingers through her curly hair to try and tidy it a bit. "Coffee?" she asked, stifling a yawn.

"Someone didn't get much sleep last night," Tom teased, as he glanced at the table top, where two of Alice's letters lay opened on top of their respective envelopes. "Been reading into the small hours, I see."

"Yes," she said, wishing she hadn't overslept. She hated to think what she must look like. "You're here rather early, aren't you?"

Tom shook his head. "If you call five-past-eight early, then I suppose I am."

Gemma stopped on her way to the kitchen and spun round. "Really? That late? Sorry, I thought, well, I don't know what I thought. You woke me from a deep sleep."

Tom tilted his head and pulled a face. "So, I gather, from the amount of banging on the door I had to do before you surfaced."

"Sorry, did you want coffee?" she asked, without waiting for an answer before going into the kitchen and lifting the kettle to check how much water was inside.

"Thank you, yes," he said. He walked up to the kitchen doorway. "Do you want me to go and fetch you some breakfast? Or, if you'd rather, I can treat you to some food in the village."

Gemma stopped unscrewing the lid of the coffee jar and turned to look at him. She weighed up his offers of food. "Both ideas are very welcome." She considered what she should do. "I think, no, I need to stay here and press on with everything. Can I give you some euros to buy the breakfast, then I won't feel so bad if you go for it?"

"No, it's my treat. I can be back here before that kettle finishes boiling."

She doubted it but nodded. "Thanks, Tom. You're a star."

She waited for him to leave before running upstairs to shower and brush her hair. Pulling on her dungarees over a long-sleeved tee-shirt and thin jumper, she tied her hair up in a ponytail, ready to go down and make their drinks.

The tyres on Tom's pick-up crunched over small stones alerting her to his return just as she reached the bottom step.

He walked in just as she reached the kitchen. "Shall I get the plates?" he asked, grinning at her as she spooned coffee into the mugs. Tom washed his hands before placing six pastries onto a large plate and carrying them out to the living room with two smaller plates.

The smell of freshly baked pastries, confectioner's custard and melting chocolate made Gemma's stomach grumble noisily.

"I wasn't sure what you'd like best, so bought a selection," he said. "Tuck in. There's enough for us to have some for elevenses later."

"Elevenses?" Gemma pulled the plate towards her with a wide grin on her face. "Who even says that anymore?" she asked, liking how it sounded.

"I do. Now hurry up and choose, I'm hungry, too."

She picked up a pain au chocolat and breathed in the sweet smell, taking a bite before lowering it to her plate. "Mmm, heaven."

He laughed. "My turn, now," he said placing his left

index finger against his lips and pretending to contemplate which one he should eat first.

Gemma couldn't help giggling. She thanked her lucky stars, or whatever it was that had brought her and Tom to the hardware store at the same time. "Thanks, Tom," she said before taking another mouthful.

"My pleasure," he said, his eyes twinkling as he smiled. "I always think people work better with a full stomach. A growling belly can be most distracting when you're trying to concentrate."

"I presume you're thinking about your own," she teased, aware that it had been her stomach that had been making all the noise before she had eaten something.

He took a bite from the pastry in his hand and smiled at her, the skin around his eyes crinkling in amusement.

"I like having you around?" she said, not meaning to voice her thoughts.

"Err, you do?" His smile vanished, and he stopped chewing for a couple of seconds.

She hadn't meant to take him off guard. "Yes," she said, determined to try and rectify her faux pas. "You're fun to be with."

"I am?" He thought for a few seconds and shook his head, looking rather bemused.

They ate in silence for a while, each avoiding looking at the other.

Eventually Tom broke the awkward silence. "I can picture how incredible the farmhouse and outbuildings will look, once the work is done," he said. "I was wondering what you intend doing with the field at the top of the yard? It seems a waste not to use it for something."

Gemma had been thinking the same thing only the day before. "I agree, but I can't decide what. Do you have any ideas?"

He thought for a moment, before replying. "You could lease it out to a local farmer. You'd only get a peppercorn rent, but it'd be something. Mind you," he said frowning. "It would have to be a short lease, if you're selling the place."

"I thought I could grow something there, maybe." She pictured a meadow filled with wild flowers, birds circling overhead and bees dipping from one flower to the next. "Wildflowers, if there isn't time to grow anything I could eat."

"It's a pleasant idea," he said, "but you probably won't be here to see the results."

He had a point.

They finished eating and Gemma, having checked that Tom had eaten enough, took two remaining pain au raisin to the kitchen. She put them back into the paper bag ready for them to have as a snack midway through the morning.

"What do you want to focus on today?" Tom asked, as they washed their sticky hands at the kitchen sink.

She dried her hands and pushed her feet into her boots as she dragged on her coat. Waiting for him to do the same, she tried to think what work was most urgent

They were going to the back yard through the kitchen door, when Tom said, "We've done all the basics for the house and I've checked most of the work on the outbuildings."

"I'm not sure whether to do anything with the barn," she admitted "Or the two small connecting buildings. "You know how people around here like to live. Can you tell me if you think it's worth spending money on that part of the farm?"

He looked out of the window at the area in question and thought. "If your market is to families, then I'd make one of the small buildings an office, the other could be a workshop, and," he hesitated. "You could paint the barn walls, at least. Clean up the floor so that it could be used for summer parties, birthday meals, that sort of thing."

Gemma had been thinking more about making the outbuildings into one or two small gîtes. She preferred his suggestion to keep it simple. "I like that idea," she said picturing a family with several children, their parents and grandparents, sitting on mis-matched chairs either side of a long rustic table. The table laid with an eclectic mixture of plates and glasses, with jam jars used to hold small posies of wild flowers. Adults laughing, while children nudged each other and giggled at silly jokes.

"Hello?"

She realised Tom was speaking to her. "Sorry," Gemma said shaking her head and clearing the vision from her thoughts so that she was back to the cold March morning staring at a dismal, dusty barn, old oil cans and oil stains on the cement floor covered with broken branches and leaves.

"I was in a world of my own."

"I could see that." Tom smiled at her. "Nice, was it?"

"Beautiful," she said, wistfully.

She realised for the first time that she'd moved on from her lifelong ambition to be the best nurse she was capable of being. Now, without being aware of its passing, she had a new dream. One filled with her own children, a gorgeous husband with whom she could share them, and a farm filled with rescue dogs, cats and maybe the odd alpaca or two. "It was perfect."

"Care to share it with me?"

Gemma stared at him for a moment. Tom was more than a contractor, he had become her only friend in France. "I've worked so hard with my nursing ambitions," she said. "But I don't think I can go back to that life now."

"Don't you?"

She shook her head. "Although living here hasn't exactly been the cosy home I'd one day like to own, it has shown me that I don't want to live in a city again. Not for a long time, anyway. I like living on the edge of a village."

"I can understand that," he said. "Living in a place like this you have the choice to mix with people if you feel a bit lonely, yet you can stay in, or go for a walk in the countryside if you want space."

Gemma smiled. "That's it exactly." She couldn't help wondering if this was behind Tom's reasoning for setting up his new life in France after being invalided from the Army. "I do like it here."

"You wait until spring arrives and the days become longer

and warmer. It's magical. I love being here then and wouldn't swap it for anything."

Without thinking, she glanced at his leg. Then, aware she had done so, Gemma quickly averted her eyes to the barn pretending that she was contemplating what to do with the place.

"It's alright," Tom said, touching her arm lightly making her skin tingle. "I'm used to it, I don't mind."

Assuming he meant his leg, she looked back at him. "You're so brave," she said, looking down at her feet. "I have a meltdown because of my job. Your life changes forever, but you carry on."

Tom cleared his throat. "Look at me Gemma," he said. She did as he asked, too ashamed not to. "I'm not as brave as you think. I crumbled when I first discovered what had happened to me and my friends. I was a mess. It was nurses like you who helped me come to terms with how my life needed to change."

"Not nurses like me."

"Yes, exactly like you," he argued. "They weren't repulsed by my injuries. If they were they never showed it. They did their job. They jollied me along and encouraged me to see my fiancée and family, when all I wanted to do was hide from the world."

His fiancée? She felt as if she had been punched in the stomach. "You're engaged?" she asked, not wishing to hear the answer if it was the one she was dreading.

"Not anymore," he said, kicking a stone lightly with his foot.

"Why not?" Gemma asked, immediately aware how rude and intrusive her question must have sounded. "Sorry, I didn't mean that to come out the way it did."

He shrugged. "No, it's fine. Amber called it off about five months after I'd been injured."

Gemma was furious on his behalf. "How could she do such a dreadful thing?"

He shook his head and began walking towards the barn. "No, it wasn't her fault."

"Well, it wasn't yours," she retaliated, following him.

Tom stopped and turned to face her. "You don't understand. I was different back then."

"That's hardly surprising," she said, wondering why he was determined to defend someone who had let him down at the worst time in his life. "You had a lot to contend with. The least she could do is support you through it."

Tom rubbed his eyes. "Really, she did try."

Gemma watched his face, saddened by how difficult it was for him. Still, she didn't think there was any excuse for his ex to leave him just when he must have felt he had lost everything else that mattered. "Not hard enough, in my opinion."

Tom glared at her. "You don't know her, Gemma. You didn't know me, back then. Amber is a good person." A shadow of sadness crossed his face as he hesitated. "I know she loved me."

"I'm sure she did." Who wouldn't, she thought, wishing she had been the one to care for him back then.

He frowned briefly. "I didn't feel that I could be the

person she wanted anymore. If I'm honest, I think I wanted her to leave me."

"Why?" she asked, aware of his answer as soon as her question had crossed her lips.

He shrugged. "It was difficult enough coming to terms with how much I'd changed physically, without feeling guilty about my part in her dreams vanishing. It wasn't fair to let her stay with me, she deserved more." He turned away from her.

Stung by his defensiveness of his ex, Gemma had to concentrate on not letting her emotions run away with her. He always came across as being capable and strong, but the Tom she was seeing now seemed vulnerable. She wanted to hug him, not fight with him. Not caring if she was being inappropriate, Gemma stepped forward and standing behind him, flung her arms around him. He stiffened, but she didn't let go.

"I'm sorry," she said. "I didn't mean to upset you. I just hate to think of you being alone at such a dreadful time."

She felt his body relax. Slowly he turned. Slipping his arms around her, he reciprocated her hug. "It's fine," he said, his voice soothing. "I know you were only trying to be a friend. Amber is a good person though. I can't hold it against her that she made a brave choice for both of us. I see that now."

Friend. Gemma's heart sank. She breathed in his freshly laundered sweatshirt and the soapy scent of his neck. It dawned on her that she would prefer him to be rather more than just a friend.

"Gemma," Tom whispered into her hair. "I appreciate your concern, but I really should be getting on with my work. I have another job I need to go to by the end of the week."

Shocked to still be hugging him, Gemma let her arms drop away from him. "What job? You didn't say?"

He smiled at her. "I didn't know until this morning. It's for the client who was away," he said. "The one I put off to come here and help you with your urgent work. Remember?"

She did. Trying not to show how disappointed she was, Gemma pushed up the sleeves of her jacket. "Oh, right. Sorry," she said hoping she didn't sound as desperate as she felt. It was time to be brave, like Amber had been. She needed to stop relying on Tom so much. "Yes, I understand."

She tried and failed to resist adding, "Will you be back soon?"

"I'll be about two months on that job, but by then you should be ready for me to begin working on any decorating here."

Two months? She pushed away her panic. "That's fine," she lied, determined not to let him see how upset she was. "It'll give me time to work out a plan for this place. I need to source a few things, like bookshelves for the office space, that sort of thing."

"Exactly." He smiled at her and picked up a hammer. "You'll do an amazing job."

Gemma couldn't miss the relief on his face when she reacted so well to his announcement.

"While you still have me here," Tom said, "Maybe you could think about what you want me to do," he indicated the barn area. "Or would you rather I focus on the spare room? It would take that cloying mildew smell from the upstairs of the farmhouse."

She liked that idea. "Yes, please do that first."

She left Tom to his work inside the house and went into the smaller of the two outbuildings. It was going to be lonely here without him. She decided that the time spent by herself would be a good thing. She wasn't exactly sure why that was just yet, but after flinging herself at him earlier, she realised she needed to step away from the poor man. Before she did anything even more alarming.

Chapter 7

Alice

1916

Alice checked her watch. The corporal had been in surgery for nearly an hour. Mary had warned her not to become too involved with the patients and usually this wasn't a problem, but there was something about Corporal Healy and his desperation to return home to his family that appealed to her.

"We do the best we can," Alice recalled her saying the previous evening in their tent. "We don't have the strength to cope with being upset each time one of them might not make it."

She knew Mary was right. For some reason though the thought of the corporal losing a leg due to an infection that she was responsible for looking after disturbed her. Maybe it was the thought of his baby daughter, Kathleen or his other children reliant on him back home, but Alice wasn't certain why it mattered to her so much.

"I just wish the amputees didn't have to face such uncertainty when they return home," she said. "There'll be many men returning to Great Britain when this is over, and I've read they're employing women over these limbless ex-soldiers. It's worrying, that's all."

Mary sympathised, but Alice couldn't shake her concerns. She helped settle one of the new patients who had woken abruptly from a sedative induced sleep and was about to take a tea break when she heard Dr Sullivan's voice outside the ward. Alice went to find him and once he'd finished speaking to one of the orderlies, she followed him to his office.

"Sorry, Doctor Sullivan?" she said, knocking lightly on the doorpost.

He turned to her and Alice noticed his pale pallor and the dark shadows under his eyes. She wondered how long it had been since he had taken any leave.

"Nurse Le Breton," he frowned, thoughtfully. "Ahh, I imagine you wish to know about your corporal's operation?"

Taken aback by him referring to Corporal Healy as 'her' corporal, Alice scowled at him. "I'd like to enquire about the success of his procedure, yes," she said, aware how officious she sounded, so added, "It's just that he has five young children and a wife to support, and I—"

"I'm of the opinion that your conscientiousness bringing his situation to my attention has probably resulted in the infection being stemmed before it took hold." He rubbed his eyes. "At least, that's what I hope to be the case." His expression softened. "You did well, Nurse Le Breton." He stared at her silently.

Alice was unsure if he was waiting for her to thank him for this information. She opened her mouth to speak, but he turned to reach for a book on his untidy bookcase.

"I'd catch up on some sleep before the next onslaught arrives this afternoon, if I were you."

"Yes, of course. Thank you, doctor," she said, hating the feeling of being dismissed. He seemed more distant than the other day, she thought.

He raised his hand in the air in a wave to her without looking back.

Alice kept a close eye on the corporal's foot, relieved each day to note that it was healing well, and any indication of infection had not returned. Doctor Sullivan had done a perfect job, once again.

"A letter from your family?" she asked finding him reading a missive one morning. "I hope they're all keeping well."

She was cheered to see that he appeared to be in good spirits today. He seemed to be well on his way to good health and had made a huge improvement over the past three weeks. Alice liked the corporal and enjoyed chatting to him about his adored family. She hoped that one day she would be lucky enough to be married to an equally besotted husband.

"You're looking a little peaky, Nurse Le Breton," he said. "I hope you don't mind me saying so."

She shook her head. "Not at all. A bad night's sleep, nothing more.

She had planned to catch up on her letter writing during her three-hour break earlier, but she'd fallen asleep instead, waking only moments before her shift was about to begin. She knew she needed to buck up if she didn't want Matron coming to the same conclusion as the corporal.

"They're well, thank you Nurse," he said, holding up a photograph. "Here's a picture of my brood," he said proudly, pointing out his daughter and four small sons. "That's my Katherine. She's praying for my return home, so that she can look after me."

Alice sighed happily. "I can imagine they're missing you terribly," she said. "They'll be relieved to have you home and be able to spend time with you, I shouldn't wonder."

"They will. She writes that the baby is walking now," he beamed proudly. "No doubt she'll be into everything. Troublesome little angel."

"Your wife will be rushed off her feet."

"She will, nurse, that she will." He went back to studying his photograph and Alice turned her attention to Captain Woodhall.

"Good evening, Captain," she said, pulling a screen around his bed. "Do you need me to plump up your pillows for you?"

"You can remove one pillow and help the captain lie flat, Nurse Le Breton," Sister Brown snapped behind her. "I need to examine his hip."

Alice hadn't heard Sister's footsteps behind her and she

immediately did as she was asked, not daring to return the captain's half smile.

"Pull a screen around the captain's bed, Nurse."

Again, Alice did as Sister Brown ordered, standing silently at the end of the bed.

"I changed the captain's dressing earlier, Sister," she said. "I doubt it needs to be looked at again so soon."

The sister hesitated for a moment. "I'll be the judge of that, Volunteer Nurse Le Breton," she said putting Alice firmly in her place. Alice watched as sister folded back the blanket and sheet to expose his pelvic area. Then undoing his pyjama bottoms, she focused on removing the old dressing. Alice took the used dressing from sister and dropped it onto the trolley next to her, relieved to note the lack of infection.

Sister Brown was unfriendly at the best of times, but Alice knew that losing two men from her ward earlier in the day, both with minor original wounds, would bring out the worst in her. As had happened many times since Alice's arrival, both injuries had become infected from the men lying on filthy soil. There was nothing that could be done about the fetid earth around the trenches, secreted with rotting flesh and blood. All the medical knowledge the staff possessed, could not save some of the men when their injuries became infected.

Alice watched as the captain was examined. She forgot to focus on what the sister was doing and looked up at the captain's face, only to see him staring at her. Alice immediately looked away, but unable to help herself glanced back at him. The captain gave her a reassuring smile and Alice smiled back, soothed by his comforting gesture. She wondered if maybe his experience looking out for his men was what made him want to reassure others at such an awkward moment.

"Nurse Le Breton," Sister Brown hissed through her gapped teeth as she slowly retied the captain's pyjama bottoms and covered him. "Help me with the pillow."

Alice took a moment to react.

"Now, Nurse."

She stepped forward. When the sister helped the captain to sit up, Alice quickly arranged his pillows to allow the older woman to carefully lower him against them.

"Remove the screen," she said, her voice low, but threatening. "Then follow me."

Alice did as she instructed, but her hands were shaking and her heart pounding. She was unsure whether it was more from her acute embarrassment, or from fright at what Sister was about to say.

"Thank you, Nurse Le Breton," Captain Woodhall said, adding, "If you need me to vouch that you weren't acting in any way that could be considered inappropriate, please, do ask."

"Thank you," she whispered, not daring to catch his eye again. "I'd better go."

She looked over to where Sister Brown was waiting by the ward entrance.

Groaning inwardly, Alice braced herself. "You wanted to speak to me, Sister?"

"Follow me."

Alice walked behind the sister, irritation at her behaviour building up inside her.

A few steps away from the entrance, Sister Brown rounded on Alice. "You are a voluntary nurse. You are not a formerly trained nurse and I doubt you ever will be."

Confused, Alice retorted. "I wasn't correcting you about anything medical," she said, doing her best to remain calm. "I was merely trying to reassure you so that you didn't waste your time reapplying a new dressing."

Sister Brown took a step closer to Alice. She couldn't escape the sour stench of the woman's breath and had to concentrate on not flinching or moving backwards.

"You need to remember your place here, Nurse Le Breton," she spat. "You might be used to people kowtowing to your every need at home, but you're here to do a job of work."

Alice held back from answering, not wishing to infuriate the woman further. She was desperate to take in a deep breath of fresh air and alleviate the taste of the woman's foul breath.

"Do you understand me?"

"Yes, Sister Brown."

"I will be watching you, and don't you forget it," the sister said. "Now, carry on with your work. If you are insubordinate one more time, mark me, I'll report you."

Alice didn't doubt it for a moment. "Yes, Sister," she said, turning and inhaling deeply as she returned to the ward.

"She didn't give you too much of a blasting, I hope," the captain said as she passed his bed.

Alice looked over her shoulder to the doorway to check the sister had not followed her inside, before stopping. "No."

"I'm sorry for causing you trouble. It was unintended."

"It's not your fault." Changing the subject, Alice said, "You're making good progress, Captain, that's the most important thing."

"I am," he said. "It's a relief. Of sorts."

"It is."

"I'll soon be out of here and fit enough to take you dancing."

Alice laughed, shocked by his forwardness. Not wishing to be caught having an inappropriate conversation with a patient, she bent as if to pull his immaculate blanket straight. "Is that right?"

"Why, are you rebuffing my invitation?" he teased.

She couldn't hide her amusement at his cheekiness. Enjoying their banter, she asked, "Do you dance well?" She was aware she was not nearly as good as she should be after all the dancing lessons her mother had insisted on her taking over the years to help make her a good catch for a prospective husband.

"I like to think so. You?"

She shrugged. "Fair, but I'm no expert by any means."

She hadn't noticed his hand moving closer to hers, so when the tips of his fingers grazed the side of her hand, Alice flinched.

"Sorry, I shouldn't have done that," he said, mistaking her reaction.

Alice didn't want him to feel guilty. She shook her head. "It's fine. I hadn't expected it, that's all."

Smiling once again, he said. "By your lack of refusal, Nurse Le Breton, am I to take it that you will agree to escort me to a dance one of these days?"

She was the one to be surprised now. She opened her mouth to put him in his place, while hiding her amusement. Alice realised by the twinkling in his brown eyes, the exact colour of her favourite Fry's chocolate, that he was teasing her.

"No, I'm your nurse and forbidden to fraternise with a patient." She stood up straightening her shoulders. "Now behave yourself, Captain, or I'll ask Sister to come back."

He reached out and took her hand. This time Alice didn't pull back.

"One of these days, whether you like it or not, I'm going to thank you for all you've done for me."

"Will you?" she asked encouraged by their rapport.

"Yes. I'll take you out to tea first, and then we can go dancing."

Alice tilted her head. "There's a war on, Captain. Or hadn't you noticed?"

"There is, and maybe I won't be able to take you dancing for a while yet. I have, however heard of others taking tea in one of the hotels in the village. I don't see why we can't do the same," he smiled, his brown eyes twinkling in mischievousness. "That is, if you wish to." He cleared his throat. "What do you say, then Nurse?"

Alice straightened up. Her back ached from

the excessively long hours bending over beds, changing dressings and nursing the men. How could she ever complain how she felt after what these men had suffered in the trenches, and continued to cope with now?

"About what?" she asked absentmindedly.

"Coming out for tea with me."

Alice gazed at the handsome captain and wished they'd met under different circumstances. She liked him, she couldn't help herself.

For once there was no laughter in his eyes, just gentle affection. "Nurse Le Breton," he said quietly, distracting Alice from her concentration.

"I'd love to, Captain" she said honestly. "But it's not allowed." She lowered her voice further. "If it was discovered that I was out with you, I'd be sent home."

"But that's ridiculous."

She agreed. "It's the regulations, and I have to abide by them."

"Naturally," he said. "Then we'll have to think of something else, won't we?"

For once, Alice noticed a chink in his confidence. "Here, let me help you get comfortable."

She helped him sit and plumped up his pillows, lowering him back. Alice caught his eye, once more. There was something appealing about him and she couldn't help feeling an attraction, but she wasn't going to allow herself to become involved with one of her patients. She'd worked too hard to come to France in the first place. Where else would she go if she was sent from here? The thought of returning to her parent's home and her mother's constant attempts to marry her off, was not something she relished.

She liked Captain Woodhall, very much though. And if they were very careful, surely no one would discover they had stepped out together. If their circumstances were different, she wouldn't hesitate to accept his invitation.

"Yes," she said, a little startled by her acquiescence. "We will."

She didn't know who was more surprised by her acceptance of his offer, her, or the captain.

His mouth pulled back into a wide smile and his chocolate brown eyes showed his delight. "I can't quite believe my ears, Nurse Le Breton," he said, pulling up his sheet, as she folded away the screen. "But I won't push my luck. I don't want to give you the chance to change your mind."

"You have to get well enough to leave here first." She hoped her offer would be encouragement enough for him to do his best to behave. "Although you're healing very well, so it shouldn't be too long now."

The thought of him leaving saddened her. More than she had expected it to. Alice happily devoted her time to all her patients, but for some reason there were men who tugged at her heart. The corporal was one and Captain Woodhall another. Both for completely different reasons. She wondered if she would ever see either man after they were discharged.

"My name is Edgar," he said. "Ed. May I know your first name, Nurse Le Breton?"

She looked around to check no other medical staff were

in ear shot. "I shouldn't say, really," she said. "But it's Alice." Her whisper was barely audible.

"Alice," he murmured, smiling up at her. "Thank you. That's a beautiful name."

"I must press on now," she said, wishing she hadn't given in and been unprofessional enough to tell him. If Sister Brown ever got wind of what she'd done, Alice knew she'd be in serious trouble.

He had indeed made progress though and that was what she'd focus on. Alice felt a pang to the pit of her stomach. She wanted him to get better. However, it would mean that the time was drawing near when he'd be given the all clear to return to the Front. She hated the thought of him being sent back.

She'd rather the captain return to a sweetheart, or even a wife, than go back to the hell of the trenches. She found it hard to bear the thought of him being sent to be used as a target, once again. Alice yawned and looked at her watch. Only half an hour until her shift ended and she could barely wait. She needed to be alone to close her eyes and think a bit more about Ed. She had agreed to go out with him. What was she thinking?

She was finishing tidying up the nurses' station at the back of the ward, when the sound of a plane's engine disturbed her. Alice was used to hearing bombardments, even the ground trembling beneath her feet, but planes didn't often come overhead like this one sounded as if it was about to do.

She noticed Edgar signalling her over to him. She reached

the side of his bed when an ear-perforating bomb exploded nearby, shaking the ground. Pots in the ward rattled, men cried out. Then silence for a split second before a second bomb crashed through one of the closer huts.

"Take cover," Doctor Sullivan bellowed from the walkway to anyone listening.

Alice wasn't sure where to go. Hearing the scream of a third bomb as it descended towards them and unsure what else to do, she determined to protect at least one of the patients. Captain Woodhall was closest to her, so she threw herself across his upper body, shielding him with her own.

Instinctively, he grabbed hold of her, turning, so that Alice's body was half under his torso. Stunned by his actions, she held her breath, waiting for the inevitable explosion.

A white flash then an ear-splitting thud. Splinters of wood flew from the tent poles like bullets. Fragments of the exploding bomb hit pots, sending jugs and phials crashing from shelves and tipping trolleys over their contents smashing onto the floor.

Seconds passed. Captain Woodhall tensed, the heat from his chest and arms filtered through Alice's uniform, forming a comfort blanket around her, as she gathered her wits. The world around them appeared to have stopped.

"Are you all right?" he whispered moments later, his voice shaken.

Alice breathed in his warm soapy smell, relishing the few seconds she was in his arms, the pressure of his body on hers. She felt safe lying under him. Screams diverted her attention back to her surroundings. She took a deep breath and pushed him gently away. Standing up, she smoothed the skirt of her uniform and straightened her apron.

"Yes, thank you Captain," she assured him, as she straightened her cap. "I'm fine. You are unhurt, I hope?"

"Only a little scratch, I believe," he said.

Their eyes locked. Alice struggled to tear herself away from his gaze.

"Let me have a look", she said forcing herself to focus.

He shook his head. "I'm sure it's fine. Please, go and see to the other patients."

"If you insist," she said, hurrying away, not looking back.

She scanned the ward looking from one patient to the other. They seemed unharmed, which was nothing short of a miracle, she thought with relief.

She calmed one of the younger patients, who was trembling violently in a corner bed.

"You're safe, now Lieutenant," she said, smiling at him and straightening his sheets. "Please try to relax a little."

Happy that none of the patients seemed badly injured, she tidied up the obvious damage and then ran outside to see what she could do to help.

Doctors, orderlies and nurses were carrying beds out of the next ward. Doctor Sullivan pointed over to the lawn area in front of Ward 3 where Alice had just been. "Line the beds up there and we'll take stock of the situation."

Seeing flames rising along the side of the next ward, Alice followed the others inside to rescue more patients. Two men hobbled out, each with an arm over the other's shoulders. She manoeuvred passed them to see what she could do to help. Noticing that the orderlies were busy carrying beds with patients still inside, she noticed the flames closing in on a part of the canvas wall where an unconscious patient lay.

Seeing one of the younger volunteer nurses standing doing nothing, Alice shouted at her. "Come here, quickly," she said, waving her over. "This way." The nurse followed Alice in to the depths of the ward. "This bed over here. We have to move it, before the flames reach him." She saw two more patients, struggling to move. "Do your best to get out," she said. "There will be others to come and help soon."

They each took one end of the bed between them. Alice would have preferred to carry the patient out on a stretcher – the combination of the unconscious man and the metal bed was heavy – but with adrenaline pumping through her body, Alice managed to lift her end. But they had only walked a few steps before they had had to put the bed down.

"It's no use," the younger nurse cried. "It's too heavy."

Doctor Sullivan ran over to them. "You two take that end," he shouted, looking to his left. "Quickly, the fire is taking hold."

They did as he said and with his help were soon able to reach the outside. As they continued carrying the bed to where the others had been placed, he called out to several orderlies. "Inside, quickly, more men need help."

Alice left the bed and followed the doctor and orderlies inside. Assisting one of the last patients out of the burning ward, she helped him sit on the edge of the wooden walkway where there was space.

"Wait here," she said. "Someone will soon settle you in one of the other wards," she said before running back to help in the damaged ward.

"All out, Nurse," the doctor said coming out to join her, his face streaked with soot. "You did an excellent job in there."

It was high praise indeed and after her telling off from Sister Brown earlier, Alice could not help feeling a little better having received it.

"You're all right?" he asked.

Grateful for his concern, she nodded. "You?"

Doctor Sullivan smiled. "Don't you worry about me," he said. "I'm fine."

She looked around, realising she hadn't seen Mary since the bombing raid. Praying silently, she hoped her friend was safe.

"Here, help me," an orderly shouted, waving Alice to go with him. Realising that he wanted her to go into the nurses' station at the back of the ward closest to the fire, Alice followed reluctantly "What are we doing here?" she shouted above the noise of exploding bottles and burning canvas. He didn't answer. Alice wasn't sure whether to keep going. Nervously, she looked around to see if anyone else was near them. She lost sight of Peter as he crouched down behind a desk. What was he doing, she wondered? Alice stepped closer with trepidation, gasping when she spotted Helen, one of the other VADs, unconscious on the floor bleeding from her head.

"I saw her come in here, but not leave," he explained. "She's bleeding heavily. We need to stop it if we can."

Alice could see blood pooling around Helen's head. Lifting her head carefully, she assumed the volunteer must have been lying there since the bomb landed. Alice looked around for dressings on the bare shelves. "There," she said, indicating a pile on the floor. "Bring me those, quick as you can."

As she knelt, her arm began to feel hot as the ferocity of the fire increased. She looked up to see it was moving rapidly towards them. Alice quickly took the dressing from the orderly's hand.

"Unwrap the bandage," she said, pressing the dressing against Helen's blood-soaked blonde head. "Right, now pass it to me." She carefully wove the bandage around the girl's head, securing it with a pin.

The orderly yelled, leaping back from her as pieces of burning canvas began to break away from the tent roof and land near them. "We have to go. Now," he shouted. "Move away from her. I'll carry her outside."

Alice stood carefully, holding Helen's head between her hands to keep it as still as possible, as the orderly lifted her. "Right, let's go," she said.

They stepped carefully over fallen packets and instruments, both sighing with relief as they made it to the outside. Alice wished Helen would regain consciousness.

"I think we should take her to find a spare bed. She can't be left outside in this condition."

"Take her to my office," Matron Bleasdale said from

nearby. "I'll get one of the other orderlies to bring a bed through for you to make up for her. I'll ask one of the doctors to come and examine her."

Alice nodded and accompanied Peter into Matron's office, passing shocked patients and medical staff busily settling them, as they worked to regain a semblance of order.

She realised for the first time how close to danger she had come. Alice focused on keeping Helen's bloodied head still as a bed was brought in for them to lie her on opposite Matron's desk. She settled her colleague down and covered her with a blanket. Alice could not help wondering whether any of them would manage to witness the ending of the war. How many of us will have the chance to return to a normal life back at home? She wondered?

Chapter 8

Gemma

2018

It took Gemma a few days to get used to having no one to talk to. She didn't mind her own company; for most of her life she had enjoyed a solitary existence. But she was missing Tom. She'd become used to hearing him singing as he worked and eating lunch with him. She even missed their companionable silences, as she sneaked glances at his muscular torso when he was concentrating on something.

She leant against her front door frame, sweater sleeves pushed up to her elbows despite the dreary day outside and her coffee in hand as she stared out at the messy front garden. Tom would be back, and she should use this time putting her issues with her ex into perspective. He might not have been the person she believed him to be, but how could you resent someone who was dead? It was pointless.

She had only known Tom a few weeks, and despite him being closed off about his past, she still felt like she didn't have to be the guarded person she usually was. Feeling comfortable enough to open up to someone was a new experience. She even held back with her parents, having learnt from an early age that they were more interested in their careers than their "ruddy great surprise".

She had seven weeks before Tom returned and she'd planned to do as much painting of the inside of the house as she could in that time. Before she knew it, April would be here, and Tom would be back.

So far Gemma was relieved to have decorated her bedroom and started work on the spare room. She had been so tired at the end of the day that she had not given any time or thought to Alice's letters. After a week decorating, Gemma was beginning to think that she was losing the power of speech. It was time to put on clothes other than her paint covered dungarees and go into the village for some shopping.

Washed and changed, Gemma walked along the peaceful road. It amused her to think that only a year ago, socialising to her had meant joining in the occasional get-together with her workmates at a bar. She even managed a meal with them when she couldn't think of a plausible reason to excuse herself. How surprised they would be now to discover her here, she mused. Then again, maybe they would think it perfectly understandable that she had ended up alone renovating an empty farmhouse.

"Bonjour," she said, walking into the small café opposite the market. "Un café au lait, et une tarte à la crème," she said relishing the thought of eating one of Marie's delicious custard tarts that Tom had introduced her to a couple of weeks before.

Gemma paid Marie and noticing two ladies getting up from a window table, went and sat down. She looked forward to the weather warming up enough to be able to sit outside. Watching people going about their business in the village was something Gemma had enjoyed on the brief occasions she had had the chance to do it. Maybe she could invite some of the villagers for a few drinks and nibbles, once the house was renovated? The idea appealed to her.

For now, though, she had to press on with the decoration work. She had to remember the reason she had come here in the first place.

Marie brought over her drink and a plate and small fork with the appealing looking tart.

"Merci," Gemma said, lifting the plate to breathe in the sweet, creamy smell. She realised that Marie was waiting for her to taste the confection and picking up her fork, dug it slowly into the creaminess, before popping a piece into her mouth. Gemma closed her eyes as the gentle vanilla taste filled her mouth. Swallowing, she smiled. "Délicieux."

"Bien," Marie said, resting her hand lightly on Gemma's right shoulder for a second before returning to serve the next customer.

Gemma wasn't used to cafés having such a personal touch. She presumed it was this extra dedication that was behind the cakes being so exquisite. She finished eating her food and sat quietly drinking her coffee, noticing for the first time a sticker on the window advertising free WiFi.

Gemma withdrew her phone from her coat pocket. Maybe it was time to check on the outside world, just for a moment, or two. She pressed on her mobile and connected to the internet. Immediately emails, Facebook notifications and missed calls alerts pinged up on her phone. The other customers turned to see who was disturbing their morning's coffee, so she hurriedly switched her phone to silent.

"Pardon," she said, hoping to placate them and Marie.

Her father had sent two emails.

Just a quick email to see if the work is coming along to schedule. What schedule was that, Gemma wondered, reading on. *I've decided that, if possible, I'd like to put the farm on the market sometime in May.*

May? Impossible, thought Gemma, upset at the thought of the project, and her association with Tom, ending that soon. She closed his email and opened the following one from him.

Hope you're coping and not finding it all too difficult over there. Dad

"Very matter of fact, as usual, Dad," she murmured, quickly typing a reply.

Hi Dad, I still haven't had a chance to change my phone to a French sim card and I don't want to run up huge roaming charges. I'm fine and the renovations are coming along well. I have contracted a reliable decorator and am enjoying the work. A May deadline is impossible, suggest July, maybe August. Please give my love to Mum, I hope you're both well and not working too hard, Gemma. x

There, she thought, hoping he would leave her to know

best when the right time would be to put the farm on the market.

Gemma doubted her father would reply any time soon, so hurriedly switched off her mobile and dropped it into her coat pocket feeling free, once again.

"Good, that's done," she said, picking up her cup to finish her tepid coffee.

Gemma stood up to leave, giving Marie a smile and a wave before leaving the café. Her next stop was the hardware store.

"Bonjour, Marcel," she said pointing to the paint section. "Deux—" she couldn't think of the word for pots, but he appeared to understand what she meant. Picking up two five litre pots of white paint, Gemma placed them on the counter to pay for them.

She was pushing the change into her pocket when the brass bell jangled on the shop door alerting them to the arrival of another customer.

"Gemma," Tom cheered. "Good to see you." He walked over to her and nodded a hello to Marcel. "I dropped by the farm, but you were out. Now, I know why," he smiled.

"Hi, Tom," Gemma said, surprised at how fiercely her heart was pounding to see him so unexpectedly. "I thought you still have several more weeks to go at your current situation?"

"I do," he said, raking his hair through his sun kissed shorter hair. "But I needed to make an urgent call to another client. She lives nearby, so I thought I'd pop in and see how you were getting on."

Gemma couldn't help smiling. It was good to know he

had thought of her. "Well, I'm glad you caught me here." She looked pointedly at his hair. "Someone's had a haircut, I see. Suits you."

"Thanks. I was sick of my mother nagging me to get it tidied up. Now it's been done I can see what she means," he laughed. "It was a mess before."

"It was a little," she teased, enjoying the easy rapport with him and realising how much she'd missed him. "This shorter style suits you."

"Enough about my hair," he laughed. "If you've finished here, I can give you a lift back."

Gemma winced. "I'd love a lift, those things are heavy," she admitted. "But I still have to do food shopping. I've pretty much run out of things to eat and drink."

He feigned horror. "Can't have that happening," he said. "I'll take these to the pick-up, it's only parked in front of the boulangerie, and I'll wait for you there."

"If you're sure? That'll be wonderful."

She thanked Marcel and hurried off to the small super-marché. Grabbing a packet of chocolate digestives, she knew Tom enjoyed, she added them to the other items in her basket and went to the counter.

Joining him minutes later, Gemma got into the pick-up and closed the door.

"That was quick," Tom said, taking her shopping bag and lifting it over their seats to place in the back of the truck. "It's good to see you again, Gemma," he said.

"Thank you, it was a lovely surprise to see you at Marcel's, too."

They drove back to the farmhouse, catching up on the small amount of decorating Gemma had done.

"Marcel was telling me about the field at your farm earlier." Tom said, changing gear. "Apparently in the summer the field is filled with poppies."

"I've read about fields of poppies, like from those First World War poems, but I've never seen one," she said.

"I've seen a few," he said. "Marcel said that if you sit at the top of the field and look down across the poppies as the ground slants downward, it looks like a sea of scarlet."

Gemma visualised the scene. "That sounds incredible. I can't wait to experience it."

"It does sound amazing, doesn't it?" He slowed down and indicated to turn into the farm entrance.

"I stopped off at Marie's café," she said, wanting him to know that she was trying to cultivate a few friendships with the locals. "I practically breathed in one of those custardy cream tarts you bought the other week."

"I don't blame you, they're delicious."

She nodded. "I also noticed she had free WiFi. I've enjoyed being disconnected with my old life while I've been here but was beginning to feel a bit guilty. So, I dared to turn on my phone."

"Everything okay at home?"

"Seems so," she didn't add that her father had plans to sell the farm so soon. "How are things going on at your current job?"

"Fine," he said, turning into the farmhouse driveway. "I'd rather be working here though."

"You'll soon be back," she said to cover her delight at his words. "Come inside. I'll make us coffee and show you my handiwork."

Tom followed her to the kitchen leaning against the counter as she put on the kettle.

"Right," said Gemma, pushing the plate of biscuits towards him. "Let's enjoy some of these, shall we?"

They drank their coffee and made small talk about the village and the shops, and when they had finished, Gemma stood up.

"Come along, then," she said leading the way upstairs. She showed him into her freshly painted bedroom. "What do you think?" She stepped back to let Tom see her work.

"It looks great," Tom said. "The floorboards okay?" he asked. "No further problems with that window?"

"All fine, thanks."

"You're doing a grand job in here," Tom said. "I look forward to being back here."

"So do I," she said, without meaning to say it out loud.

Chapter 9

Alice

October 1916

Alice walked into the ward to see Mary administering to the captain. Worried something must be wrong, she hurried over to check.

He was lying on his front grimacing, as Mary dabbed antiseptic soaked cotton wool gently onto an inflamed area. "A piece of shrapnel is embedded his buttock," she said looking concerned.

Alice bent to take a closer look and saw that the area needed urgent attention. "You said you weren't hurt," she said, angry at him for lying to her. "Why would you lie about that?"

"I preferred the idea of one of the other nurses dressing my backside, Nurse le Breton," he said without looking at her.

Alice studied Ed's firm buttocks.

"I'll see to the captain," Mary said, waving her away. "You take a break. You look like you need one."

Disgruntled at Ed's dismissal of her, Alice did as Mary suggested and went to leave, almost being knocked over by Doctor Sullivan on his way in to the ward. He grabbed hold of her to steady her. "Apologies, Nurse Le Breton," he said. "I trust you're unhurt."

"I am," she said, smiling to reassure him. "However, I believe Captain Woodhall might be in need of your attention."

"The captain is the reason I find myself here," he said, leaving her standing, stunned.

She watched him go to Ed's bed and check him. Not wishing to miss his diagnosis, Alice made herself busy tidying the beds of nearby patients. She smiled at each, but didn't engage in conversation, all the time trying to hear what the doctor was saying.

One of the sisters called her over to the other side of the ward. "Fetch clean sheets for this patient's bed, Nurse," she said. Anxious for Ed, but not daring to ignore an order, she nodded, leaving immediately to do as she had been asked. Maybe if she was quick, she'd be back at the ward in time to find out whether Ed's injury was badly infected, Alice thought hopefully.

She selected the bedding she needed from the store room and was on her way back when Matron gave her a message to give to one of the other sisters. Finally, after a slight delay, she arrived back at the ward. Alice went to the patient's bed needing to be changed. Glancing over at Ed's bed when sister's attention was diverted, she noticed he was no longer there.

Trying not to fret, she finished what she was doing and asked Sister if she could take a break. Sister checked her watch, seemingly taking an age to do so. "Yes, you may."

Alice walked out of the hut and went towards the theatre tents. Spotting Mary coming in her direction, she ran over to her. "How is he? Are they operating on him?"

Mary put her finger up to her mouth. "Shush, calm down." She frowned at Alice. "What's wrong with you today?"

Not in the mood for a lecture, Alice, took hold of her friend's hand. "Will you just tell me?"

"The captain's being operated on now."

"He is?" She covered her mouth, taking a deep breath attempting to regain her composure.

"I've never seen you like this about any of the patients," Mary said. "You're ashen." They walked together for a little longer.

Alice had never felt so deeply for any man, let alone a patient, and she admitted her feelings to her friend. "I don't know what's come over me."

Mary stopped her and smiled. "Do you think you could be falling in love with the captain?"

Alice glared at her and continued on her way. She regretted saying anything to Mary, if she was going to begin questioning her. "Don't be ridiculous, Mary. I'm probably tired, that's all," she insisted. But as she said the words she suspected it was not the case. There was something about the man that connected deep within her. It was a new, and not altogether joyful experience.

They spent their break in companionable silence, returning to the ward straight afterwards.

Sister Brown spotted them. "Nurse Jones, come with me," she said. Alice wondered if the woman ever smiled. "Nurse Le Breton," she added. "You are to go to the recovery tent. Doctor Sullivan wants you to sit with a patient who has just had surgery."

Trying not to show her relief, Alice immediately left the ward. She had to concentrate on not running to the small side ward, where she found Ed, still sedated and looking very pale. She carefully lifted a nearby chair and placed it by the side of his bed before sitting and beginning her watch over him.

She didn't hear Doctor Sullivan enter the canvas room. "The captain should be fine," he said, his deep voice quiet. "I've removed the slither of wood from his muscle and giving the area a good clean. Hopefully, it should heal quickly."

"Yes, Doctor," she said. "How long shall I stay with him?"

"Until he regains consciousness. When you believe he has recovered enough to walk, then you may escort him back to the ward and his own bed."

"Yes, doctor."

She waited for the surgeon to leave before placing the back of her hand against Ed's forehead. His temperature seemed fine, she noted with relief. She watched his broad chest rise and fall under his hospital blues as he slept. His fair hair slicked back looked darker. She wished she could lean forward and press her lips against his perfect mouth.

138

Shocked at her thoughts, she sat up straight and glanced at the door. It's fine, she reassured herself, no one could see into her mind.

A loud bombardment shook the ground causing the captain to stir. "It's nothing to be worried about," she soothed, aware that it was another explosion like this that had caused him to be lying here.

His eyes moved back and forth under his eyelids and he groaned. He was about to come around, she thought nervously hoping she hadn't uttered any of her most private thoughts for him to hear. His eyes flickered and then opened. He stared at her for a moment before his mouth drew back into a wide smile.

"There you are, Nurse Le Breton," he said, his deep voice croaky from sleep. He took in his surroundings. "We're here alone?"

She nodded, happy, but shy for once.

"Good."

Taken aback, Alice frowned. "Why?"

"I've been waiting to speak to you privately."

Alice's heart pounded. "What about?"

His hand moved, taking hold of hers. "I wanted to thank you for saving me."

"I didn't. You were saved by a team of medical staff. I was only doing my duty looking after you." She wondered why she couldn't simply take his compliment?

He raised his free hand to touch her lightly on her left cheek. "No, for saving my spirit when I thought all was lost."

She didn't understand what he meant. Alice frowned. "I don't follow."

He removed his hand from her cheek and cleared his throat. "The last letter I received from home before being injured, was from my brother." Alice waited while he hesitated. "He informed me that he had fallen in love with my fiancée and that she was breaking off our engagement to marry him." Shocked, Alice opened her mouth to speak but he continued. "I had suspected there were feelings between them," Ed said. "I must admit, even I could see she was more suited to him, than to me."

"That's no excuse for jilting you," Alice snapped, horrified to think of anyone treating a brave soldier in such a way, yet aware that it happened only too often.

"When I was injured and lying in No Man's Land, it occurred to me that maybe it was meant to be."

"However, do you mean?"

"Only that, if I was dead, then any scandal would be averted and after a reasonable time, my brother and she could be married."

Alice stared at him, aghast. "How could you even think such a thing?" she asked trying not to show her upset, both at his words and the fact that he was in love with this unfaithful woman.

He closed his eyes briefly. "My mother will be devastated, both for me and as there's bound to be a local scandal. She values her reputation and that of the family most highly."

Alice thought of her own mother and how much she valued her reputation on the island. "More highly than your life?" Alice replied, regretting her haste instantly. It wasn't his fault her mother put Alice's feelings about marriage behind what the neighbours expected. "I'm sorry, I take that back."

He took her hand in both of his. "This isn't why I'm telling you," he said, calmly. "I want you to know that I believed all was lost, that I had no reason to fight to recover." She opened her mouth to argue, but he placed a finger on her lips. "Hush. What I'm trying to tell you, in my clumsy, feeble way, is that when I opened my eyes for the first time afterwards and saw you gazing at me, with such concern, I knew that there was still more waiting for me in this life."

Choked by his words and that she had made a difference to him fighting to survive, Alice took a deep breath.

"You gave me hope. I consider you to be my very own angel."

It was a strange thing for him to say and Alice wondered if it had something to do with him still being under the effects of the anaesthetic.

Before she could say anything, the canvas door was pushed back. Doctor Sullivan entered, noisily. He glanced at her briefly and then addressed the captain. "I see you've come back to join us."

Alice immediately stood, picking up the chair and turning her back on the doctor. She placed the chair in the corner of the room while the doctor was addressing Ed. Smoothing down her apron, she returned to Ed's bedside.

"You may accompany the captain back to the ward now, Nurse."

"Thank you, Doctor," Ed said.

"Yes, well, next time you receive an injury, my man, be sensible and tell a member of the nursing staff. We must deal with injuries as soon as possible. Leaving them to fester does none of us any good."

"Understood," Ed said, looking, Alice thought, suitably chastised.

The following week, Alice was walking to her bell tent when she heard her name being called out. Turning, she saw the captain walking as quickly as he could towards her. He waved at her, wincing momentarily.

Alice didn't miss his valiant attempt to hide his split-second show of pain, with a smile. "Slow down," she insisted, walking in his direction. "There's no need to rush."

"It's wonderful to be outside on such a glorious day," he said looking up at the cloudless sky. He took a deep breath, savouring the clean air. "I find I can almost pretend that there isn't a war going on nearby on days like these."

"Me, too," Alice admitted. "Although it's becoming less often."

He reached her. "Join me for a stroll?"

Alice nodded. She had intended spending her break catching up on a little reading but spending time with Ed was much more preferable.

"How are you feeling, Captain?"

"Please," he said, gently. "As we're alone, can't you call me Ed?"

The subtle change in their friendship, although not

entirely unexpected after his admission to her after his operation, nonetheless made Alice feel awkward. "I'm not sure."

"We're friends, aren't we?" he asked his smile slipping. "At least, I'd like to think we are. I'd like to hope we could keep in touch when I'm discharged."

Shocked, Alice stopped walking. "I was only doing my job, err, Ed." She didn't want to appear unkind, so added. "You shouldn't feel that you have to thank me or keep in touch. It really isn't necessary."

Ed smiled. "It's nothing to do with gratitude, I can assure you," he smiled. "I'd like to correspond with you when I leave here. Would you mind if I did?"

She thought about it and shook her head. "Not at all." She was so used to focusing on her work and having distanced herself from the friends she had in Jersey, Alice only exchanged letters with her mother and occasionally her younger sister. "But I'm afraid we can't correspond, it isn't allowed."

His smile disappeared. "I wouldn't want to cause you trouble," he said as they resumed their walk.

They reached the wooded area at the back of the casualty clearing station. Distant muffled gunfire interrupted her thoughts. She didn't want to lose contact with him but was unable to think how to move forward with their friendship.

"They don't encourage closeness between the patients and staff," she explained. She had experienced two nurses being sent home in disgrace when they had fallen in love with patients and another with one of the surgeons and told Ed. "It's always the woman who's punished and sent home."

He frowned. "That's unfair, but it does seem to be the way of things, I'm afraid." He bent stiffly to pick a poppy and handed it to Alice.

Embarrassed, but touched by his gesture, she took it and smiled. "Thank you," she said, gazing at the perfect blood red petals. She'd have to place it between the pages of one of her books if she didn't want the poppy to shed its petals by the following day. "I love poppies," she said. "They're my favourite flowers."

Ed placed a hand on Alice's right forearm. Surprised at the physical contact, she stared at him, waiting for him so speak.

He cleared his throat. "This is probably forward of me," he took a deep breath. "Ordinarily I wouldn't presume to address you in such a way, but these are exceptional times and our circumstances are unusual."

Alice suspected he was worried about leaving soon. She waited for him to continue.

His hand dropped from her arm and he stared at his feet. Then, looking into her eyes, he said. "The thing is, Nurse Le Breton."

"Please, call me Alice when we're alone."

With a bare hint of a smile on his lips, he said. "Alice, the name suits you."

Aware she didn't have long before she was returning to the ward, Alice resisted the urge to hurry him.

"Well, the thing is," he stopped and thought for a moment, before adding. "May I kiss you?"

"I beg your pardon?" Stunned, Alice stepped back. "Captain, um, Ed." She was about to rebuff him. Then it occurred to her that now wasn't the time to play coy. She had developed feelings for him and he would be leaving soon. Maybe forever. Alice could feel her face reddening. She couldn't believe that she was about to give him permission to kiss her.

"I'm sorry," he said, taking her hesitation for refusal. He turned to walk away. "I should never have asked such a thing of you. It was wrong of me. Please, forgive me."

"Yes," Alice whispered, unsure if he was close enough to hear her.

Ed stopped and turned to face her. "I beg your pardon?"

Alice shrugged, enjoying the new experience of flirting with a man. "You may kiss me." When he didn't react, she glanced at her watch. "You'll need to be quick though, my shift begins in two minutes exactly."

For someone who'd recently had surgery, Ed took a mere second to reach her. He stopped in front of her, his lips drawing back in a smile. "I find that suddenly I'm nervous," he said, before bending his head and kissing her.

Alice had only ever kissed one other man and that had been her ex-fiancé. That was only because she desperately hoped to find something appealing about the man her mother insisted she marry.

This was different though. Very different.

Ed took her in his arms; their kiss deepened. Alice's legs

barely held her as she lost herself in the moment. His lips pressing against hers as he held her against his hard chest, was something Alice knew she would never forget. Nor wished to.

She heard someone shouting in the distance. She pushed him away gently. "I have to go," she said breathlessly. Giving him a brief smile, she straightened her cap and broke into a run. She daren't look back as she raced to the ward. Try as she might, she couldn't unscramble her thoughts. She reached the entrance and closed her eyes to gather herself.

"Are you unwell?" Mary asked, in concern. "You look all off kilter. Something happen?"

Forcing a smile, Alice shook her head. "No, of course not. I was concerned I might be late for my shift, that's all."

"Hmm, I'm not so sure," Mary said tilting her head to one side.

Alice sighed. Her friend knew her a little too well to see through her denials. "Come along," she said, hoping to distract her. "We don't want to be late to start our shift."

The following day Alice received a letter from her mother begging her to come home. "She says she's unwell," she grumbled to Mary as they rested on their beds that evening.

"Do you think she isn't then?" Mary rubbed her eyes before lying back and closing them.

Alice wasn't sure. "She's used to getting her own way," she said suspicion increasing that her mother was playing mind games to make her return to Jersey. She re-read the brief letter, trying not to fret. "She's not averse to using emotional blackmail. I almost married a man I didn't love because of her persistence. Coming here has given me a freedom I've never known before."

Mary's eyes snapped open. She turned on her side, resting her head on the palm of her left hand.

"Almost? You're brave. I doubt I'd be able to stand up to my father, if he tried that on me." She chewed her lower lip. "I'm here because he kept going on that I should do my bit." Mary shrugged. "He's always blamed me for being the cause of my mother dying and the reason he never had any sons to take over his business."

Forgetting her mother's wiles for a moment, Alice reached out and placed her hand on Mary's arm. "I'm sorry. That's horrible of him to blame you for such a thing. You like working here, though, don't you?"

Mary nodded. "I do. It's been better than I ever expected. I assumed I would be going from one controlling situation to another."

"But at least this one is away from our parents."

"Exactly. My days back at home were mostly spent with him barking orders at me in our confectioner's shop. I don't know what I'm going to do when this war is over. It's not as if I have any excuse but to go back."

Alice felt the same way. "Maybe you'll meet someone and get married before then," Alice suggested hopefully, although unsure where her friend was supposed to meet anyone when they spent most of their time either working or catching up on sleep.

Mary lay back down. "I'll only marry, as long as he

doesn't dictate how I live each day." She groaned. "Why is it so difficult for women to be in charge of their own lives?"

"I don't know," Alice answered. She was certain that her life would have been filled with many more choices if she had been born a man. "I'm only ever going to marry for love. My mother is distraught that I'm a spinster and feels that my situation reflects badly on her. She's horrified that I didn't get married when she expected me to, but I'm not going to spend the rest of my life with a man I don't love. I'd rather never marry."

Mary giggled. "Funny how it's all about how our parents feel."

"I know. Mind you, if we were men, then we'd have probably been conscripted by now. We'd be out there fighting. At least here we're behind the lines and for the most part out of danger. Is it that dreadful if we end up returning to the lives we had before the war?" Yes, she thought, it would be.

"Maybe not," Mary said. "I don't know."

Hoping to change the subject, Alice asked, "Have you heard from your aunt again?"

Mary visibly cheered. "Yes," she patted the pocket in her dress and pulled out an envelope. Unfolding the pages and scanning the words, Mary said, "She says how more and more women are going to work in munitions. They're even making the aeroplanes," she giggled. "Can you imagine that?" She stared into space for a moment. "I'd probably be more suited to doing that sort of job. At least I wouldn't have to listen to the pain these poor patients have to bear."

Alice agreed with her. "Maybe, but I'm glad you're here, otherwise we'd never have become friends," she said.

"Thank you, that's a good point." She looked down at her letter again before lying down and staring up at the tent roof. "When you think of all the effort some of us put into the suffrage movement. Now it's all forgotten about and men and women are fighting the Hun together."

Alice thought about what her friend was saying. "I have to admit that I've never been prouder of what I'm doing than now. It's exhausting, and often heart-breaking, but I feel like I'm helping make a difference by being here."

"Me, too." Mary looked at her and winked. "Gone are the days that women were only expected to look pretty on a man's arm."

Alice hoped so. Surely, she thought, this war and their efforts during it meant that women would now be allowed to make more choices about their lives. "I suppose we ought to try and sleep, while we have the chance," Alice said.

She lay back and tried to decide what to do. If her mother was unwell, then she should be at home looking after her. What sort of daughter was she if she ignored her mother's request for her to return home? She would speak to Matron in the morning and request leave. Fear coursed through Alice. If her mother was truly sick, then would she ever be able to return to France? What about Ed? If she left, would she ever see him again? She took a deep breath to reduce the pressure building up inside her chest.

"It's fine," Mary whispered. "You'll come back, you'll see. We'll find a way."

Chapter 10

Gemma

May 2018

Distracted from reading Alice's letter by the sound of the metal mail box jangling, Gemma turned her head to see an envelope land on the floor. She went to pick it up, just as the door opened and Tom peered inside.

"Let me get that for you," he said picking it up and handing it to her.

Surprised and delighted to see him again, Gemma beamed. "Well, this is an unexpected treat."

"I like that you think so."

"Come in, then," she said waving for him to enter the room. "I have a sneaking suspicion I know what this is." She waved the official looking envelope in the air before inserting her little finger through the gap at the top and tearing it open. Pulling out the folded piece of paper, she read it quickly.

"It's from work," she said quietly, re-reading the words

she'd been expecting for a couple of weeks. They want to know when I'm going back." The time had come for her to decide. Coming to France to take on this project had been a promising idea of her father's but they both knew it was a temporary placement. She stared at the neat font on the letter.

"Will you be going back?"

"Either I return to what I know, but have lost my passion for, or find something else to invest my time and emotions in." She looked up at him, glad he was here to discuss her thoughts with.

"Go with your instincts."

She wanted to, but Gemma wasn't certain what her instincts were telling her. She studied her ragged nails. "The thing is, I don't think I want to go back. I've loved it here." She noticed Tom's lips draw back, very slightly. The movement was so subtle she wasn't certain whether she imagined it. "It's been refreshing doing something completely different."

She spotted two paper bags in his hand. "What have you got there?"

"I thought you could do with a break from whatever it was that you were doing, so I bought lunch."

Gemma smiled. "You see? That's why we get along so well. You feed me when I forget to eat. I like this arrangement."

Tom laughed. "Right, well leave that letter on the table and let's go and make the most of this exceptionally warm May day and have a picnic."

She didn't need to be asked twice. "I won't argue with that suggestion."

They walked up towards the five-bar gate and Gemma let her hand glide across the heads of the colourful weeds along the hedgerow as she made her way up the slope.

"If you did stay in France, would you remain in Doullens, do you think?" Tom asked breaking the silence.

Would she? Gemma wasn't sure. "The only thing connecting me to this place is my friendship with you really," she said. "I don't know anyone else. I feel more at home here than I expected."

"Was Brighton ever home for you?" he asked, lifting the wire from the top of the gate and pushing it open. "Or, I suppose Jersey, seeing as that's where you grew up."

She gave his question some thought. "To be honest, I'm not sure. Thinking back to my flat in Brighton, it doesn't seem as if it was ever a home, more of a place to sleep and eat." She considered what she had just said. "I love Jersey, always will. Obviously, I feel connected to the island, but I think home is where you choose to settle."

He stopped at a small patch of grass where fewer poppies would be damaged if they sat down. "Here?"

"Perfect," she said.

They sat, and both stared thoughtfully at the expanse of green, with the occasional red headed poppy standing proudly. "I can't wait till this field is awash with poppies," she said.

He undid the top of one of the brown paper bags and

held it out to her. "I know you don't eat much meat, so both baguettes are cheese and tomato."

Gemma breathed in the scent of freshly cooked bread. "They smell heavenly. Thanks very much." She lifted one of the baguettes from the bag and took a paper napkin.

"How do you know this wasn't just my excuse to come to enjoy eating my lunch in this beautiful spot?"

"I don't care," she giggled, truthfully. "You're feeding me. I like your company, so this suits me too."

"If you did stay here," he said, folding his napkin around the base of his baguette. "What do you think you'd do, workwise?"

She sighed as she finished her mouthful. She had no idea. "I'm not sure, which is why I might just have to go back."

"Would your parents want you to continue with your nursing?"

It was time to open up a little to him. He was her friend, after all, and if he was going to understand her in any way then he would need to know more about her family.

"To be honest, I'm not terribly close to my parents."

He looked saddened by this information. "I assumed that as you were an only child, you would be a close little unit," he said shaking his head. "I'm not sure why, but that was the picture I had of you all."

Gemma crossed her legs and forced a smile. "I would like to say you were right, but it isn't the case. My mother is a lawyer," she said proudly. "She's been involved in all sorts of high-profile cases. Her career comes before anything,

Dad, or me. She's always been that way. Dad's a businessman and his life is all about making money and supporting Mum. I don't know anything different and so I don't hold it against them. It's just how it is, I guess."

"Where do you figure in it all?" he said narrowing his eyes thoughtfully.

Gemma sighed. She didn't want sympathy from him. "Look, I'm only telling you this because I want you to understand why it doesn't matter to them where I live." She stared at the peaceful view in front of her. "I suppose I'm luckier than some, in a way. My parents never make me feel beholden to them or ask anything of me." She smiled to soften her words. "I probably wouldn't mind being needed just once or twice in my life," she admitted. "But they have each other. I was an unexpected baby, to say the very least."

Tom looked sad. "You must have spent time with them growing up?"

She shook her head. "Not much. They're real socialites. I was always well looked after, but it was by babysitters, or nannies. My parents aren't very close to their own families, so I didn't really mix with cousins, or anything."

Tom stared at her. "It sounds like a very lonely childhood."

It did, even to her own ears. "It wasn't as bad as it seems. Don't forget I didn't know any better. And I did learn to appreciate books and being by myself."

"Friends back in Brighton?"

She shook her head. "I pretty much kept myself to myself,

apart from the odd occasion when I had to attend an event."

He continued to eat his baguette, staring at her thoughtfully.

"What?" she laughed. "I must sound like a right Billy-no-mates."

He shook his head and finished his mouthful. "No, I was thinking how friendly you are for someone who's spent most of their life enjoying their own company."

"Thank you, I think," she said taking a bite of her baguette and smiling at him over the top of it. "At least my parents are honest about their feelings," she added. "I'd rather that than people pretending to feel deeply about me and lying."

He reached forward and brushed a crumb off her cheek. "Has someone done that to you?"

"My last boyfriend."

"Want to tell me more?" He finished his food and leant back resting his hands on the grass behind him.

Did she? She wasn't used to sharing her feelings with anyone. She looked at Tom, who was watching her intently. The gentle expression on his tanned face made her want to confide in him. What was the worst that could happen? He could laugh at me, she thought. No, Tom wouldn't do that.

"We were seeing each other for a few months. I knew he'd been married but he swore he was legally separated from his wife and living apart from her."

"And he wasn't."

She shook her head.

"How did you find out? Someone at work tell you?"

"Nope." She cleared her throat, wondering if opening up this wound would bring back all the shock, humiliation and devastation, or if sharing it would help heal her. She took a deep breath. "He was injured in a pile-up on the motorway and brought into the trauma unit with several others." She pictured the chaos of that day. "It was manic. The team were rushing about trying to deal with the stream of accident victims being brought in by ambulances. I was helping work on him, when I noticed his watch." She hesitated, determined to finish what she was telling him."

"Go on."

"I barely recognised his face, he was that battered. His phone rang, and I was handed it and told to answer it."

"It was his wife?" Tom said quietly.

"How did you know?" she asked, her heart pounding with the tension of reliving the events of that life-changing day.

"A good guess. What happened next?"

"She asked who I was, which was understandable. I told her gently that he'd been involved in an accident and where he was." She exhaled sharply. "She told me she'd need to find someone to look after their baby, but that she would be there as soon as she could."

"Did he make it?"

Gemma shook her head, miserably. Tom leant forward and took her in his arms, hugging her tightly. "I'm so sorry you went through that, Gemma. It must have been horrendous on so many levels."

Chapter 11

Alice

1916

Several days later, Alice was called to Matron's office. She stood in front of Matron's desk, trying to imagine what she could have possibly done wrong. Her stomach contracted nervously at the thought that someone could have spied on her with Ed. Had they been seen kissing? The thought made her mouth go dry. Was she about to be sent home in disgrace? She stared at the top of Matron's head waiting for her to finish writing notes.

Eventually, Matron placed her fountain pen down on her desk and blotted her work. She looked up at Alice and clasped her hands together.

"As you're aware Nurse Le Breton, I'm obliged to read all my nurses' incoming mail." Alice nodded. "I note that you have received several from your mother, who appears to be ailing somewhat." She waited for Alice's reply.

"That's correct, Matron."

The older woman frowned, thoughtfully. "I don't understand. If this is the case, then why haven't you come to me to request leave to return to the Channel Islands?" Alice nodded guiltily. "If your mother is ill, then you must surely go to her?"

Alice tried to form a coherent sentence. One that wouldn't end up with Matron seeing her as a selfish, unfeeling woman.

"Well?" Matron tapped her two index fingers together impatiently.

Alice took a deep breath. "I'm unsure if my mother is in fact ill," she said, cross that her reply hadn't come out the way she had intended.

Matron stiffened. "Not ill? Are you insinuating that your mother has fabricated this information?"

Alice fidgeted from one foot to the other. "No, but," she hesitated, trying to find the words. "My mother didn't want me to come here," she explained. "I suspect she may be feigning illness to ensure my return."

"And you do not wish to go." It was a statement rather than a question. Her words made Alice wonder if maybe Matron had her own issues with her family. Could she understand the position Alice found herself in better than she was letting on?

"I'm needed here, Matron," Alice tried to explain. "We're desperately short of nurses, as you know," she added, hoping Matron wouldn't find her reply patronising in any way. "I worry that if my mother is exaggerating her health issues, which I have to admit she has done several times in the past, then I believe I'd be wasting time going home."

She didn't mean to sound nasty towards her mother. She loved her, very much. But she also knew what her mother was capable of and this seemed too familiar for Alice to be fooled.

"The journey alone takes a couple of days, both ways. I have to go via the south coast of England, you see."

"I'm well aware, Nurse Le Breton. However, you must go." Alice opened her mouth to argue, but Matron narrowed her eyes and stopped her before one syllable could escape. "There's an ambulance taking two of the patients back to England. You'll accompany them to Dover and from there other nursing staff will take over. You may then travel to Southampton to catch the ferry on to Jersey. I've signed a leave pass and travel warrant." Alice didn't bother arguing. "You have two weeks before you're expected to return. Naturally, if your mother is worse than you fear, then write to me and I shall extend your leave."

Alice nodded, unable to hide her disappointment. "Thank you, Matron," she said, more miserable than she could recall being since the start of the war.

Matron took a breath to speak, but before she could utter a word, shouting from the yard interrupted her. She immediately stood, handing Alice the dockets, which she slipped it in her apron pocket. She opened the office door, holding it back for Matron to hurry through.

"What's going on?" Alice heard Matron demand as she closed the door and joined her.

"In Ward Three, Matron." An ashen-faced probationer pointed in the direction of the ward.

"I know the way," Matron snapped, pushing past the girl's arm and going to the ward.

Hearing screams and scuffling coming from inside, Alice peered into the tent. Staring momentarily at the chaos inside the large tent, she gasped as Ed and Corporal Healy were struggling to restrain one of the newer patients. Alice spotted a nurse lying on the floor in between two upturned beds, holding the side of her face. She recognized her as another volunteer.

Matron helped with the hysterical patient and Alice rushed over to the prone nurse.

"Are you all right?" she asked crouching next to her. When the stunned girl didn't reply, Alice took hold of her wrist and carefully pulled her hand away from her cheek. Her face had been cut, she was horrified to notice, and quite badly. "Quick, over here," she shouted at the probationer who had run up behind her. "Help me."

Alice could hear Matron telling another nurse to bring a sedative to calm the struggling man. Alice glanced up at him. His eyes bulged, and he was baring his teeth using every ounce of strength he had left trying to pull away from the men restraining him. As Matron tried to restore order, Alice assisted the nurse, helping her to her feet. She wobbled for a moment, probably from shock, Alice assumed.

"Come with me," she said. "We'll go somewhere quiet and I'll fetch you a cup of tea."

She could feel the girl's body trembling. "Bring me a blanket," she whispered to the young probationer. "I'll fetch disinfectant."

"I'll take her to the dining tent. We need to give her a little time to gather herself and check any damage she's sustained."

They walked slowly with her along the wooden walkway to a large tent where they all congregated for meals.

"Here," Alice said, pulling back a chair at the table closest to the entrance. "Take a seat." She asked a probationer to bring the nurse some tea and then sit with her. I'll fetch disinfectant and a dressing."

The wound wasn't as deep as she had first feared, Alice was relieved to note as she cleaned it carefully with antiseptic. "Sorry, it does sting, doesn't it?"

The nurse nodded. "Like the devil."

Alice then covered the cut with a dressing. She was pretty sure the poor girl would need stitches and resolved to speak to Doctor Sullivan as soon as she had the opportunity. Alice hoped he'd agree to tidy the edges of the cut to leave the nurse with as little scaring as possible.

"What happened?" Alice asked.

"He went berserk," the nurse mumbled after a few mouthfuls of the tepid tea. "I thought he was going to kill me." Her voice cracked as she spoke. She wiped tears from her undamaged cheek. "I only went to take his temperature." She hesitated and shivered. "He grabbed a pair of scissors and lashed out at me, screaming for me to leave him alone. I swear I didn't do anything I shouldn't have."

"I'm sure you didn't," Alice soothed. "You're in shock, and it's not surprising."

She empathised with her. Alice had witnessed several

attacks on nurses since her arrival, narrowly missing being the target of one on her second day.

"He probably wasn't aware that he was attacking a nurse," she said. "He might have thought he was back in the trenches and defending himself." She had heard it happen before and was not surprised if this was the case. Mostly, Alice did not want the girl to blame herself for the attack.

"If it wasn't for Captain Woodhall and Corporal Healy, I daren't imagine what would have happened."

Alice watched the nurse's tears flow harder. "There, there," she said. "It's all over now." Except it wasn't. They both knew that she would probably come across the patient again at some point in her working day. "He's being sedated and will have to be watched, so he doesn't hurt someone else."

The nurse looked up at Alice, her eyes filled with concern. "Is my face terribly bad?"

"No," Alice assured her. "It's slightly swollen now, so will look worse than it is for a while, but I'm sure it'll be fine."

"I'll have a scar though, won't I?"

She would. Alice didn't want to alarm her, but couldn't lie, not to a fellow professional who knew as much as she did. All the nurse had to do was quietly check her face in the mirror later to know how bad it was.

"A little one," Alice said. "I can speak to one of the doctors, if you like? Maybe he can use smaller stitches to close the wound."

The nurse began crying again. Her body trembled violently, and Alice knew it was the shock coming out of her system. It was a good thing, so she simply pulled the blanket tighter around the nurse's shoulders.

"I don't know what's wrong with me," the nurse cried. "I can handle this." Her teeth chattered as she tried to speak.

"It's the shock. Don't fight it," Alice said, aware that the nurse would be saying the same words to her if she had been the one to be attacked. "I'll stay here with you for as long as you need me to."

They sat together, the only sound coming from voices passing along the walkway outside.

"You're in here," Ed said, entering the tent. He walked up to them. "I just wanted to check you're all right," he said to the nurse. She gave a little sob and nodded. "You're not to concern yourself. Everything is under control now. The private has been sedated and taken to a smaller ward away from here. He's being watched by one of the orderlies, so you needn't worry."

"Thank you," Alice said. She studied his handsome face, wishing she didn't have to leave just when they were becoming closer. Alice couldn't believe the change in her attitude, allowing herself to become involved with a patient. Before the war, she had always followed the rules, but she liked how it felt to be bold and make her own choices – it was liberating.

He caught Alice's eye as he looked from the nurse. "How are you?" he mouthed.

Could he tell that something had happened causing her to return home, she wondered? "Speak later?"

Ed nodded, the concern on his face deepening. "If you

don't need me for anything, I'd better return to the ward. I don't want Matron on the war path. She wasn't happy when it all erupted back there."

Alice could imagine.

Ed went to leave the tent, just as Matron marched in. He stood back to let her pass.

"Return to your bed now, Captain, if you please," she said glancing from him to the nurse. "Ah, there you are. I'm relieved to see Nurse Le Breton has been tending to you."

Carefully pulling the dressing back from the nurse's face, Matron Bleasdale examined the injury. "Ah, Doctor Sullivan," she said, holding her hand up for him to see her. "This nurse has been injured by one of the patients."

He glanced at Alice, then bent to inspect the nurse's face.

Matron turned to Alice, seemingly oblivious that Ed was still standing at the doorway and checked her watch. "Nurse Le Breton, if you haven't already packed, I suggest you do so now. The ambulance will be leaving for the docks in half an hour. If you miss your lift, there isn't another one today. Now, hurry along."

Alice noticed Ed's eyes widen in surprise. He left the tent and her heart dipped. "Yes, Matron."

"You're leaving us?" Doctor Sullivan asked without looking up from what he was doing.

Taken aback by his interest, Alice cleared her throat. "Yes, doctor, my mother is unwell."

"I hope we see you back here in the not too distant

future then nurse," he said. "Hand me those tweezers, Matron?"

Matron glared at Alice, so she hurried outside, glancing to her right towards the ward to see if she could see Ed. She couldn't bear to leave without saying goodbye to him. Disappointed and aware she didn't have much time, she ran in the direction of her tent. Turning the corner after the last ward, she slammed into him.

"Oof, sorry," she said, winded slightly after being stopped by his muscular chest.

He didn't speak but took her hand and led her a little way into the woods. Looking around to check they were alone, he stared at her. "You're leaving? You didn't say."

"Yes, my mother's ill. Matron has given me two weeks' leave."

Ed nodded solemnly. "I'm sorry about your mother."

"I suspect she's fine. She just wants me back home again. She does this sort of thing to get her own way." She hated seeing him looking so sad. She ached at the thought of leaving him.

"I'll miss you, Alice," he said, putting a finger under her chin and lifting it. He bent his head until his lips were pressing against hers and kissed her, hard.

All the anguish Alice was feeling at being separated from Ed was reflected in his kiss. Saddened to have to leave him so soon, but relieved he was demonstrating how much she meant to him, she flung her arms around his neck and kissed him back.

"I'll miss you, too," she whispered when their lips parted.

"I tried to argue with Matron about being sent home, but I suppose she feels I ought to go in case my mother really is ill."

Ed's face softened. "I'm sure you could do with the break from here. You nurses work immensely hard and for such long hours, it'll probably do you good."

Alice swallowed the lump forming in her throat. Why did she have to leave just when she had every reason to stay?

Ed pulled her into a bear hug. "You'll soon be back." He patted his hip lightly. "And, I'll still be here. Doctor Sullivan said it'll be a few weeks yet before I'm fit enough to resume fighting."

"But we'll be spending most of those weeks unable to see each other," she argued. "I'm fairly positive my mother's acting, she's used to being demanding and getting her own way."

He put a finger against her lips to stop her from ranting. "Hush, it's fine. You'll do the right thing and I'll be here, waiting for your return." He pulled her close again, soothing her with his gentle Scottish lilt. "My father sounds a little like your mother. I remember his brother saying, 'Stuart the world doesn't revolve around you and your whims, you know.'"

Alice couldn't believe what she was hearing. Amused, she looked up to him.

"What?" he asked.

"My grandfather. He was also called Stuart. How odd is that?"

Ed threw his head back and laughed. "I wonder if they were both cantankerous old miseries."

Alice smiled. "Well, my grandfather wasn't miserable, but I think he could be a little cantankerous at times."

She heard Matron's voice in the distance and remembered what she should be doing. "I have to go. I need to pack my things and change out of this uniform if I'm to make that lift."

"One more kiss?"

"Yes," she said, thrilled he had asked. They kissed, each putting their mutual need into their love, until eventually she pulled back. "I really must go. Take care, and do as you're told," she said. "I don't want you damaging that hip while I'm away."

"Yes, Nurse Le Breton."

The skin around his dark eyes creased as he smiled. It took all Alice's will power not to kiss him again. She was late though, and if she didn't get a move on she would either have to travel without any of her belongings or miss her lift. She ran off towards her tent, turning to see if he was still waiting there, delighted when he smiled and waved.

"I'll miss you," she mouthed, glancing around to check that no one was around to see.

Within moments, Alice had changed, roughly packed up the few things she'd need and glanced around her tent. She'd miss this place, even though she was returning to her comfortable bedroom at her parent's beautiful farm.

"Right, time to go," she said buttoning up her coat and

putting on her hat. Alice lifted her small tan leather suitcase and went to locate the ambulance.

"We're all loaded up here. Hop in the front with me." The driver said and Alice did as she was told.

"Don't look so miserable," the driver laughed. "Most people would be happy to leave this place and be going home to Blighty."

Alice forced a smile as he turned the ambulance in the courtyard. She stared out of the window hoping for one last glimpse of Ed and saw him step out of the shadows and give her a discrete wave. He was right. She would be back here soon.

bedroom. Showered and changed, Gemma got into bed and arranged her pillows against the newly painted metal bedstead. She made herself comfortable, enjoying being in her freshly decorated bedroom. She picked up the last letter she had been reading and carried on. She felt more and more compelled to know what had happened to Alice with each letter.

Their lives seemed connected in many ways, yet they lived a century apart. Gemma was aware that her emotional investment into Alice and Ed's lives was deeper than she had intended when she first began reading their correspondence. Maybe Tom would find her intrigue a little odd? She doubted it. He seemed so understanding.

Gemma lay back and closed her eyes and pictured Tom. He was nothing like her usual type. He was athletic, muscular and more at home in the outdoors than inside. He didn't seem very academic either and that was refreshing. A warm feeling came over her. Her guilt at her part in what her ex had done had lessened since confessing all to Tom. She mulled over their conversations and tried to imagine how he saw her. Was he just being friendly? She hoped not. What was she going to do when he finished working here, she wondered? Could she find a way for them to stay in contact? Would she want to, or would it be easier to move on and start again without a reminder of Tom and the time they'd shared during this project? She leant over and placed the letters carefully on her bedside table, before turning off the lamp. Lying in the dark, with rays of moonlight coming through a gap in the top of her curtains, Gemma tried to picture the next owners of the farmhouse. She hoped it would be a couple or a small family – two people in love with one, or maybe two small children. This place would make a perfect home. She was going to miss the farmhouse when the time came for her to leave and return to the real world.

Gemma closed her eyes and pulled her duvet up over her shoulders. What was she going to do after this episode of her life ended? She still couldn't imagine returning to nursing, but she wasn't qualified to do anything else. She hadn't ever wanted to be anything but a nurse. How things changed, she thought as she drifted off to sleep.

The following morning, sunlight had replaced the moon's rays waking Gemma slowly as it shone into her bedroom. She rubbed her eyes and stretched, taking a while for her to wake up. She threw back her duvet and sat up. It was going to be another gloriously sunny day, she thought happily. She got out of bed and pulled back the curtains to look at the view outside. Standing at the open window, she tilted her head back closing her eyes as the sun warmed her face.

"When you're quite ready," Tom shouted from outside. "I've only been waiting an hour for you to surface."

She squinted down at him, noticing him trying not to laugh as he tapped the face of his watch with his finger.

"Coming," she giggled, running down the stairs, pulling on her dressing gown. She unlocked the front door. "Isn't it a gorgeous morning?"

"It is," he said walking inside and leaving her taking deep rosemary-filled breaths on the footpath. "It's Sunday, so I thought I'd come and help you here, if you like?"

"I'll get us coffees," Gemma said, pushing her sleeves up her arms as they went into the kitchen.

He leant against the wall and watched as she prepared their drinks. "So, how is the letter reading going? Discovered anything else interesting?"

"Yes, but only because of the little notes on the backs of the letters," she said, filling a cafetière she had brought for his coffees. "The letters say very little, but the notes tell me much, much more about her daily life. I'm still a little confused about why she's writing letters to the Lieutenant, when the notes are all about her affection for Ed."

"Ed?"

"That's the captain."

Gemma set the cafetière down on the table and turned on her phone, checking her emails. "I have to take photos for Dad," she said, reading an email from him. "Apparently, my mother said that if we don't get a sale this summer, then we should rent out the farmhouse." Gemma's heart dipped at the thought of someone else enjoying this place during the summer.

"Couldn't you live here instead of selling?" Tom asked.

"I told you he was a business man," she said reading through the rest of her dad's email. "He'll want to make money out of it as soon as possible." She skimmed through the words. "He wants me to find a management company to look after the place for us if we do rent it."

"It's a shame. Let's get out and take these photos for him." Tom said as he downed his coffee.

"Do you think we should put it on the market soon, then?"

He shook his head and stood up. "No, but it'll buy you time while you work out what to do next."

She liked his way of thinking. "Good plan." she said, as she followed him outside, carrying her coffee mug with her.

Tom stepped out of the way when necessary to give Gemma a clear view of the cobbles, doorway, or unpainted wall that she was attempting to capture on her phone.

"Pick up that broom," she said, pointing for Tom to stand in the barn.

"Why?"

She could see he wasn't sure if she was joking, or not.

"It'll give more perspective to the room, so that we can see how large it is."

He frowned and then did as she said. "Do I get paid extra for my modelling?"

She shook her head, glad that she would have a photo of him to keep, if she did have to move soon. "No, I thought you'd be happy to give your time for free as it's Sunday."

Tom threw his head back in laughter. "That is the weirdest argument I've heard for a long time. He picked up the broom and posed for her. "Like this?"

"That's right. Now, lean on the broom with your elbow and smile at the camera." He did as she instructed. Gemma knew she'd remember today, with or without the photos in her phone.

Chapter 13

Alice

October 1916

Alice stood on the freezing deck of the ship. Pulling her hat down further over her ears, she took deep breaths in an attempt to dispel the nausea caused by the rough sea. Her shoulders hunched against the biting cold, she held the front of her winter coat tight with one hand, pushing the other into her pocket. She was in desperate need of a cup of hot tea and a warm bath. She wasn't a good sailor at the best of times and this journey had been the worst one she could ever recall taking. It seemed to be lasting forever.

She spotted the familiar sight of Noirmont, with its openness and lush greenery above the cliff face, and her mood lifted. Until now, all she could think of was how heart-breaking it had been to leave Ed behind. Now with the coast of Jersey up ahead, she felt a little comforted. She had missed this place.

The trip hadn't been too bad between Calais and Dover, probably Alice thought because she had been concentrating on looking after the two patients she was accompanying. It had been a relief to hand them over to waiting nursing staff at Victoria and be able to catch her train to Southampton.

Her feet ached. She was used to spending hours each day on them, but for some reason the tiredness seeped into her bones. Maybe it was the concern for her mother playing on her mind, she thought, or the sadness she felt from saying an unexpected goodbye to Ed.

She had booked a carriage for the overnight crossing, but it was cramped, and she found it difficult to sleep. She stifled a yawn and straightened her hat, not wanting to arrive at the docks looking unkempt. Her mother was already irritated with her for not agreeing to return home earlier, she didn't need to upset her further by making a show of herself.

The wait for the ship to be tied up was interminable. Alice shivered as she paced back and forth, desperately trying to build up a little body heat, willing the dockers to hurry up.

She peered across the New North Quay and waved to one of her father's oldest friends, a master stevedore called Edward Troy. She could see him talking to someone standing with his back to her. Alice leaned forward over the railings but couldn't see if it was her father. She hoped he was waiting for her with his horse and trap. The wind was making her eyes weep, but that was preferable to feeling queasy. She heard the thud of the passenger ramp as it connected with the boat. Lifting her case, Alice slowly made her way towards the exit with the rest of the eager passengers.

"Miss," one of the dockers shouted to her. "There's a gentleman over there. I think he's trying to attract your attention."

Alice looked over to where the man was pointing and saw her father. She smiled for the first time that day.

"Thank you," she said, hurrying as quickly as she could to get off the boat.

Reaching their family horse, Phantom, Alice stroked his silky chestnut neck.

"Hand that valise here, dear," her father said, reaching down to take Alice's case from her hand. He placed it behind him and patted the leather seat. "Climb up next to me, so we can get you home. It's bitter out here today."

Alice did as he said, grateful to be away from the boat and almost back at the family farm.

"Here, put this over your legs," he said, covering her lower half with a thick plaid blanket. He smiled at her fondly and kissed her on the forehead. "It's good to have you back home, Alice. We've missed you very much."

"It's good to be home, Father," she said. "I didn't realise how much I'd missed this place until today," she added, honestly. "I've been so busy at the CCS that I've barely had a chance to think of anything much apart from my work."

"That's how it should be," he said patting her leg. "We're

very proud of you, your mother and I. Very proud indeed."
He raised the reins, "Come on Phantom, time to go."

The horse slowly wended its way through the crowds of people walking on the quay, breaking into a trot as soon as they reached the road.

"How is Mother?" she asked, hoping her suspicions had been correct and there was little wrong with her apart from some attention seeking.

He hesitated briefly. "I have to admit I believed her to be putting on an act initially."

Alice tried not to panic. "You mean, she really is unwell?" she asked guiltily.

"I think so, yes." He glanced at Alice giving her a comforting smile. "Not terribly ill. Not enough for you to concern yourself unnecessarily, my love, but we've sent your sister to stay with her friend's family in St Peter, to give your mother peace to recover."

Alice was sad to hear her sister wouldn't be at home, but it was good to know that her mother wasn't as bad as she had dreaded her being. "I'm glad Mother is not dangerously ill." She sat back and enjoyed breathing in the familiar salty air as the horse trotted along the waterfront to the avenue towards their home near St Aubin.

She couldn't help willing the weather to be better in the morning. Now she was home, she couldn't wait to see something of her beloved island in the sunshine. It was how she always pictured the place when she was in France. She recalled one of the patients saying how all the soldiers lived on memories when they were away, and he was right. Alice smiled to herself, thinking how funny it was that whenever she thought of Jersey it was always sunny. She never pictured it raining, or cold and windy like it was today.

They waved to several friends on their way home and forty minutes later Phantom trotted into the spotless yard at the farm. Alice stepped down from the trap.

"You go inside and warm up," he said. "Your mother will be waiting. I'll settle Phantom and bring your case in soon." He lowered his voice. "I think she'll be looking forward to having a little time alone with you."

Alice forced a smile on her face. Happy for the opportunity to get warm after such a long overnight journey, she almost ran inside.

"Hello, Miss," said Jeanette, the youngest daughter of neighbouring farming family. She beamed at Alice, hand outstretched to take her coat.

"I didn't realise you worked for my parents, Jeanette?" Alice said, pleased to see the cheerful girl, her rosy cheeks shining. She knew that the girl's family struggled financially. They were one of the poorer families in the Parish and Jeanette was the youngest of twelve children, and her parents would no doubt be delighted to have Jeanette helping her family by working for her parents. "It's good to see you," she added. "Will I find my mother in the drawing room?"

"Yes, Miss," she said. She waited for Alice to remove her hat and gloves and then carried them along the hallway to hang them up in the cloakroom. "She's been unwell this past fortnight."

"So, I gather," Alice said.

"Madam said I must bring in tea and the fruit cake my mother baked for her as soon as you arrive."

Alice's eyes lit up. "I love your mother's fruit cake," she said honestly. "What a perfect welcome. I can't think of anything I'd rather eat right now. Thank you."

She went to the drawing room door, patted her hair in place, and smoothing down her skirts, took a deep breath before walking in. "Mother," she said, a little taken aback by how much weight her mother had lost. "I'm so sorry you've been unwell."

Her mother gave a little cough, delicately holding up a lace handkerchief to her mouth as if to make a point. "I'll be much improved now that you are here to keep me company." She indicated the chair facing hers. "Sit there, next to the fire. That dear girl, Jeanette has been a godsend since you left. She works hard to keep up with everything. Did I mention in my letters that we lost Mrs Le Brun?"

Alice nodded. "Yes, I was sorry to hear about her bereavements."

"Two boys, dead." She shook her head. "And only her daughter left. It's too cruel, that's what it is." She gave a sob. "I always wanted a son, as you know, but after all the dreadful news coming from this war, well, I'm relieved I don't have to worry about my son being sent to be killed."

Alice leant forward and took her mother's hand in hers. "I was thinking how relieved I was not to have a brother to fret over."

Jeanette knocked before entering the room carrying a tray. It looked heavy, but Alice didn't want her mother to think she might not need Jeanette now she was back at home. The poor girl needed this job. She was going to have to ensure her mother understood that she would be returning to France in just under a fortnight. Alice cleared several novels to the side of the table, to enable Jeanette to lower the tray.

"Thank you, Jeanette," her mother said. "By all means, fetch another plate. Alice will cut you a slice to take and eat in the scullery. You must be due for a break by now."

Alice couldn't help smiling at the skinny girl's delight as she almost ran out of the living room. "That was kind of you, Mother," she said. Her mother must be fond of the girl to be so pleasant towards her, she thought happily.

"She's been a dear. She works terribly hard and I can't help liking her."

Jeanette returned seconds later, placing the spare plate next to the tray. "Thank you, Madam," she said, bobbing slightly.

Alice cut her mother a piece of cake and poured her a cup of tea. "Please pass these to my mother for me."

While Jeanette did as she asked, Alice cut the girl a thick slice of the moist cake and handed the plate to her. "Here you are."

Jeanette did her usual bob and left.

Pouring herself a cup of tea and cutting her own slice of cake, Alice went back to sit next to the fire. "Why does she bob like that?"

"I think it's a form of curtsy," her mother said between mouthfuls. "I keep meaning to tell her that it's not necessary, but every time she does it I worry that I might embarrass her by correcting her."

Alice could see what her mother meant. "Would you like me to have a quiet word with her?"

"Oh, yes, please, Alice. Would you?"

Alice could feel her hands and feet slowly warming up. The tea and cake had done masses to restore her energy levels and it was heavenly to sit in a comfortable chair for once. After she had tidied their crockery away to the tray, Alice sat back.

"It is good to be home," she admitted. "I almost don't remember what it's like to be sitting somewhere this pleasant."

Her mother studied her for a while and then said, "Tell me all about your work. Have you made friends there?"

Alice was aware that her mother was fishing but didn't mind. It was good to speak without having to watch who might be listening in on the conversation. As she spoke she pushed away thoughts of Ed lying in his hospital bed and how close they had become since he had kissed her.

"Are you still cold?" her mother frowned.

"No, not at all," Alice reassured her. "I was just thinking about the patients. There are many dramas each day and night. I think I'll take a few days to fully understand that I'm back here and not on call for emergencies."

"Why don't you tell me all about it," her mother suggested. Alice was surprised at her mother's interest in her work, but did as she asked, leaving out any mention of Ed.

Initially Alice was happy to dutifully accompany her mother to visit relatives and neighbours, but the novelty of having little to do soon wore off. Her initial misgivings about her mother's health passed. She couldn't miss how spritely her mother was when they were out socialising and how good her appetite seemed to be. She also looked as if she was rapidly gaining weight. She suspected her mother had simply not eaten for a few weeks to persuade others that she was unwell.

"How has my mother's appetite been while I was away?" she asked Jeanette one morning before her mother joined her for breakfast.

"The madam was off her food for some weeks," Jeanette said, setting places at the dining room table ready for them to eat their breakfast. "I don't know what caused it, but she suddenly went off her food and took to her bed. It made me worry terribly, it did. I even asked my Ma what she thought I ought to do."

It had been as Alice had presumed. She listened to Jeanette's concerns determined to reassure her. "I don't think we need to worry now though, do you?"

Jeanette stared at her before moving along to the next place setting on the table. "Are you certain, miss?"

"Yes," Alice said, angry that her mother's selfishness had upset the young girl.

"I was worried she'd need someone to nurse her and that I might be dismissed."

Anger increasing, Alice shook her head, desperate to console the troubled maid. "No, you mustn't think that," she said. "Whatever happens here, I'm sure my parents will need you working for them, probably for years, or until you marry."

Jeanette giggled at the mention of marriage and turned her back on Alice briefly. Facing her once more, her cheeks red with embarrassment. "Do you think I'll be wed then?"

Alice had always liked Jeanette and pitied her life at the same time. Now, all she saw was a young girl who until working for Alice's parents had very little in her life. She obviously had not been encouraged to think that she should hope for much in her future.

"Yes. You're a hardworking, kind girl," Alice said, truthfully. "Is there anyone you've noticed?"

"Well," Jeanette looked down at the floor. "There is one boy—"

Several days later, Alice gave in to her mother's insistence and lacking any excuses not to, accompanied her into St Helier. They walked along King Street and Queen Street and Alice wondered if, despite her mother's annoyance at her working as a VAD, that maybe she was secretly proud of her. Each time they met one of her acquaintances, she insisted Alice told them a little about her work at the casualty clearing station.

They stopped at the Central Market to collect several jars of jam her mother had ordered. Then, after dropping in to see a friend of her mother's who lived on Hill Street, strolled towards Weighbridge near to the docks where they had arranged to be collected by her father.

Alice spotted a group of men working near the docks. "Who are they?" she asked her mother pointing discretely at them.

"They'll be German prisoners of war," she whispered, putting her gloved hand up near her mouth. "They bring them here early each day from Les Blanches Banques camp in St Ouen's bay. I don't like to think of them being here."

Alice doubted they enjoyed being kept on the island, either. She imagined Ed being captured and wondered if he would be treated fairly. She peaked from under the rim of her felt hat. They looked thin, but relatively healthy. She wondered how many of them were being held down at the camp below the sand dunes in her favourite bay. She thought back to the many times she'd accompanied her father down to the beach on the road the locals knew as the Five Mile Road, sitting next to her father on the cart pulled by Phantom. She'd paddled in the warm sea, looking for tiny crabs in the rockpools while her father and his farmhands harvested the seaweed ready to be spread on his Jersey Royal potato crop.

She spotted her father waving them over and linking her arm through her mother's they each carried a basket in their free hands as they hurried to join him.

"You two have been busy by the looks of it," her father laughed. "Here, let me take those from you." He smiled as he took the baskets and lifted them onto the trap.

Alice took her mother's right hand and assisted her up onto the leather seat. Once she was settled, Alice climbed onto the back of the trap, sitting on one of the cushioned side seats. She moved the baskets placing them between the back of her parent's seat and her legs, so that they didn't move about and fall over on the ride home. The horse moved on and when they were out of earshot from anyone Alice decided it was safe to ask her father a few questions about the prisoners.

"How many of them are kept at the prison camp, Father?"

"I've heard that it's about 2,000," he said. "Your mother frets about them escaping." He winked at his wife over his shoulder.

"Oh, stop teasing me," her mother grumbled. "You know how much the thought troubles me."

It worried Alice now that her father had brought it to her attention. "Have any of them escaped then?"

He laughed. "No. A few have tried, or so I've heard, but no escapees yet."

Her mother nudged him sharply in his side. "Enough of that scaremongering. I'm not the only one who's concerned about them being here. Anyhow, we've had a pleasant day and I don't wish to taint my mood with such nonsense."

Alice was happy to change the topic of conversation, too. "You seem much better today, Mother," she said, taking a chance that her mother would not use this reminder to have an instant relapse.

Her mother gave a feeble cough. "A little, dear. I've been

putting on a brave face, so we could venture out and give you some fresh air. You must be rather bored at home after all the excitement of your work."

"A little," Alice admitted, taking the opportunity to remind her mother that she would soon be returning to France. "About that, Mother. Please don't forget I'll be leaving in three days. I'm needed in France."

"You're needed here, young lady," her mother snapped. "It would make a welcome change if you remembered your priorities occasionally."

Not wishing to cause a drama, Alice bit back a retort. "More wounded soldiers are brought in daily, Mother. I've gained a huge amount of experience and they'll want me back as soon as I'm able to return."

The following morning, Alice was woken by a loud banging on her bedroom door. She forced her eyes open and sat up. "Yes?"

"It's the madam, miss," Jeanette called through the door. "She's taken poorly again. The doctor should be arriving shortly."

Alice lay back down on her pillows and stared miserably at her white ceiling. "Thank you, Jeanette," she said, concentrating on keeping her voice light. "Please tell her I'll be with her presently."

Alice supposed it served her right. She had given in to her compulsion to remind her mother about her return to France, so naturally her mother would suffer a relapse. Irritated with her for being so selfish, Alice turned on her side and punched one of her pillows.

Ten minutes later she was dressed and trying to remain composed in her mother's bedroom. The curtains were closed as their family doctor chatted sympathetically to her mother. "I'll call again tomorrow morning," he said, closing his leather case and going to the door. "Do not hesitate to call me before that time should you need me."

Alice followed him silently out to the hall. She waited until they were by the front door and he had put on his overcoat before speaking.

"My mother's illness. Do you know when it will subside?"

"It's her nerves, Alice," he said. "I understand you must be impatient to return to your voluntary work, however, your mother needs you here."

"Yes, of course," she said, wondering if he couldn't see through her mother's charade, or if he was wanting to keep feigning ignorance and be able to go on to his next patient.

Despondent, Alice opened the door and accompanied him outside. She was tired of her mother's emotional blackmail. It was time she stood up to her. Alice took a deep breath. It wouldn't be easy, even her father still found it nigh on impossible at times. But she wanted to be back in France and more than anything, to see Ed again.

She cleared her throat, her heart pounding with nerves. "Doctor, we both know she isn't as delicate as she professes, don't we?" She willed him to be honest with her.

He swapped his case from his right to his left. Alice could see he was finding their conversation awkward, but she was desperate to stop the pretence and return to where she truly was needed.

"I can't stay here on my mother's whim," she explained. "You have a son in the Jersey Pals. Surely you think it's a good thing that I go where I'm most needed?"

He glanced up at her mother's bedroom window and then back to Alice. Sighing heavily, he shook his head. "You put me in a difficult position, young lady."

"I apologise," she said, honestly. "But I need your help to do what's right."

After some hesitation he said, "I'll speak with your father. I'm afraid you will have to delay your return, but shall we compromise and agree that you'll remain here for a further week?"

Aware she had little choice, Alice agreed. "Thank you. If you tell my father I'll no longer be needed here after then, he'll persuade my mother that there's little choice but to let me return to France. I can then write to my superiors and request a week's extension to my leave."

He turned and walked away from the house and down the driveway without saying anything further. Alice realised that although she wasn't able to leave immediately, she would only have to remain here for another seven days. She had done it. She had finally stood up for herself against her mother.

Everyone in the household knew her mother was giving a great performance. Ordinarily Alice would go along with it, as the family had always done. This time though things were different. Finally. She hoped it was the start of her being more assertive when it came to her home life. Now, she would visit her sister and then all she had to do was wait one more week before seeing Ed. She could not wait. Humming, she hurried inside to pen a letter to Matron Bleasdale.

Chapter 14

Gemma

2018

"I'm not sure who Alice Le Breton was," Gemma said to her father during a brief catch-up call, as she put away shopping she had bought in the village. "Like us, she has a connection to Jersey."

"Do you suspect she could be my late cousin's mother?" her father asked in contemplation.

"Possibly."

Tom knocked on the front door, and Gemma smiled and waved him in. She pointed at her mobile phone wedged between her right shoulder and ear and he nodded

"Was your cousin's last name Woodhall, by any chance?" Gemma asked, trying not to get excited at the prospect yet willing her father to say that it was. She loved the idea that Alice and Ed married and brought up their family in this farmhouse, living happily ever after.

"I'm ashamed to say I don't know," he said. "I'll look up his name when I get home and let you know."

"That would be great, thanks." She was desperate to glean as much knowledge about what had happened to Alice after the war. Gemma was excited at the prospect that maybe she and Alice actually were related. She hoped they were.

"You could simply read through the rest of the letters, you know," he said. She could tell her dad was irritated with her for giving him something to do. "Maybe you'll discover what happened to her by reading the final one."

Gemma had thought of that and resisted from groaning. "The final letter is still addressed to Alice Le Breton, Dad. That's why I'm asking."

"Don't forget you need to get that place ready to put on the market."

Gemma groaned inwardly at his reminder of the inevitable. She wasn't ready to think about packing up and leaving this place, let alone cheerily showing prospective buyers around her current sanctuary.

"Yes, I hadn't forgotten."

He sighed. "Right." There was a brief silence and then just when Gemma thought he might have cut her off, he said. "I'd better go. Your mother and I are off to some function at her law firm. Damn dreary evening it'll be, no doubt, but one has to make the effort."

"No problem," Gemma said. "Have a good time." She ended the call and turned to Tom. "The letters really are very romantic," she said dreamily. She leaned against the sink and closed her eyes briefly. She dreamt of having a love as beautiful as Alice and Ed's although supposed that a love like theirs probably only came about with the uncertainty of a war.

"Daydreaming?" Tom teased. "I'm going to leave you to it." She opened her eyes to see him pass her on his way to the back door, stopping when his hand grasped the Bakelite door handle. "I'll be fascinated to know how Alice's letters came to be hidden here."

Gemma smiled, paying attention once more. "Me, too." She could see he was wanting to say something more, but clearly wasn't sure how to put it.

"Go on, what's bothering you?" Gemma folded her arms and waited, amused. She wondered if Tom wanted to read the letters, too? She hoped so.

"I was thinking," he hesitated "About Ed's injuries."

Gemma stiffened. "What about them?" she asked quietly.

His pensive expression exuded sadness. "I can't help comparing the treatment of the injured soldiers back in the First World War to now," he said. "Men shouldn't have suffered so badly in the name of serving their country, but they still do."

"I agree," Gemma said, touched by his sentiments. She watched him walk outside, shoulders back and a determined expression on his face. She thought about how kind he'd been to her, stepping in at the last minute to take on the work at the farm. Gemma's heart swelled to watch him. She stood at the open back door.

He was unaware how much he was helping her heal and

move on with her life. Maybe one day, she would be able to trust her own instincts and have another intimate relationship with a man. She wished that man could be Tom, but as friendly as he was, there was still something haunting him. She wondered if it was the loss of his friends in Kabul. An experience like that was bound to change someone mentally, she mused, let alone Tom who was living with the physical consequences of that day.

Tom noticed her watching him. He looked over to her and smiled. "You're welcome to help anytime," he teased. "Get your wellies on. Come and do something useful."

Gemma made a big show of rolling her eyes heavenward, before doing as he suggested. She pulled on her coat as she crossed the courtyard and zipped it up. "What needs doing first?"

The morning passed quickly as Gemma handed Tom sheets of plasterboard so that he could fix them to the wall in the small outbuildings. By the time they returned to work after a bite to eat at lunchtime, Tom had explained that a plasterer friend would be coming by within the hour to do the walls in each room.

"That's quick," she said, surprised.

"I thought you'd be pleased," he said stopping what he was doing.

"I am," she fibbed. "I just didn't expect it, that's all."

You'll be able to paint the rooms in a few days," he said to Gemma. "Then I can get on with the partitions for the attic space, if you decide you want it converted."

"Maybe. I've been thinking about the stairs up to the attic rooms," she said. "I think a spiral staircase will probably work best, don't you?"

Tom considered the option. "There is another way," he said. "I'll get my phone and show you an idea I discovered last night when I was trawling through the Internet."

Gemma could not envisage another way to fit stairs up from the open barn area without taking up too much room.

Tom scrolled through his phone until he found what he was looking for. "There," he said pointing to what looked like a narrow wooden staircase. "If you're happy with that I can build it myself. We won't need to order one, so there'll be no delay waiting for it to be delivered. It'll be bespoke for the space, too."

"What about the cost?" she asked. "It looks good, but I know Dad won't want to spend a fortune."

"The supplies shouldn't be more than a couple of hundred," Tom said, pushing his phone into his back pocket. "Then my time. I guess it'll take me a few days."

"Great. Leave it with me to check with Dad, then I'll let you know."

Anything that delayed him at the farm was welcome to her. She would simply have to persuade her father that there was no option but to choose this staircase and hope that he trusted her enough to agree to pay for it.

Chapter 15

Alice

November 1916

This time Alice didn't care about her bumpy, cold journey back to the casualty clearing station. All she wanted was to see Ed again. It had been just over three weeks in reality but had felt like a lifetime. Three hours would be too long the way she felt about him now.

She dropped her suitcase into her tent and quickly changed into her uniform. Then, going to Matron's office, she knocked on the door.

"Enter," Matron said, her voice sounding strained, Alice thought.

She walked into the silent room, feeling a little nervous.

"Ah, Nurse Le Breton, you're back," Matron said, looking a little less severe than usual. "As I'm sure you expect, much has happened since you've been away." She checked her watch. "Your mother. She is better, I assume?"

Alice didn't like to admit that her mother had never

really been unwell and that her visit had not been a necessary one. "Yes, thank you. Much better now."

"Very good. I'm relieved to hear it," she straightened several sheets of paper on her desk. "I'd like you back on the wards as soon as possible. We're rather short staffed."

"Yes, Matron," Alice said, delighted to oblige. "Thank you, Matron."

She returned to Ward Three, eager to see Ed.

"Oh, you're back," Mary said, as she reached the ward entrance.

Alice could tell by the furrows of concern on her brow that something was amiss. "Is everything all right?" Alice asked, concerned for her friend.

Mary went to say something when Matron walked around the corner and spotted them chatting. "Nurse Le Breton, Nurse Jones. There is much work to be done. Go to your wards, immediately."

Alice pulled an apologetic face at Mary. She would have to ask her about her woes later when they were in their tent.

Striding into the ward, a smile on her face, Alice saw that there was a stranger in the bed where Ed used to be. Maybe they've rearranged the room, she thought, aware that it had happened many times since she'd begun working there. She scanned the room for sight of him and her heart raced when she couldn't see him anywhere. Surely, he hadn't relapsed? Trying to control her panic, she spotted a probationer and went over to her.

"Captain Woodhall," she said quietly. "Do you know where he's been moved to?"

The nurse frowned. "I'm sorry, which one is he?"

Concerned, but trying to remain professional, Alice pointed to where she had last seen him. "That was his bed, there."

The young girl thought for a moment. "Oh, yes. Injury to the head and hip, fair-haired, good looking," she smiled. "Is that the one?"

Alice wanted to throttle her for taking her time. "Yes."

"He was a nice man"

"Was?" Alice's heart plummeted. Exhausted from two days travelling and her rising panic was threatening to overwhelm her. "Please, what happened to him?"

"Oh, he's gone." She turned to walk away, but Alice stepped in front of her.

"Gone?" If he left, then he was fit. Relief flooded through her. But it meant that she had missed him. "When was this?"

"Two days ago," she said, folding her arms in front of her chest. "You all right?"

No, Alice thought, I'm not. She nodded. "Was he discharged, or sent home, do you know?"

"The Major deemed him fit to return to his unit. I gather he was sent back to the Front with about twenty other of the men." The girl smiled wistfully. "It always saddens me to think of them going back to those rat-infested trenches. After all the effort we put in to ensure they're kept clean and warm. When you think—"

"Yes," Alice snapped. She couldn't bear to think about Ed being posted back to the trenches. Then feeling badly for her reaction, added, "Thank you. I'm sorry, I'm a little tired. I've only just arrived back here."

"Don't worry," the nurse said. "I'd better press on anyway."

Alice marched off to go and find Mary. How could she have missed him by only two days? Two days. Her throat constricted with tears. No one must be allowed to see her cry though. The last thing she wanted was for anyone to discover their closeness.

"Have you seen Nurse Jones?" she asked a passing orderly as she rushed to the next ward. He shrugged and pulled out a cigarette and matches as he walked away from her.

"Was yer lookin' for that pretty nurse with the red 'air?" a patient asked from one of the wicker chairs on the lawn.

Relieved, Alice went over to him. "Yes, have you seen her?"

"Yeah, she's fetching me a tea. She should be back anytime now." He peered in the general direction that Mary would use coming back. "She 'as bin longer than I expected though."

Unsure whether to remain where she was and wait for Mary there, or go and look for her in the canteen, Alice thanked him. She paced back and forth, relieved when Mary re-appeared.

Alice's brain raced. Why had she not thought to swap addresses with Ed? What did she really know about him? Thanks to him being surrounded by other patients, either as he lay in the ward, or outside in the fresh air, the entire extent of their conversations consisted of information that wouldn't draw suspicion to their closeness.

"Ahh, you know, don't you?" Mary asked unnecessarily. "Come along," she said, linking arms with Alice. "I need you to come and fetch supplies." They began walking. "A convoy will be arriving in about an hour, so we need to stock up."

Once far enough away from the ward and any patients, Mary stopped. She hugged Alice. "I'm so sorry you missed him."

Alice couldn't hold back her tears of disappointment and frustration. "I can't believe it. Two days, that's all." She pushed away ill feeling towards her mother for being so selfish.

"I know, it's cruel."

Alice withdrew a handkerchief from her sleeve and blew her nose. "Sorry. It's just a bit unexpected, that's all. I've been looking forward to seeing Ed so much." She took a deep breath. "I haven't even asked how you are yet?" she said, wiping the tears from her wet cheeks with the bottom of her clean apron. "Any unexpected dramas that I should know about?"

"Never mind that," Mary said, walking on again towards the supply room. Once inside, she scanned the room to check they were alone, and said, "He's going to write to you."

"He mustn't. He knows I'm not allowed to correspond with him."

"That's true," Mary whispered. "But you can receive letters from your cousin."

Alice looked at her wondering if Mary had lost her mind. "But I don't have one. At least, not a male one."

Mary took Alice by the shoulders. "I know that, but no one else does. He said he'll find a way. Also, that if he mentions someone called Stuart in his letters, then that's him sending a personal message to you."

Alice stared at her friend in stunned surprise. She should have known Mary would not let her down, nor Ed. How typical of them both to collude in this way.

"Maybe he'll write letters as Stuart somebody-or-other," Mary added, giving Alice a satisfied smile. "You see, there is a way."

Relief that she hadn't lost contact with Ed, coursed through Alice. "Thank you, Mary," she said, hugging her friend tightly. "You're a good friend. I should have known you'd come up with an idea."

"He was the one who addressed me about it," she confided. Alice could see Mary was impressed with Ed. The thought that the two of them had become friendly made her happy. "He insisted I should tell you he'd find a way. He was desperate not to lose you." Mary beamed. "Those were his words, not mine. He's in love with you, Alice. You do know that, don't you?"

Alice had hoped it was the case. "I hadn't wanted to presume," she admitted. It was a joy to discover that the man she had fallen in love with, reciprocated her feelings and was happy to admit them to her friend.

Not wishing to be caught slacking, Alice began tidying the messy counter. Her mood dropped as a dreadful thought occurred to her. "He can't, Mary," she whispered.

"Can't what?"

Alice swallowed away the lump in her throat. "His letter. It will have to come from him. How can he post a letter from a fictional man? He's in the Army, he'd never manage it."

Alice felt sorry for Mary watching as her cheerful expression vanished.

"Oh, I'm so sorry Alice," she said covering her mouth with her left hand. "I truly thought it was a clever plan."

"It's fine," Alice lied. "I'm grateful to you for trying. Never mind."

But it did matter. It mattered very much. Pretending to carry on with what she was doing, Alice turned her back on Mary so that her friend wouldn't witness her heartbreak.

The door flew open and crashed noisily against the wooden wall of the hut. The women shrieked in shock.

"For pity's sake," Mary shouted at the white-faced probationer. "What do you think you're doing barging in here like that? You could have given us apoplexy."

"Sorry Nurse," the younger woman said, her cheeks reddening.

"Well?" Alice asked, relieved for something to take her mind off her misery. "What's the matter?"

"I've been looking for you everywhere," she said, not looking at Mary, who Alice could see from the corner of her eyes was glaring at the girl. "Matron said we need all those on duty to come to her office, at once. That was five minutes ago."

"Goodness," Mary said, "Leave this lot, we can fetch it later."

The three of them hurried to Matron's office.

"Look," Alice grabbed Mary's right wrist outside the office door as they slowed to a walk. "Over there." She pointed at a large tent being erected in a nearby field.

"It looks like they're setting up another ward," Mary said. "Come along, we'd better get a move on."

"I hate this war," Alice said, her voice cracking in emotion. "There's far too much death. I don't know how much more of it I can stand."

Mary put her arm around Alice's shoulder. "I know. It's beyond anything I could have imagined, too. My aunt wrote just yesterday telling me that almost a quarter of the men who joined up, or were conscripted, have fallen. Their poor families will never recover."

Both women smoothed down their skirts and checked their caps were straight before knocking on Matron's office door.

"Enter." Matron shouted.

Alice put her hand up to turn the door knob, when another nurse inside opened the door and pulled her in.

"Come inside and close the door," Matron snapped. "Where have you two been? We've been waiting," she lifted her watch to calculate how long. "Six minutes."

Alice led the way into the packed office. She looked around at the other faces, trying to work out what they were all doing in there.

"Sorry, Matron," Alice and Mary said, in unison.

Matron glared at them. As soon as they were standing behind the other assembled nurses, she began, "Now that we're all here, I can tell you that there's been a big push. We have a substantial number of casualties being brought down the line to us. I need everyone to be prepared. Do as much as you can for the current patients, naturally. However, be aware that we will be kept busy overnight with the men on their way to us now."

"Yes, Matron," they said in unison.

"I'm advised that there's a badly burnt pilot among them." She looked at Mary and Alice. "You two nurses have more experience than most of the volunteers here. I want you to assist Sister Brown with his care. He's in a bad way." She took a deep breath. "I want a report as soon as Sister has settled him in the ward."

"Yes, Matron."

Matron went on to give further instruction to the other nurses and volunteers assembled in her office. Alice couldn't help worrying that her lack of knowledge, was going to be an issue. She reminded herself that Sister Brown might be a tyrant to those under her, but to the patients she was an angel, albeit a formidable one and would give them any necessary instructions.

They knew not to try and remove any part of the sedated pilot's uniform in contact with his skin. Silently, Alice and Mary concentrated as they took off the outer layers under Sister Brown's watchful eye and settled him in a bed.

"There's no spare room in any of the wards. I want a

screen kept around him at all times." She handed Mary a clipboard with his report sheet on it. "This is a good opportunity for the pair of you to show your mettle," she said. "Now, what do you see?"

"Apart from burns to his face and hands," Alice said, as Mary wrote up their report. "Both his femurs and left tibia appear to be broken, as well as his left forearm."

Doctor Sullivan walked in, closely followed by one of the other doctors.

"How is he, Sister?" the doctor asked.

"We're doing all we can to make him comfortable."

They waited silently while the doctors examined the man, who Alice was saddened to discover was only just twenty-one. She could see that the airman's chances were slim.

The doctors discussed their thoughts quietly to one side. Eventually, Doctor Sullivan said, "We'll aim to operate in the morning. We need to stabilise him as much as possible, Sister." He looked from Alice to Mary. "I need him to be watched around the clock until further notice."

"Of course, Doctor," Matron said.

The doctors left, and Matron said, "Nurse Le Breton, go and find an orderly. Tell him we need a frame to cover this man's body. I don't want sheets touching his damaged skin."

"Yes, Sister," Alice said, relieved to be able to do something constructive.

Chapter 16

Gemma

2018

Sitting outside the front door on an upturned bucket, Gemma slammed the letter onto her knee, wincing as it tore on one side. She couldn't bear reading that Alice had returned to the casualty clearing station after Ed had been sent back to the Front. She could only imagine Alice's shock discovering he wasn't there.

Did she and Ed ever manage to meet up again, she wondered? "They have to find a way," she groaned, wishing Tom wasn't busy in the barn. She hated to disturb him but was tempted to go and share her concerns with him about this couple who had grown to mean so much to her. Unable to help herself, she read on. "Poor man." Gemma said, transfixed by the latest note on the back of the letter.

"You okay?" Tom asked, alerting her to his arrival. His eyes narrowed in concern. He noticed the letter and nodded. "Ah, Alice's letters. What's happened now?"

Gemma sighed. "She only made it back to the CCS after Ed had been discharged. Do you think they ever saw each other again?"

"I hope they did," Tom said, looking as saddened by the news as she had been.

"There was a young pilot, who was admitted." She sniffed. "Oh, Tom, it's horrible. The unfortunate man was badly burnt when his plane was shot down." She thought of how basic the burn treatment must have been one hundred years before. "How on earth did they look after men in that condition back then?"

Tom shuddered. "I hate to think." He walked up to her and placed a soothing hand on her right shoulder. "They didn't have the luxury of antibiotics either, did they? I've read that they achieved some incredible work reconstructing soldiers' faces, but that was mainly for shrapnel or bullet wounds." He shook his head. "I've no idea about burn victims."

"Nor me. I'll have to investigate a bit about it, when I have access to the Internet."

"I'd rather not know," Tom shivered. He stared at the letter. "Did he survive?"

"I don't know yet," she said, carefully folding the thin paper and sliding it inside the yellowed envelope. "I hope so." She stood up and stretched. "Did you want me for something?"

"No rush. I just thought you might have some ideas about where you want the electric points and lights in the attic space above the barn area."

Gemma had not thought about it and admitted as much. "I haven't given it a thought," she said, feeling ridiculous. "Is it big enough to fit a couple of rooms?"

He looked surprised.

"What?"

"You haven't seen it?"

"No, when would I have gone up there?"

Tom took the envelope from Gemma's hand and put it inside on the dining room table. "Sorry, I assumed you must have done at some point. Right, you're coming with me."

Gemma took his hand. It was only when his step faltered that she realised she'd been talking about war wounds again and she hoped she hadn't upset Tom. She went to pull her hand away, but Tom tightened his hold and pulled her along through the house to the back yard.

"I'm not taking no for an answer," he smiled, misunderstanding her reluctance to go with him. "You can't make a decision about the electrics if you haven't seen the place." He stopped and pointed up at the roof of the barn.

"Do you see that tiny window?" He asked, and Gemma nodded. "I'm going to show you a fantastic view. When you see it, I'm sure you'll agree that the area can be made into a large party room, or flatlet, or something else. With a couple of large sky lights in the roof, the space up there will be airy and bright."

Gemma liked the sound of his ideas. She couldn't hide her excitement and ran towards the stepladder. "Is it safe to go up?"

"Yes, perfectly safe. I put that ladder against the first floor earlier.

"No wonder I've never thought to go up there, if this is the only access."

Tom took his hand from hers and smiled. "Go on, I'll make sure you don't fall."

She groaned and climbed up the stepladder taking each step tentatively. Her stomach contracted in fear as she stepped higher.

"I hate heights," Gemma admitted. "I'm not sure this is going to be worth my efforts."

"It will, I promise you," Tom assured her. "I've left a torch up there; can you see it?"

"Yes," Gemma said, gritting her teeth and wishing she had never agreed to this. She grabbed hold of the sides of the opening on the floor above and carefully stepped forward. "How am I going to get down?" she asked breathlessly.

"I'll help you," Tom said, his head appearing in the opening of the floor behind her. "Never mind about that now." He stood up next to her. "Here, take my hand again," Tom said, picking up the torch. "I've laid plywood on the beams, so you don't have to worry about where you're walking. Come on, this way."

Focusing on the distraction of her hand held tightly in his, Gemma did as he asked.

"Right, through here." Tom said, and Gemma let him pull her along, following the beam of light coming from the torch in his hand. "Oh, I see it," she said, spotting the shaft of sunlight glinting through the tiny window in the roof.

They reached the tiny window and Tom stepped back to let Gemma have a look. "It's not as clean as it could be, but you should get an idea of the view across the fields."

Gemma pressed her hands on each side of the window and standing on tiptoes peered out of the grimy window. He was right, the view across the poppy field was stunning. "I can see the fields and a wood beyond that," she said, awed at Tom's discovery. "It's glorious."

"I'm glad you agree," he said; and Gemma could tell he was smiling as he spoke. "Obviously, it depends on how much you have left to spend on this place after all the main renovations have been made. However, if you don't make the changes up here, you could always point them out to a buyer when the time comes to sell the farm."

Gemma felt another pang at the thought of leaving the farm. She wondered if her growing attachment could have anything to do with her growing attraction to Tom. She turned to face him, unable to hide the delight on her face. "That really is a brilliant discovery of yours," she said smiling up at his tanned face lit by the shard of sunlight. "Thank you."

They stared at each other silently for a moment. It was as if nothing else mattered as she stared into his navy-blue eyes. They seemed to bore into her soul and for a split second she imagined she was Alice and he was Ed and they did have their happy ever after at the farm.

Tom was the first to move. He held out an arm waiting

for her to step forward. "Come along. I'd better press on if I'm to get everything done before I leave," he said, shattering her romantic thoughts.

"Yes, sure," she said walking forward towards the opening in the floor. She stopped suddenly, her heart pounding as she tried to work out how to get down to the ground without falling. "I don't think I can do it."

Tom stood behind her and took her by the shoulders. "Don't fret," he said.

"I'm serious," she panted, her mouth dry. "I can't move."

He gave her shoulders a light squeeze. "I'll move past you now and climb a few steps down."

Unable to see how that would help, she held her breath as Tom slowly manoeuvred around her. He placed first one foot and then the other on the ladder.

Stepping down a couple of rungs, he reached out to her. "Take my hand," he said. "Go on, I promise I won't let you fall."

"I'm very clumsy," she argued, picturing herself tumbling head first onto the concrete below. "I'm always tripping over things. I know I'll do the same going down."

He stared at her, his hand still outstretched. "I said I won't let you fall, and I won't. Now, inch forward," he said, waiting patiently as she did so. "Good, now, take my hand."

Gemma grabbed for his hand and held on tightly. She wasn't sure if he winced as she clung on, but when he nodded to her she felt slightly reassured.

"Turn around, so that your back is against me," he said, his calm assertive voice soothing her fear enough for her to be able to do as he asked. "Well done. Now take a step down, that's it." Gemma concentrated on finding the first rung with her foot and then the next.

Tom slipped his arm around her waist, holding onto the ladder with the other hand. "Okay, now let's take one rung at a time."

She did as he asked, comforted by his tight hold around her waist. His warm body pressed against her back distracted her enough to enable her to make it to the bottom of the ladder and onto the cobbled barn floor.

"There," he said, letting go of her.

Gemma's joy at being back on terra firma was lessened by his sudden release of her. She turned to face him, forcing a smile. "Thank you, Tom. I'm sorry to be such a baby about that, but I really am terrified of heights."

"No problem at all," he said, pushing his hands through his hair to push it off his face. "We all have things that frighten us."

She couldn't imagine what his fears might be. If he did have any, he kept them well hidden.

"I feel such a fool," she admitted, gazing down at her feet.

Tom took her face gently in his hands. "You're not a fool, Gemma," he whispered.

She barely had time to register where his hands were before he bent his head and kissed her lightly on her lips. It was so unexpected that she was unsure how to react. He moved back slightly, and she could see he was unsure about whether to continue. Gemma gave him a shaky smile, relieved, when Tom took her in his arms and kissed her so perfectly, her knees seemed to lose their strength and she had to focus on staying upright.

Gemma slid her arms around his neck and kissed him back. Her mind went blank as she lost herself in the blissful kiss. Sensing someone nearby, she ignored it, relishing the closeness with Tom and the discovery that his expertise at kissing was better than anything she had experienced before.

There was a deep cough behind her. Tom dropped his hold on her at the same moment Gemma realised it was the plasterer making his presence felt. She swung round, feeling like a naughty teenager being caught snogging her boyfriend late on a school night.

"Hello?" she said feeling awkward.

He held up both hands. "Don't mind me," he said glancing at Tom. "I thought you said two o'clock, Tom."

"Yes, of course. Sorry," Tom said, stepping away from her. "This is Gemma, she's renovating the farm." Gemma nodded. "Follow me and I'll show you what needs doing." He turned to Gemma. "I'll catch up with you later?"

"Yes, fine," she said, leaving them and walking back to the house. "I'd better get on."

Deciding that now was as good a time as any, Gemma went to grab her phone hoping her father was around to take the call.

He answered almost immediately. "What's the matter?" he asked impatiently.

"Nothing, Dad," she said, annoyed that he acted as if

she was constantly harassing him. She told him about the upper floor of the small barn. "I think we could make use of the loft by turning it into a couple of rooms, or studio flats, or enclosing down below and building one or two gîtes. What do you think?"

There was silence as he gave her idea some thought. "It all depends on the cost and whether or not we'd get our money back in a sale." He hesitated. "However good an idea is, you don't want to spend more than you'll make back on a property."

"I thought the same thing, but I do like the idea."

"So, do I," he said. "Let me give it some thought, and I'll get back to you."

Gemma, happy not to have received an immediate rejection for Tom's idea, walked up the slope towards the field. She stopped at the gate, transfixed by a sparrow hawk circling overhead before swooping down to grab its prey. Taking in the scene in front of her, Gemma felt the atmosphere of the history to the place. She assumed Alice had lived here, but for how long? Did she come to live here with her beloved Ed, she wondered? She pictured the two of them walking hand in hand in the long grass, wild flowers brushing against their legs, then stopping to kiss.

Her thoughts returned to Tom. What happens now between us? He'd go to his other job, she thought miserably. His kiss had altered things between them now. At least it had for her.

"You're miles away," Tom said, giving her a gentle nudge. "It's peaceful up here, isn't it?"

217

"Yes, it's difficult to imagine that there was ever a war going on near here."

"It is," he agreed. "To think that there are men and women still fighting out there somewhere in the world, still dying," He studied her face. "We're very lucky to have this time here, Gemma," he said, looking serious.

"You say that as if it's about to end," she said, dread seeping into her mind.

Gemma looked at him lost in thought.

"I was always carefree, before this happened," he said tapping his prosthetic leg. "I've learnt that you have to live in the moment without being fearful. Take opportunities when they arise, without thinking too far in advance."

"I'm learning a lot from you, Tom Holloway," she said. "Spending time here with you has made me question so much about my life."

"Good for you," he said. "I think that as long as we're learning and making the most of things, then we're doing the best for ourselves."

"I think that makes a lot of sense." She watched him and wondered how long they would have here together. She needed to take charge of her life. She'd shown herself that she had more guts than she had ever imagined before. So, why stop now?

Chapter 17

Alice

December 1916

"I'm sad he died," Alice whispered to Mary as they congregated with the others, waiting for the pilot's coffin to be carried out of the mortuary. She fought back tears. "I know he was dangerously ill, but his bones would have mended eventually."

"Yes, but what about the burns to his poor body?" Mary signed. "He was in terrible pain and only regained consciousness once."

"I was hoping there was something they could do for him," Alice said keeping her voice low. "They're making incredible progress medically now."

"Not so much for burns, they are something else entirely."

Alice agreed. "I have to admit they're the worst. It breaks my heart to see these poor pilots coming in, although most of them die when the plane goes down."

They stopped speaking when Major Phillips stepped out

of his office, followed by Matron, two other senior officers and a priest, all with sadness etched on their faces. The coffin was carried outside and Monseigneur Jacques, the priest who had become part of the daily order of the place, stepped in front of it. The solemn cortège began its brief journey to the clearing station cemetery.

Alice clasped her hands together in front of her uniform. She walked in silence, head down, with the rest of the mourners. She had made this journey many times now and it never got any easier. Each death stung and reminded her painfully how fruitless this war had become. They had been at war for over three years, and still there was no end in sight. At least the staff and those patients able to join in the procession, were able to give the fallen men the respect and honour they deserved. She felt it gave them all a sense that they were giving the dead one last act of respect, where their family were unable to do so.

The procession reached the edge of the cemetery and stopped in front of the freshly dug grave. Alice pulled her cape tighter around her shoulders, as if it was able to give her some comfort. She listened to the priest, his face a mask of sadness, as he held his worn bible, speaking for them all to another life lost.

At the end of the short service, each member of the congregation made the sign of the cross and bowed their heads. The drizzle fell as the casket was lowered slowly into the ground. After a moment of reflection, Major Phillips began walking with Monseigneur Jacques back to his office.

"They're brave men, those pilots," one of the probationers

said to anyone who would listen. "My friend was courting one of them a few months ago. She said that those planes are only made out of wood. Wood? That's no protection against bullets, is it?"

"Shush," Mary said. "Keep your voice down."

"Sorry," she said, taking a breath to continue. "Did you know they're only covered with Irish linen. It's dipped in something, although I can't recall what, but that sounds flimsy to say the least."

"It sounds horribly fragile," Alice agreed.

"The pilots can't see straight ahead of them either," the girl added, her volume increasing as she imparted the information. "I heard that their line of vision is blocked by the engine and propeller. If they want to keep an eye out for any enemy planes coming for them, they have to keep moving about."

"Can that be right?" Alice asked, shocked. "Imagine flying at speed and not being able to see directly ahead of you?" The thought terrified her. "It adds to their bravery, I think." She pictured the dead pilot. How dashing must he have looked in his blue uniform and leather jacket? She wondered who would be grieving for him at home.

The drizzle turned to rain and everyone moved faster. Alice and Mary reached their tent.

Checking no one was near enough to overhear, Mary said, "I was told that the average life expectancy of a pilot is only seven days."

Alice shuddered. "That's dreadful," she said, hoping Mary was wrong. She was relieved Ed wasn't a pilot. Then again, hearing Mary's comment made her wonder about the statistics for an infantryman. She couldn't bear it if he was hurt again. The thought of anything worse happening to him than what he'd suffered forced her to stop her train of thought and focus on something else.

"I suppose we'd better take these off," she said undoing her cape and shaking it near the entrance to the tent. "We need to get back to work." She yawned. She needed more sleep but worrying about Ed did not help. When was she going to hear from him? She needed to know he was safe.

The following morning the mail was brought into the yard. As usual, all mail addressed to the nurses was taken to Matron's office to be checked.

"I hope she doesn't take too long," Mary said, as she crossed paths with Alice. "My aunt promised to send me more socks and a pair of gloves. It's getting cold and I know I haven't enough to keep me warm this winter."

Alice had been so preoccupied with Ed's situation and the deteriorating condition of the pilot that she had given no thought to her own winter wardrobe. She would write to her mother later. Maybe ask for her to send a few things to make another winter in the leaking bell tent more bearable.

"Good idea," she said, wishing she was focused on practical things, like Mary. "We'd better return to the ward."

An hour later, Alice was called into Matron's office.

"You've received a letter from a Lieutenant Peter Conway," Matron said taking Alice off guard.

Alice wasn't sure who this person was, or why she would receive a letter from him. But then she thought about Ed. Could this be a letter from him? Distracted by her thoughts she struggled to come up with a reply.

Matron looked as if she had taken Alice's hesitation as concern, and said, "You haven't received any mail from your cousin before now, have you, Nurse Le Breton?" she asked.

"No, no Matron," Alice answered, her heart beating faster and faster in her chest.

"Well, you have now."

"Yes, Matron."

"He's requested that you're given an afternoon's leave to meet up with him."

"He has?" Alice didn't dare hope that this was Ed, trying to conjure up a way for them to meet.

Matron handed Alice her letter.

"Tomorrow afternoon, at two o'clock." Matron stared at Alice, her face solemn. "I am happy to oblige with his request."

Alice couldn't help smiling. "Thank you, Matron." Her heart pounded so hard that she was sure Matron might hear it and suspect what was going on.

"I don't like my nurses travelling off the camp alone," Matron added.

Alice's excitement waned slightly.

"You will need a lift into town. I have arranged for an ambulance to collect three of the patients to take them to the docks. It should arrive at one-thirty, which leaves more than enough time for you to make your way to the village for your appointment." She smiled, thoughtfully.

She straightened two pieces of paper on her desk. "I have given permission to Nurse Jones to accompany you," Matron said, finally. "You both must ensure to be back at the grounds by five o'clock."

"Thank you, Matron," she said, trying not to show her excitement.

"Do not let me down now, Nurse Le Breton." Matron stared at her for a moment.

"No, Matron," Alice answered, trying not to show how guilty she already felt to be leaving under a false pretext. "Would you like me to ask Nurse Jones to come and see you now?"

Matron shook her head. Alice noticed the dark circles under the older woman's eyes. For the first time, it occurred to Alice that however tired they were as nurses, Matron Bleasdale had to keep order of them all. The stress of her work was beginning to show.

"Here is your permission slip," Matron said, handing two slips to Alice. "The one for Nurse Jones is with it." She gave Alice a smile. "And here is a letter addressed to you from the Lieutenant. I hope you have a pleasant afternoon with your cousin."

Alice took the proffered slips and Ed's letter, noticing that the stamp was not stuck onto the envelope neatly. "Thank you, Matron," she said, leaving the office before the redness building in her cheeks alerted the older woman to her deception.

"I knew he'd manage it somehow," Mary giggled when they were alone in their tent later.

"I felt a little mean," Alice said. "Especially when she was so friendly and kind about my time with my cousin." She handed one of the slips to Mary. "I have to admit I am excited to see him."

"Clever Captain Woodhall," Mary said, giggling.

Alice lay back on her bed and closed her eyes, clutching her permission slip to her chest. She was grateful to him for being bold enough to try such a tactic. She didn't think she had felt this happy for months.

"I can't wait," she said, placing her slip into her purse, so that she didn't mislay it. "It's going to be a little strange to meet him socially though. I've only spent time with him being a patient here."

"Where are we meeting him?" Mary asked, sitting down on her bed, staring at the piece of paper in her hand.

"Hotel du Nord," Alice said, scanning her letter from Ed. She couldn't wait to read it in its entirety. However, she wanted to be alone to do so to relish every nuance and curve of his slanted writing. "In the village. We should arrive there at about two o'clock, I suppose. He's asked us to take tea with him." She realised his letter made no mention of Mary at their meeting. Alice looked up to see Mary smiling at her.

"I wonder how that will taste," Mary giggled.

"It could taste like brine for all I care," Alice sighed, longing to see Ed again.

"You don't want me playing gooseberry. I'll take myself

off for a walk around the town. I love exploring new places."

Mortified to think of her friend making herself scarce so she could spend time with Ed, Alice shook her head frowning. "Absolutely not. You deserve tea and cakes, or whatever we will be served, as much as we do," she said. "I don't know much about Ed, but he is a gentleman. I can't imagine he'd allow you to spend the afternoon by yourself in a strange place, whatever you say." She thought about how she could find some time alone with him. "We can all go for a walk afterwards, if the weather stays fine. Ed and I shall walk a little behind you, we can talk then."

"If you're quite sure," Mary said, unconvinced.

"Absolutely," Alice said, determined not to push her friend aside. "You simply mustn't wander around the village alone, it wouldn't be seemly."

"You don't know when you'll next be able to see him. Let's not make too many definite plans about tomorrow, shall we?"

"You're a good friend, Mary," Alice said, grateful for her friend's understanding.

She stared at the envelope longing to read the letter inside. "He has beautiful writing, don't you think?" Alice said. "The stamp confuses me though."

Mary laughed and picked up her wash bag and towel. "Perhaps he's sent you a message."

"What do you mean?" She stared at the crooked image of the King's head.

"Depending on which way the stamp is stuck on to the envelope will depict the message he's trying to send to you."

Delighted for this extra surprise, Alice, held up the envelope for her friend to see. "What has he said to me with this one?"

Mary shrugged. "I don't know, sorry."

Disappointed, Alice frowned. "You really don't know, or are you teasing me?"

Mary placed her hand lightly on her friend's shoulder. "I'm afraid I really have no clue. You'll have to ask Ed when you see him."

Alice didn't want to wait that long, but knew she had no choice. She didn't feel comfortable asking anyone other than Mary about it, in case her friend had made a wrong assumption.

Later when Mary went to the ablution block to wash, Alice read her letter.

Dearest cousin,

I have taken it upon myself to write to your Matron. I have requested permission for you to meet with me for afternoon tea. We have not seen each other in such a long time and I thought that as well as catching up with my dear cousin, Alice, I very much hope that we will be able to spend the afternoon together and look forward to hearing about how Aunt Cecelia and Uncle Frank are coping in Jersey.

I look forward to hearing from Matron, and you, too,

dearest cousin. Stuart sends his best love and wishes his auntie well. He hopes she isn't working too hard, or missing home too much. I am assured he is looking forward to a time when his aunt can hug him once more.

Well, dearest Alice, I have less enjoyable letter writing to which I must urgently attend.

I hope my request is granted and that we are able to meet.

Sincerely,
Your cousin,
Peter

He had sent his love and wanted to hug her. She folded the sheet of paper and slid it back into the envelope. The thought of being in his arms again so soon made her feel energised. Alice hugged herself pretending it was his arms about her. How clever of him to think of this and to mention Stuart in such a way. She was much happier now, knowing that she would soon be back in Ed's arms.

The following day was humid. The sun beat down on the dry grass, but Alice didn't mind because she was treated to another letter from her fictional cousin. This time the stamp was upside down. Intrigued, she wished she could decipher this message. Never mind, she'd be seeing him soon.

"How is it that my hair looks all messy, today of all days?" Alice moaned, dipping two fingers in her half-empty glass of water and dampening a few unruly strands.

"It's always the way," Mary said, pulling on her hat and checking her reflection in her small hand mirror.

"Oh, this will just have to do," Alice said, fed up with her wasted efforts. "Quick, we're going to have to run if we don't want to miss our lift into town." She hurriedly pushed her arms into the sleeves of her coat and making a grab for her hat and handbag, ran out of the tent.

Alice pulled on her hat as she ran, dropping her bag and having to stop to retrieve it. "Don't let him go without us," she shouted.

Mary waved to stop the ambulance driver from driving away. "We're on our way," she yelled.

By the time Alice reached the auto ambulance, Mary was already making herself comfortable. She pushed the door open with her foot. "Come along."

"Thank you," Alice said, a little out of breath. She squeezed onto the passenger seat next to her friend. "I'm sorry if we kept you waiting."

"Yer didn't, love," the driver said, smiling. "I don't do waitin', for no one. Thirty seconds later and you would 'ave bin walking in ter the town."

"Well, we're relieved we made it to you in time," Mary said widening her eyes as she glanced at Alice and shuffling over slightly to give her more room.

Alice tried to ignore the butterflies fluttering around in her stomach as the ambulance reached the town. The first thing she noticed was the high belfry that overlooked the town and then passed the impressive brick town hall with its wide steps in front of the entrance. She had missed Ed enormously, but now felt nervous and was unable to think of anything that she would talk to him about.

"Right, ladies," the driver said, pulling over in front of the town square. "I will be back 'ere at five on the dot. If you're 'ere I'll give yer a lift back to the 'ospital. If not, then that's yer look out."

He seemed rather aggressive to Alice, but the smile on his face made her think that maybe it was just his way. The women got out of the ambulance and thanked him.

"We'll be here," Mary said. "Goodbye."

"Enjoy yerselves."

They watched him drive away and scanned the area around them. "Look," Alice said, the fluttering in her stomach going into overdrive, as she pointed. "There's the Hotel du Nord."

"Are you all right?" Mary asked quietly. "You've gone awfully pale."

Alice took a deep breath. "To tell you the truth, I'm terrified," she admitted, pushing her shoulders back and checking her hat was on straight. "Do I look presentable?"

Mary reached out and smoothed down one side of Alice's coat collar. "There, you look perfect."

"Thank you," Alice said, looking across the square at the clock on the church spire. "It's nearly time to meet him." She shivered. "I'm relieved you're here. I can't think what I'm going to say."

"You'll forget your nerves when you see him," Mary assured her as they walked in silence to the hotel entrance. Inside, Mary gave Alice a gentle nudge. "Just remember that this is Ed, the man you've seen at death's door. He isn't a stranger you're trying to impress. He knows you and has seen you in many stressful situations."

She was right, Alice realised. This was Ed. The same man who she had given bed baths to and who had shielded her body with his own, being grazed by a shard of wood that would have otherwise caught her. There was nothing to be frightened about.

Alice took a calming breath and smiled. "Let's go and see if he's inside, shall we?"

Happy muted voices could be heard leading them to the dining room without them having to ask the way. They reached the doorway and Alice looked around the light-filled room, smiling in anticipation of seeing Ed for the first time in months.

It was difficult to make him out in the sea of faces, but then Mary coughed quietly to get her attention. "There he is," she murmured.

Alice looked in the direction of Mary's gaze and saw Ed and another man stand up. Ed beamed at her and unable to help herself, Alice returned his smile. He looked thin and pale, she decided, giving him a little wave. Trying to retain her decorum, Alice led the way passed a seemingly endless line of chairs to the table where the uniformed men stood.

Their eyes locked. Alice looked at him properly for the first time, relieved when she noted that he seemed as delighted to see her as she knew she was to be with him again. Her heart raced. She hadn't seen him in his uniform before, not standing up and looking so immaculate.

"Good afternoon, Mary," he said giving her a slight nod. Then turning to address Alice, he took her hand and lifting it to his mouth gave it a gentle kiss. "Alice. I've been looking forward to this afternoon since you left for Jersey." He indicated the dark-haired officer standing next to him. "This is Lieutenant Peter Conway."

Alice and Mary gazed at the handsome man, but Alice was certain their reasons for staring at him were very different.

"Lieutenant Conway," Alice said extending her arm to shake his hand. "I believe you're my cousin. Thank you for inviting me to afternoon tea."

"Please, call me Peter," he said. "It was my pleasure, cousin Alice."

"This is my friend and fellow VAD, Nurse Mary Jones," Alice said unable to help smiling when she saw how wide Mary's eyes were, as she stared at the man in front of her.

"I'm very pleased to make your acquaintance Nurse Jones," he said.

"Please," Ed said, grinning. "Take a seat."

They sat down. Alice, aware that they only had two and a half hours before having to meet the auto ambulance, decided that she was not going to waste any of her afternoon by being coy.

"It was very clever of you to arrange this meeting, Ed," she said allowing him to take her hand under the small table. It felt soothing to have his hand holding hers. "And kind of you, Peter."

"Were you confused at all?" Peter asked. "Or, did you

know immediately that my friend here had come up with the idea?"

She shook her head and gave Ed's hand a squeeze. "I have to admit that when Matron called me in to see her and told me about my cousin Peter writing to me, it took a couple of seconds to work out what must be happening. I was excited to think that Ed might be behind the letter in some way, but hardly dared hope his plan would work."

It felt surreal being in the same room with him, and when Alice turned her attention to Ed she saw him gazing back at her. They stared at each other in silence.

"I've missed you," he said. "Very much."

Alice could only imagine how horrified her mother would be right now to witness her forwardness with a man she barely knew. "I missed you, too," she said, vaguely aware that Mary was talking to Peter to give them some semblance of privacy. "I was devastated when I arrived back at the CCS and discovered that you had returned to your unit."

Ed nodded. "It came a little out of the blue," he said. "They needed the numbers and I was just about fit enough to go back, so off I went."

"If only I hadn't let the doctor persuade me to delay my return by a week," she said, wondering when her resentment towards her mother would diminish. "I knew she wasn't ill, almost as soon as I arrived home in Jersey."

"She's your mother," he said squeezing her hand. "She loves you. I can understand her wanting to find a way to spend time with you."

"You can?" She thought he was being rather noble and

generous with his feelings towards the woman whose self-ishness had kept them apart.

"Naturally," he said, smiling at her. "Isn't that what I've done, by roping in Peter to pretend to be your cousin?"

Alice mused over his sentiments. Her irritation with her mother softened. "I hadn't thought of it like that. Poor Mother. I'm so desperate to make my own decisions from now on, that I suppose I've been the selfish one in this instant."

"Let's not concern ourselves with unpleasantness. How about we order tea and then I thought we could take a stroll by the river."

"That sounds heavenly," Alice said, nodding. She hadn't walked along the River Authie before but had heard it was very pretty. "I'm famished."

They ordered a tier of home-made pastries and it occurred to Alice as she sipped at the weak tea that this wasn't the British tea she had initially expected. What a fool to expect this to be something different. She asked the others what they thought about it.

"I think," Peter said quietly. "That there's someone running this hotel who has very good business acumen. They are trying to accommodate us, I'm not so sure we would be so generous if it was the other way around."

"What better way to ensure the British soldiers stationed nearby come and frequent this establishment though," Ed said, his fingers grazing Alice's. "Mind you, the tea is pretty dire."

"It's near enough for me," Mary said, refilling their cups

with the weak amber liquid. "And anything is welcome in this heat."

"It certainly is," Ed agreed.

"We've been desperate to try these pastries," Mary added. "We've heard the baker is the best in the area."

"Yes," Ed said, drawing his gaze reluctantly from Alice's face. "I've heard the same thing said about this place." He looked from one to the other. "You both seem well. Matron not running you ragged then?"

"We're surviving," Mary joked. "It's great to get away from the place though, especially Sister Brown."

Alice was aware that she needed to snap out of her dreamlike state and nodded. "Yes, it's a relief to have some time away."

"No more issues with the Hun flying over recently?" Ed asked, frowning.

"No, thankfully. How about you two? Or do you not wish to discuss it?" Alice added after she spotted Peter glance at Ed.

"The usual organised chaos," Peter scowled. "I do wonder if—"

"I think we change the subject to more brighter topics," Ed suggested giving his friend a pat on the back.

"Absolutely." Peter smiled at Mary and Alice apologetically.

"How is Corporal Healy?" Ed asked. "When I was discharged they were about to send him back to Blighty to be looked after by his family for a few months."

"He's gone home," Alice said. "He was so excited to see

that baby girl of his. It was all he talked about." She laughed at the thought of the man with the lovely Irish lilt telling stories to anyone who would listen about his family. "Her and his strapping boys, he was so proud of them all."

"Good, I'm glad," Ed said. "He was a fine chap and I'm pleased to hear he is home with his family."

A shadow crossed his face and he looked down at his half-eaten cake. Alice didn't like to see him sad. "One of these days, we'll look back at this time differently, I suppose."

Ed looked at her. "I'll remember my time at the CCS fondly. How could I not when it was how I met you."

"Me, too," she said, not caring that she was blushing.

"Eat up Captain," Mary said putting on her best nursing voice. "We don't want to miss out on our stroll, do we?"

Ed laughed. "No, we don't."

Alice watched as he finished his cake. He was still very thin, and she had a feeling that something was worrying him. Was it the big push that they were preparing for? She hoped not. The thought of Ed going over the top terrified her. She shivered.

Ed noticed. "Are you all right?"

"I'm fine," she lied. "I just wish I didn't have to say goodbye to you today, that's all."

"Me, too," he said. He glanced at Peter and Mary as he put the last forkful of cake into his mouth and chewed. Swallowing, he dabbed his mouth with his napkin and placed it down on the table. "Finished, Nurse Jones," he joked. "I'll go and settle this and we can go for our walk."

"Thank you," Alice said, wishing that she could stay with Ed and never leave him.

Alice and Mary excused themselves and went to the bathroom to freshen up before their walk.

"He's jolly nice, isn't he?" Mary said, grinning at Alice.

"I assume you're referring to Peter," Alice teased, brushing her hair and pinching her cheeks to ensure she looked healthy. "Yes, he is. It makes this afternoon so much more fun now that you have someone to accompany you, especially as you like him."

Mary straightened her hat and grinned at her reflection. "My tummy is all fluttery," she whispered, glancing to check they were still alone in the small room. "I like him rather more than I probably should do, having only met him today."

Alice straightened her hat and linked arms with her friend. "This is turning out to be a treat of an afternoon," she said, thinking that it was far more than that for both of them.

They left the bathroom. "I shan't be a moment," Alice said realising she had forgotten her handkerchief on the wash stand. "I'll catch up with you. You go ahead, I'll only be a moment," she giggled, going back and grabbing it. Alice stuffed it into her small clutch bag and pushed opened the door. Fastening the clip on her bag, she rushed out into the hallway without looking and slammed straight into Doctor Sullivan's chest.

Shocked she gasped. "I'm so sorry, Doctor. I wasn't looking where I was going."

"Please don't concern yourself," he said, looking her up and down. "No harm done?"

"No, I'm fine, thank you," she said certain she must have hurt him.

"I noticed you across the dining hall earlier," he said.

He seemed cold and less friendly than usual. Alice didn't like the steely glint in his dark eyes. "Yes, I, well—"

He glanced over his shoulder towards the entrance and lowering his voice, said, "I don't wish to presume anything about your situation, Nurse Le Breton, but I recognised Captain Woodhall. Matron mentioned that you were meeting your cousin? I don't know the other gentleman accompanying you and Nurse Jones, so I'll assume that must be he," he said.

Alice could see he was not fooled by their charade but was giving her a way out of being discovered deceiving Matron. Why had she and Ed ever thought they could get away with this, she wondered?

"We met for afternoon tea," she said, stating the obvious but unhappy to think that the doctor might think the worst of her, or Mary. "We're going for a stroll before going back."

He nodded slowly. "It's a perfect day for a walk," he said. "Mind you're both on time for your lift." he said. Alice nodded and stepped forward to leave. "Alice," he said, quietly.

Stunned to hear him use her first name, she spun round. "Yes, Doctor?"

"I had hoped," he cleared his throat. "That is to say, I—"

He hesitated and smiled. "No, it's nothing. Please, take no notice of me."

Alice was unsure what to make of his change of heart. What was he trying to tell her? He seemed so unsure of himself. It was the first time she had seen him like this. "Are you sure?"

He frowned. "I just wish for you to be careful, that's all."

Irritated with him for telling her what to do, Alice took a deep breath and straightening her shoulders she looked at him with as much dignity as she could muster. "Are you going to report me, Doctor Sullivan?" she asked wishing to be prepared, in case that was what he was intending.

His eyes widened and then hurt registered on his face. "No. Forgive me, I didn't mean to sound threatening. I only wish for you to be careful, Nurse Le Breton. Nothing more."

She nodded, feeling guilty for upsetting him. "I see," she said, still confused by his behaviour. "I hope you enjoy your afternoon."

She walked as calmly as she could manage outside to meet the others. Mary was talking animatedly to Ed and Peter. Alice focused on hiding how shaken she was from her confrontation with the doctor as she went to join them.

"Sorry for taking so long," she said, keeping her voice as level as she could manage. "I've just bumped into Doctor Sullivan, quite literally."

Ed's eyebrows knitted together. "Let's set off," he said, as the four of them walked along the pavement and away from the hotel.

Alice was relieved to see that a few white clouds were

masking the intense heat of the sunshine. She tried to push all thoughts of Doctor Sullivan to one side. He was usually so confident and in control but had seemed rather discombobulated earlier. But nothing was going to get in the way of her enjoyment of being with Ed today, she determined, linking arms with him.

Alice was relieved when Peter invited Mary to walk with him, and he seemed to reciprocate Mary's feelings, she was relieved to note. How perfect it would be, Alice mused, if her friend and Ed's friend began courting too. Ed held back a little and Alice slowed her steps to keep in line with his.

"Is everything all right?" he asked quietly. "If you wish, I'm happy to speak to Doctor Sullivan about today. I wouldn't want him causing trouble for you, not on my account."

Alice shook her head. "No, I don't think he will. He knew I had said I was meeting my cousin and remembers you, so knows you aren't a relative of mine."

"Did he assume Peter was your cousin then?"

Alice thought it would be better to be honest and said, "He said he did, but I think he was saying that so that I didn't worry."

They walked on in silence for a few steps. "He seemed a decent enough fellow, when I met him those times at the hospital," he said. "I doubt he'd cause you trouble by reporting you to Matron."

"I thought the same," she agreed, relieved to hear Ed echo her own thoughts and reassure her that it wasn't simply wishful thinking that had brought her to the conclusion that Doctor Sullivan was merely looking out for her as a colleague.

Ed smiled at her and began whistling.

"May I ask you something?" Alice said, unsure whether she should.

He smiled. "Anything, sweetheart."

"It may be an odd thing to say."

Ed laughed. "I'm fairly sure it won't be. Ask me."

"I was wondering about the stamps on your letters." She stared down at the ground. "Mary suspected you might be sending me coded messages by sticking them on the envelope in different ways."

"She was right," Ed said. "Some call it the language of stamps."

Alice beamed, delighted to hear that his letters meant even more to him than what was written on the paper inside.

"How you place them on the envelope gives a different meaning." They walked on again. "My first letter to you, my message was, 'I am longing to see you'."

Delighted that her instincts had been right to nag at her. "And the second?"

He stopped, checking that no one was looking, before pulling her into the shade of a tree. "It said, 'I love you truly'."

Alice could not hide her delight that he had taken such trouble to tell her how he felt. "And do you?" she asked, confident of his answer.

"Yes, to both." He took her in his arms and smiled down at her. "And, what would your message be to me?"

Without hesitation, she said, "It would say that I love you, too and that I wish we didn't have to part again."

His smile vanished, and he hugged her tightly to him. She could feel his breath on her hair. "Dearest darling, I wish this war had ended. More than anything I want to spend the time together that we crave. However, for now, at least, we must do our best to carry on. It won't be forever."

"No," she said, unsure if he was right to be so certain. "It won't." Not wishing to waste a precious moment with him, she changed the subject.

He kissed the top of her head, eventually letting go of her.

Not wanting their time to be marred by regrets, she distracted him by fanning herself with her clutch bag. "If I was at home, I'd be delighted with this heat," she said, thinking about the large pond on her parent's land that she swam in on days like these.

"I agree," Ed said, linking arms with her. "I long to discard this uniform, once and for all. It's uncomfortable at the best of times, but in this heat, it's not very pleasant. Enough grumbling," he said. "We're together in a beautiful village, on an almost perfect afternoon."

Alice sighed. He was right. She looked up to agree with him, when a distant barrage pounded making her flinch. "That seems rather close, don't you think? Isn't that the direction of Amiens?"

Ed put his arm around her shoulders protectively. "It's

far enough away for us not to worry about it. Come along, let's ignore it as best we can."

They reached the riverbank, with its worn path meandering along the water's edge. "Did I tell you how happy I am to spend time with you here today?" Ed said.

Alice giggled. "Just once, or maybe twice."

They reached a small copse of chestnut trees and Ed stopped.

"Is everything all right?" Alice asked, wondering what had caused him to stop.

"May I kiss you?" he asked, his deep voice cracking with emotion.

There was nothing she would like more. "I'd be upset if you didn't."

He pulled her into his arms, and placing his fingers under her chin, raised it slightly, lowering his head until their lips met.

Alice melted into him. The blissful pressure of his firm lips on hers made her legs weaken. Ed held her tightly, one arm around her waist, the other hand gently on her neck. For several moments nothing else mattered.

Ed took her hand and together they walked on, silently, each lost in their own thoughts. Alice wished this time together could last forever.

She allowed herself to consider how it would feel to be his wife. She imagined them living in a small cottage somewhere, waking each morning knowing they were able to spend the entire day in each other's company. Alice breathed in the warm summer air and smiled when she spotted the tiny white and yellow heads of the daisies along the pathway. Would this war ever end, she wondered? Could she dare hope that there might be a future for her and Ed?

Ed gave her hand a gentle squeeze. Without stopping, or looking at her, he quietly asked, "Would you mind terribly if I wrote to Matron Bleasdale and told her that we were courting?"

We are courting, Alice thought, unable to help smiling at hearing him say those words. "Dare we tell her yet?" She was unsure how Matron would take the news and was alarmed to think that she could be banned from contacting him. "She's very proper and would take it badly if she discovered we had fooled her by meeting today."

Ed turned to face her. "My darling Alice," he said, his eyes filled with so much love that she instantly knew that whatever he said she would agree to it. "We are apart most of the time. We don't know how long this wretched war will continue." He hesitated and took a deep breath. "Sweet girl, we don't know if I will even survive." She went to argue, but he placed his finger on her lips to stop her. "We both know there's a high chance that I won't. I want us to make the most of every second we have together, just in case." He gave her hand a squeeze and she could feel him trembling. "I won't let someone else keep us apart, if I can possibly help it."

Alice raised her right hand and rested it on his cheek. "Maybe leave it a little while before you write to her," she agreed nervously.

He kissed her. "One of these days, we won't need to ask

permission. We'll spend all our time together, making up for the months we've been kept apart."

She liked that idea, very much, and was thrilled Ed had been thinking the same things as her. "I dream about that time," she admitted.

"I wish you didn't have to leave so soon," Ed said, pulling Alice into a kiss, once again.

"Me, too," Alice said.

"I'll write to you, using Peter's name. If that's acceptable to you?"

Alice hated to see the concern on his face. She stood on tiptoe and kissed his cheek in the same place her hand had been. "It is. But you'll still have to be careful about the content of your letters, at least until you've written to Matron. Don't forget that for now, you're supposed to be my cousin."

He shrugged off his mood and smiled. "I'll do as you ask. The last thing I want is for you to be in Matron's bad books." He smiled. "She's a fierce woman."

"She is," Alice laughed, relieved. "Although the longer I know her the more I realise that she does have our best intentions at heart. Although to be honest, I hoped that coming to France would take me away from the confines of my parent's rules. I seem to have swapped them for Matron's."

"I feel the same way about being in the army," he agreed as they walked on. "When I do write to her, I'll do my best not to antagonise her. I do believe, though, that we need to take a little control and try to spend as much time together as possible."

"I agree," she assured him, secretly dreading Matron's reaction. "Until then, we're going to have to carry on communicating through Peter."

"It's a good thing he doesn't mind," Ed said. "Although I saw his face when Mary arrived and by the looks of it they're smitten."

Alice looked over at their friends. They did seem to be enjoying each other's company. "If that's the case, then he can simply send messages from my fictitious nephew Stuart, like you did in your letter."

"I'm sure he won't mind," Ed said. "I think he might get a little confused with our letters and the ones I'm presuming he'll begin writing to Mary after today." He watched them thoughtfully for a moment. "I'll do as you suggest." Ed said, laughing as he picked her up and swung her around before placing her back on her feet. "You're very clever, young lady," he said, kissing her on the tip of her nose. "That's a good plan."

Alice squealed. She spotted an elderly couple glaring at them disapprovingly and patted Ed's shoulder. "Better put me down," she giggled. "I think we're making a show of ourselves."

"Can't have that," he said, doing as she asked.

She gazed at her beloved Ed, relishing the precious time being close to him. Her attention was distracted by Mary and Peter approaching them. Alice was amused to see Mary laugh at something Peter was saying to her and was delighted Mary seemed to be enjoying the day out as much as she was. Alice hoped something would become of Mary and Peter's friendship. Despite Mary's cheerful countenance most of the time they were alone in their tent, Alice suspected her friend was lonely, too.

"Sorry friends," Peter said, pulling a sad face at them as a butterfly floated near his head. "It's time we returned to the hotel. We don't want these young ladies missing their lift and being banned from meeting us in the future."

Alice and Mary exchanged glances. So, he does want to see her again, Alice thought happily. By the look on Mary's face, she approved of this proposition.

"No, we don't," Ed said, linking his arm through Alice's as they turned around and began walking back in the direction of the hotel. "Why is it that when you're sitting for days in the trench time stretches endlessly ahead of you, and an afternoon like this one it vanishes in a flash?"

"I was thinking the same thing," Alice admitted sadly, hugging his arm closer to her. "We'll have to find a way to do this again, soon."

Chapter 18

Gemma

2018

Gemma set about cleaning the fireplace and preparing paper, kindling and a couple of logs to light a fire later that afternoon. She wanted to warm the place up and lose herself in some of Alice's letters to take her mind off Tom's departure.

As if he had heard her thoughts, Tom's heavy footsteps clomped down the stairs into the living room.

"Having fun there?" he asked smiling and looking rather gorgeous.

Gemma sighed, wishing he didn't have to go. "Not really." She swept up the mess that she had made from some escaping ash. She wished she could tell him how she felt. She'd never minded being alone before, but she hadn't known Tom then.

"Need help?"

"No, but thanks." She looked concerned. "We've been

getting on so well with the work, that I'm a bit down about you leaving, that's all," she admitted, surprised by her boldness.

"I understand how you feel. I'd rather stay here and get on with the renovation work, too. I can't put them off again though, unfortunately."

Realising he'd misunderstood, Gemma couldn't help feeling slightly relieved. What would she have said to him if he'd gone deeper into the conversation? She wasn't sure. "I'll just have to prove to you how much I can do in your absence," she said, smiling. She thought of Alice's letters. "I've set up a fire and will catch up with some reading first though." She glanced at the black tin box. "I'm trying to savour them."

"I look forward to you giving me an update when I get back."

She watched him walk through the living room to the back door and begin putting on his dusty boots. Gemma opened her mouth to speak, when she caught him wincing.

"Is there something wrong?" she asked, without thinking.

"No," he looked over his shoulder at her. "I'm fine, thanks."

She could see he wasn't willing to talk about it and wondered if the work at the farm was getting too much for him. If he was in pain, then she didn't mind risking annoying him. Getting up, she went to join him in the kitchen. "Sorry, Tom," she said nervously. "I know you're very private about your injury, but if the constant climbing up and down ladders is causing you problems with your leg, then you must tell me."

He straightened up. "I'm fine," he snapped. "I've lived with this for a long time and I've never let a client down yet."

Gemma cringed. "I'm sure you haven't," she said. "I was only trying to—"

"What?" He glared at her.

"Look," she said embarrassed to have caused antagonism between them. "You don't have to be defensive. I thought we knew each other well enough to be straight with each other. There's no need to take offence."

He bent down to continue doing up his boots. "You're right. I apologise."

She wished she could take back what she'd said. "We are friends, aren't we?" she asked hopefully. "At least, I thought we were."

He sighed. "Look, let's forget it. I'm sore, but fine. No need to worry, I'm tougher than you think."

"I don't doubt it," she said.

They glared at each other for a few seconds before bursting out laughing.

"Our first quarrel," she teased, relieved.

"I doubt it'll be the last," he winked, shaking his head. "I'll leave you to get on with your reading."

"It's a shame I already know there isn't a sequel."

Tom shrugged. "There might be another tin somewhere? Maybe we just haven't found it yet."

Gemma loved the idea. "I doubt it, but we can hope."

She watched in silence as he crouched down and finished tying his laces.

Tom pulled the last one tight and stood up, staring at her. "I'm sorry to leave you so soon," he said.

She didn't want him to feel guilty. If he hadn't stepped in when he had, then very little progress would have been made.

"Don't be silly," she said, slapping him lightly on the side of his arm. "I'm grateful to you for all you've done here."

"And I'll be back in a few weeks," he said. "You'll soon get used to enjoying your peace without me here." He smiled cheekily at her.

She doubted that very much. "I'm not so sure," she said, not meaning to say it out loud. "But I will focus on doing as much as I can, if only to be able to show it all off to you when you're back."

Tom lifted his jacket off the hook on the back of the kitchen door and slipped it on. "Well, that's me then." He went to say something, and then hesitated.

"What is it?" she asked, willing him to kiss her again, just once. Her lips still felt the pressure of his lips against hers from when he had last kissed her.

He looked down and when he caught her eye again, shrugged. "Nothing, I, um, I'd better get going. I'll see you as soon as I can get back here." He opened the kitchen door, but before walking out of the farmhouse, Tom turned and said. "If you need anything, call me. I can be here in no time."

Not wishing him to worry about her, Gemma shook her

head. "Yes, I know. Bugger off now. I'm a big girl and used to living alone," she said pushing him gently out of the door.

"So, we're both a lot tougher than the other gives us credit for then?"

"Seems like it," she agreed. "Right, go. I'll see you soon."

He laughed. "See you in a few weeks then. Bye."

She closed the door before he could see her staring mournfully after him. "Get a grip, Gemma," she mumbled to herself, walking over to switch on the kettle. She hoped he believed her false bravado.

When had she become reliant on others, she wondered? She had enjoyed living alone in Brighton for the last few years and had never needed anyone then. Why was she feeling so lost now? For some reason Tom had shown her that it could be fun to spend a lot of time in someone else's company. She needed to be careful not to become too reliant on him. It would be more upsetting for her when he finished working at the farm.

Irritated with herself, she thought about Alice and Mary and all that they had endured. It was time to claw back her inner strength and get on with renovating this house. Once it was sold she could decide what she wanted to do with her life, and where she wanted to go.

Gemma went upstairs to see what work Tom had done that day. Opening the spare bedroom door, she stepped inside and couldn't help smiling. Once the plastering had dried, it would be ready for her to paint the walls. She looked forward to buying a new mattress and some bedlinen for the bed and making this room look homely.

"A few pieces of furniture wouldn't go amiss," she said. "In fact, I could do with some in the living room," she mumbled to the empty room. If she lived here by herself, she thought, she would have to adopt a rescue dog. Then she would have someone else to talk to. Just as she was getting used to the idea she realised miserably that she wouldn't be living here, alone or otherwise.

Gemma thought about taking a walk to the village and asking about second-hand furniture stores nearby. It would cheer her up and take her away from the solitude at the farm for a while. She decided that first thing the next morning she would go and try to source a few pieces to brighten up the farmhouse.

Gemma was woken by the sun streaming into her bedroom. Noticing it was just after seven, she stretched and got out of bed. Once downstairs, she made some toast and coffee and sat down at the table in the living room to make a list of the furniture she might need.

She scanned the living room with its table, chairs and two old armchairs. "Definitely newer armchairs," she said, looking forward to the day when she could burn these two. "And a side table." She could do with some soft furnishings, too, she mused, like cushions and perhaps a rug for in front of the fireplace. The spare room would need at least one bedside table, a chest of drawers and if possible, a wardrobe. It wasn't all the place needed, Gemma thought, but it would be a start.

After breakfast, she showered and dressed, walking into

the village with her list. She popped in to see Marie, and unable to resist, bought a baguette and two croissants.

"Do you know where I could buy some second-hand furniture?" she asked as she delved into her purse for a few euros to pay for them.

Marie frowned and shook her head. "Pardon?"

Gemma realised she didn't understand her. She tried to think of a way of saying "second-hand" and pointed at a nearby table and chairs and said, "Old? Not new? Um," She thought for a moment, trying to recall her schoolgirl French and wishing that she had had time before coming to France to refresh herself a little. "Où, um, je acheter des tables des chambre et des chaises?"

Marie looked bemused for a moment and then began to laugh. Soon she was doubled over, tears coursing down her lined face. "Pardon, Gemma."

Gemma was not sure what could be quite this funny and was a little irritated at Marie's mocking. At least she had tried to speak French.

Marie glanced at her and shook her head, wiping her eyes. "Non." She took a deep breath. "You have asked for buying a room, table and chairs."

Gemma groaned and smiled. She really needed to work on her command of the French language. "Sorry, I mean, pardon," she said.

Marie smiled. "The market? It is mostly legumes, um vegetables. Today, it is other things. Look, over there." She pointed towards the busy market area in the square across the road from her café.

Gemma studied the stalls and noticed one at the back by a high wall looked as if it was selling furniture. "Oui, merci," she said, delighted.

Marie rang up her purchases and handed Gemma her change. "Bon chance," she said, as Gemma took the bag of food from her hand and left.

She hurried across to the furniture stall and seeing a bedroom set of a walnut chest of drawers, wardrobe and two bedside cabinets, asked the stallholder how much. His English must have been as lousy as her French, Gemma assumed, when he totted up the amount on a small calculator and pointed at the screen to show her the total cost. It was more reasonable than she had expected, but aware that he would expect her to haggle, she shook her head, took the calculator and tapped in an amount that was five percent less. He tilted his head to one side and then the other, looking as if he was trying to decide whether to accept and then reached out his hand for her to shake it.

"You can deliver?" she asked. "Sur the voiture, a la ferm, dans la Rue de L'Eglise?"

Unlike Marie, he did not laugh at her, but she could see by the glint in his eyes that he was amused. "Oui," he said.

She tapped in an amount that equalled fifty per cent of the total and showed it to him. "I will give you half the money, um de l'argent, now," she said. "The rest at la ferme."

He narrowed his eyes and gave her a lazy shrug with his left shoulder. "A sept heure."

She assumed he meant that he would deliver the furniture at seven o'clock that evening and nodded, finally shaking his hand. Opening her purse, Gemma discretely counted the right amount. She would have to stop off at a cashpoint on her way home to have enough money to pay him the balance later.

Spotting a colourful stall selling brightly coloured cushions and throws, she bought pink ones for her bedroom and a set of orange ones for the other bedroom. Then, Gemma bought a blue and red vase that she like the look of. Shopping was fun, but she couldn't do this every day simply to take her mind off Tom. She parted with her last few Euros on two rag rugs, one for beside her bed and the other for in front of the fireplace, and although she was disappointed not to find any armchairs, she decided to keep a look out for one or two over the next few weeks.

Gemma carried her bulky shopping to the bank, struggling to hold them as she withdrew her money for the furniture and extra to keep her going for the next few days with food and milk. Finally, she trudged home, tired but happy.

"Perfect," she said half an hour later having draped the pink throw over the bottom half of her bed. She positioned the cushions against her pillows. The rug would be perfect for when she stepped out of bed. "Finally, it looks welcoming," she said, happy at last with how her temporary bedroom looked.

She changed into her dungarees and set about painting the spare room. The last thing she needed to do was have to move the furniture by herself later. Better to paint it now before it was delivered and standing in the way, she decided.

By the end of the day, she was feeling satisfied with her work. She showered, changed into her pyjamas and dressing gown and lit a fire. The first day by herself had gone well. But, she reasoned, she hadn't spent much of it at the farm. It was time to make herself a hot chocolate, settle down and get cosy, to read more of Alice's intriguing letters.

Forgetting her woes, she lost herself in Alice's letters and notes and Gemma enjoyed learning about Alice's way of life through her eyes and thoughts. It was exciting to discover that Alice and Ed were becoming closer. Gemma had never fallen for any of the patients she nursed, and she couldn't help wondering how agonising it must have been back then to fall in love with a soldier, only for him to be sent back to the Front.

She tried to imagine herself in Alice's place and Tom in Ed's. How would she have coped to discover Tom's body had been shattered by the IUD? Would she have given up on him as his ex-fiancée had done? She knew she would not have done. Gemma read on, stopping only when she became aware that the temperature in the room had dipped. Shivering, she got up and added another log to the fire.

Her emotions were stretched as she envisaged Alice and Ed parting and then meeting again. How had people coped with the painful separations and loss she mused, her heart filled with admiration for Alice and those like her. All those young unworldly women leaving their homes with no idea of the hardship in front of them. And the men. At least now people had some idea of what to expect from war before signing up to serve.

Chewing her thumb nail, Gemma read on, learning how Alice and Ed made plans to meet up despite it being against the rules. She would do the same in their position, she decided without hesitation. Then again, Gemma mused, it had been different back then, with people more deferential to authority. She loved that Ed was determined to keep seeing the woman he loved, despite the odds.

Gemma was enchanted at the turn of events that had brought the couple into her own life. She felt like she knew them, or at least understood something of what they might have felt for each other.

Reading the next letter, Gemma gasped in disbelief.

"So that's why Alice bought this house," she said, wishing Tom was with her so she could share what she had just learnt. "I thought this place was special," she sighed. "And now I know why."

Chapter 19

Alice

October 1917

Alice tapped her cheek with her silver fountain pen and tried to think of the most appropriate words she could use in her note to Ed. She ached to be in his arms and wished there was some real hope that this interminable war would soon end.

"You're not still composing that letter?" Mary asked when she arrived back from her ablutions. "You do realise that we only have four minutes until we have to be on duty again?"

Alice hadn't realised the time. She would have to find a peaceful moment to write her letter to Ed later. Folding the sheet of paper carefully, she slipped it into the envelope and into her leather folder.

"This has to be the worst yet," she said, standing up and checking her veil cap in the small vanity mirror. "Using gas on men is vile. I can't bear seeing these men in such a state."

"Nor can I," Mary said, checking her watch. "Watching them clawing at their throats as they choke, or not giving in to their pleas to unleash their wrists from their beds, is unbearable."

Alice agreed, and they reluctantly left the peace of their tent. It had only been a month since the Hun had used mustard gas for the first time. She understood the men's fear of the odourless killer that took about twelve hours to wreak its damage on them. "It's shocking that there are so many gas victims that we need a new ward to house them. They say it can take men four to five weeks to die," she said, her voice breaking in a sob.

Mary grabbed her arm and pulled her to a stop. "We have to buck up. We mustn't let them know how much it affects us."

"I know," Alice said, guiltily. She took a deep calming breath. "Right, I'm ready," she said. She knew the patients were reassured by their reactions and the last thing she wanted to do was frighten any of them. "Come along, or we're going to be late."

They broke into a run. Arriving at the entrance to the ward, they stopped and took a moment to check their caps were straight and uniforms smoothed down.

"Here goes," Mary said.

Alice braced herself, fixed a smile on her face and she followed Mary inside.

Sister Brown stopped telling off one of the younger nurses and checked her watch, no doubt, Alice assumed, disappointed to find that they were on time. "These patients need to be fed." She indicated rows of invalid cups. "The chicken soup is cool enough now. You two can assist. Begin with the patients on the left-hand side of the ward."

Alice picked up a cup and napkin and walked over to the first bed. Manoeuvring the patient's pillows to raise his head slightly, she sat next to him.

"Good afternoon, Private," she said, her heart aching to see the palm-sized mustard coloured blisters on his swollen eye lids looked as bad now as they had the day before. "I've got some chicken soup for you. It'll make you feel much better."

"Not sure about that," he rasped, wincing in pain as he spoke.

"I'll pour a little into your mouth at a time, so try not to panic." She lifted the spout to his mouth and tilted the cup slightly. Despite the tiny amount of soup running into his mouth, he coughed, choking. He tried to wave for her to stop, his wrists strapped down onto each side of his bed.

Alice placed her free hand lightly onto his right hand. "It's fine," she soothed. When he caught his breath, she gave him a moment and then said, "Right, let's try again."

He moved his head away from her and clamped his lips together.

Alice closed her eyes briefly and gathered herself. "Come on," she said. "You need nourishment to help your body heal."

He seemed to think about it and then, giving in, relaxed slightly. Alice lifted the spout to his lips once more and raised the cup with extreme care. This time he managed to swallow the fluid, grimacing as the warm liquid made its way down his throat.

"Well done. I know this is difficult, but you'll feel better with something inside you."

They managed a few more mouthfuls and Alice was beginning to feel like she was getting somewhere. She lifted the cup to his mouth again when the ground shuddered as an explosion went off a couple of miles away. Shaking, Alice noticed she had spilled some of the soup onto the bed sheet.

"Nurse Le Breton, take better care," Sister Brown snapped, appearing at the end of the private's bed. "I want his bed linen replaced as soon as you've finished what you're doing."

"Yes, Sister," Alice said, irritated with herself for making extra work for herself when there was already so much to do.

The sister walked away mumbling to herself.

"Tyrant," he whispered.

"Don't try to speak," Alice said, silently agreeing with him. She wondered what made the woman so nasty. Nursing was compassionate work, but as far as she had seen, Sister Brown had very little for her fellow workmates.

After another few mouthfuls, the private shook his head. She was not surprised that he had had enough. The poor boy looked exhausted by the effort of having to swallow. She admired them all for somehow bearing the agony of liquid passing their damaged bronchial tubes. How many of these men would die, she wondered miserably? Alice wiped his face and proceeded to change his bed linen.

"There," she said, settling him back down on his clean sheets. "You try to sleep now."

He murmured his thanks and Alice went to tend to the next patient. She was relieved to see that he appeared to be breathing a little easier than he had during her previous shift. He was still covered with large yellow blisters, but at least she was able to hide her shock at the sight of him. She spoke to him gently as she fed him, wondering if he would ever regain his sight.

She was almost finished when Doctor Sullivan walked up to the other side of the bed. "How is my patient today, Nurse Le Breton?"

Sensing an awkwardness between them, she hesitated before replying, "He's doing well, aren't you Sergeant?"

He winced as he swallowed before whispering, "I am."

"That's good to hear." The doctor waited for Alice to wipe the patient's mouth. "If you're finished, nurse, I'd like you to assist me checking the sergeant's eyes. I'll need saline solution to flush them out."

"Yes, Doctor," she said, relieved to have something to do. She took the empty cup to the trolley and went to fetch the saline solution and a fresh dressing, returning to find him soothing the patient.

"We'll start by undoing these," Doctor Sullivan said, unclipping the strap restraining the patient's left hand, while Alice undid the right.

Once free, the sergeant rubbed his wrists and moved his arms slowly.

Another shell exploded nearby; and Alice flinched.

Doctor Sullivan glanced at her, raising his eyebrows questioningly. She hated that she was becoming more frightened by the noise, the longer she worked at the hospital, and wished she could refrain from reacting each time.

She watched as the doctor carefully removed the bandage and dressing from the man's sticky blistered eyes. His eyes ran with fluid and they looked so painful. She observed as Doctor Sullivan washed and cleaned them with a tenderness Alice had never noticed before. She took the discarded dressing as he inspected the damage to the eyes, all the time encouraging the man. He applied the dressing and a fresh bandage and lowered man's head carefully onto his pillow.

"They seem to have improved slightly. I'm unable yet to ascertain how permanent the damage is to your eyes, but hopefully it won't be as bad as we first suspected."

"Thank you, doctor," the man rasped.

Alice liked his honesty and knew the men did too. She had heard several patients remark that however bad the diagnosis, it was still easier to come to terms with it when they were told the prognosis.

Once the sergeant was comfortable, Alice followed the doctor outside.

"Do you think he'll get his sight back?" She knew she shouldn't ask but wanted an excuse to speak to Doctor Sullivan and see if there was a problem between them.

"It's hard to tell," he said. "I hope so." He rubbed his face, wearily and she noticed a sadness she hadn't seen in him before. "I thought the other gas attacks were dreadful, but this mustard gas is the cruellest. In the past month I've seen too many men grabbing at their throats trying not to choke. It's desperate."

Alice, shocked by his openness, rested her hand on his forearm closest to her. "At least you know you're doing all you can to help them."

He stared at her hand.

Alice blushed and pulled it away. "I'm sorry, Doctor," she said noticing Sister Brown walking away from them. "I forget myself sometimes." She hoped the woman hadn't witnessed what she'd done.

"Don't fret," the doctor said. "We all need a friendly reminder that we're trying our best and I appreciate yours." He smiled at her. "Some days are harder to bear than others, aren't they?"

"They are." She cleared her throat. "I'd better return to the ward, I have more patients to spill food down."

He laughed. It was a deep rumbling sound that she had never heard before. She liked it and relaxed slightly. Maybe after this war, they might meet up and be able to be friends.

She smiled at him and left to return to the ward.

The rest of her shift was spent taking care of more gassed men, her heart aching as the day passed. She hoped Ed didn't get caught by this vile weapon. The thought of him being tortured like these poor souls was horrendous, so she pushed it away.

"Nurse Le Breton," Sister Brown hissed from behind her. Arms folded behind her back, her large matronly chest pushed out.

Alice wondered how she could be comfortable standing in such a way. "Yes, Sister Brown?"

The older woman looked pointedly in the direction of the sergeant and then back at Alice. "Is there something you've missed?" she asked, her voice filled with sarcasm.

For a moment Alice couldn't see anything wrong. The patient was sleeping, his sheets neat and dressing clean. Then it dawned on her that his wrists weren't restrained.

"I don't think he needs his wrists bound now he's asleep."

"It is not for you to decide what a patient needs, Nurse Le Breton," Sister snapped. "You take orders. You do as you are told. Now, go and strap his wrists before he causes further damage to himself."

Alice hoped she would meet up with Sister Brown after the war was over, too. She would have a few things to say to the harsh woman. Now was not the time, or the place, she decided as she went to do as she had been instructed.

Relieved when her shift was finally at an end, Alice walked alone to her tent. Unable to get the image of the men she had nursed from her mind, she reached her tent and unfastened her veil cap, placing it carefully on her trunk. Catching sight of her reflection in the mirror, she saw her cheeks were wet. She had no idea she'd been crying. She was exhausted and unable to take any more, Alice lay down on her bed and sobbed.

She didn't know how much longer she could continue witnessing everything that happened at the clearing station. Then guilt flooded through her. How could she allow herself to wallow in self-pity, when these men suffered so badly? Some of them had a life time of pain ahead. Others would have no future at all. The thought of more unnecessary deaths brought on a fresh wave of tears.

"Good grief," Mary said, her voice filled with alarm. "What's brought this on?" She sat on the edge of Alice's bed and stroked her back.

Alice's sobs slowly calmed. "I'm sorry," she gulped in between bouts of crying. "I don't know what came over me."

"Nothing we haven't all experienced. Don't you worry about that. "You cry. It'll do you good." Mary soothed. She stood up and began to undress. "It can be overwhelming sometimes, it's nothing to feel ashamed about. I've found it more difficult to deal with recently, too."

Shocked not to have realised, Alice pulled a handkerchief from her uniform and wiped her eyes. Blowing her nose, she felt calm enough to speak again. "I'm sorry, Mary."

"What on earth for?"

"For not noticing when you were upset."

Mary shook her head and unbuttoned her uniform. "I waited until you were working on a different shift to me," she said. "I needed a blub and it did me good."

Feeling a little less guilty to learn that her friend had wanted to be alone, Alice sighed. "How long do you think this ghastly war will go on for, Mary? Surely it has to end sometime soon."

"I do hope so," Mary said, pulling on her night dress and sitting down on her bed, facing Alice. "Or we're going to run out of soldiers to fight."

Alice shivered, horrified by the thought. "Don't say such things, please."

"Sorry, that was insensitive of me."

Alice leaned forward and took her friend's hand. "We will get through this, and so will Peter and Ed."

Mary nodded, but Alice suspected her friend didn't feel as certain she did.

Chapter 20

Gemma

June 2018

Gemma lifted the thin sheet of paper to her chest, breathed in the scent of the old paper, and closed her eyes. Would her future hold something as romantic as Alice's, she wondered, envying her for a split-second.

Each day without Tom dragged at the farm. She missed his cheerful chatter and quietly watching his muscular body as he carried materials, hammered nails into walls and carried out jobs that she did not have the physical strength to do.

She was happy with what she had achieved since he was last at the farm, especially the furniture and the painting. Having no one else to talk to meant she ended up spending quite a lot of time thinking. She realised she was slowly coming to terms with her ex's death. Even her regret at not giving up her nursing training to emigrate to Australia with her childhood sweetheart, was something she was now beginning to think of as fate. After all, despite what he said about her not having the guts to leave her job, she was here now. Maybe she was toughening up and learning to share her life with other people. And enjoying it, too.

Or maybe it was just Tom that she yearned to be with above anyone else. Tom, so undemanding, calm and emotionally accepting of her. He didn't seem to mind her quiet ways and solitary behaviour. It was as if she had met her spiritual mate.

Three weeks into her solitude, she decided that she needed another walk into the village. She had run out of milk days before but had not been in the mood to leave the peacefulness of the farm.

The day was sunny and warm enough for her to wear a short-sleeved top and shorts. She reached the village, delighted to find that it was market day in the square near Marie's café. She popped in to see her friend briefly and to buy some of her favourite pastries.

"Bonjour Marie," she said wanting to make the most of what little French she was learning. She was happy to see that there was not a queue at the till. "Comment ça va?"

"Well, thank you," Marie said. "We 'ave many customers today."

She could not think how to continue and pointed out the pastries she had chosen. "Please may I have those?"

They exchanged pleasantries and she paid for her bag of treats.

Gemma could smell the sweetness emanating from the crepe stall long before she reached it, and her stomach grumbled impatiently as she watched the stallholder expertly ladle a spoonful of the mixture onto the large circular heated metal place and turn a long spatula in a circle to cover the entire area. After a minute or two, he flipped over one section, then another covering the crepe with melted chocolate sauce and dropping it into a paper container handed it to a teenager.

She would have to try one of those, Gemma thought. Seeing that she would be sixth in the line in the queue, she decided to go and check out the other stalls first. Maybe she could find something that would add texture or colour to the farmhouse.

Several items caught her eye as she walked from stall to stall. She inspected several plates, cushions and fabric, but liked nothing enough to buy it. Noticing a mahogany occasional table, Gemma pictured it in the living room and thought it would be perfect for the farmhouse. Then spotting a small oak sideboard, she haggled with the handsome stallholder until she was satisfied she had a bargain. Arranging to come back and collect the two items later, she carried on walking around the market stalls.

She lined up for her crepe and moments later, she was sitting on a low wall in the shade relishing the sweet taste, determined to come back the following week to have another. After she had finished, she walked over to the stall to collect her small table and ask about delivery for the sideboard.

Gemma spotted a stall that she had previously missed where an elderly lady was selling brightly coloured rag rugs. She selected two smaller ones for her bedroom and the spare room, paid for them and carried them over to the handsome stallholder. Realising she had got a little too carried away, she was relieved when, for a small fee, he agreed to deliver all her items after the market closed.

Gemma hummed as she walked back to the farm. It dawned on her that she felt more at home here than she had ever done anywhere. It felt odd to think that soon she would have to pack up and leave and she pushed the thought aside before her mood dropped. She would enjoy every moment of this experience while it lasted, she decided.

Later that evening, she helped the man manoeuvre her new sideboard against the furthest wall from the fireplace and stood in front of the fire on her colourful rag rug to survey the room. The roses she had cut from an old rose bush weaving its way through one of the hedges on the way to the field, stood proudly in the vase that she'd treated herself to. The sugary pink leaves gave a warm hue as the sun beamed on to them through the nearby window.

This place was feeling and looking much homelier, she thought happily. She was becoming far too comfortable here though. She would need to keep reminding herself that she was only here on a temporary basis and that this was not her house to keep.

The following day, she finished painting the spare room. It looked very different to how it had been when she'd arrived at the farmhouse. Tired from a morning's graft in the unusually hot day, she changed and went downstairs. Contemplating what to do with her day, Gemma glanced at the black tin containing Alice's letters which had pride of place on the new sideboard. She poured herself a glass of water and carrying it and a chair from the living room, set everything down in a shady spot outside the front door, settling down to read.

The hours passed in a happy haze, and as Gemma put down the letter she had been reading, her eyes felt heavy. She dozed off, waking up cold just as the sun was setting. Another day gone by without company, but she hadn't minded. She thought back to the previous year and how perfect this would have seemed to her back then from the quiet of her small living room in Brighton. It was strange to think that now perfection to her included Tom. Gemma smiled.

Gemma woke early the next day, thinking back to one of the letters she had read the previous day. "I'll go and see if the Hotel du Nord still exists," she said, wondering why she hadn't thought to do so before.

Delighted with her idea, she decided that if the hotel was still there, she would treat herself to whatever tea they served and a pastry. It would be interesting to see how much it had changed and she was excited to think that she might be able to soak up some of the atmosphere Alice, Ed, Mary and Peter had enjoyed that day they'd met as a foursome for the first time.

Deciding to make the most of the morning sunshine, Gemma changed into her dungarees, to paint the lower half of the front wall of the farmhouse. Tying a bandana around her head to keep her hair out of her face, she sang to herself as she worked. She loved mornings like this one, listening to bumble bees busily flying to and from lavender plants, between the bramble and the honeysuckle growing up to the side of the front door. Birds sang in the nearby sweet chestnut tree at the side of the house. The only interruption was the engine of an occasional car as it passed, but mostly it was her and nature working side by side.

It was a cloudless day and the sun beat down on her. Gemma thought back to the same time last year and the contrast in her life since then. No longer was she spending her days when the only glance of daylight came as she waited by the entrance of the trauma unit for an accident victim to arrive. The long, stressful days, not knowing what state the next patient would be in or fighting to make sure they survived were a thing of the past. Life then was incomparable to now. Here the biggest challenge she faced was climbing down a ladder from an attic space with a muscular builder ensuring she didn't fall.

Gemma sighed happily, distracted from her thoughts when she noticed a small area on the wall she had missed. She went to dip her paintbrush into the pot, waving a butterfly away before it landed in the newly painted area and dropped her paintbrush. Still watching the butterfly's wings careful they didn't become stuck, she reached out to grab the brush.

"Thank you," Gemma said instinctively, as it was handed to her. She stretched up to paint the missed area on the wall, as it dawned on her that someone was standing next to her. Not daring to hope, Gemma looked sideways.

"Tom," she said startled to find him standing there smiling at her. "You're back." Her heart pounded with joy to see him.

He seemed happy with her delight. "Not for good," he said, glancing down at the paint dripping from the brush. He leant forward and took it from her hand. Then, easily reaching the area she had intended to paint, he quickly did it, resting the brush on the tin lid next to her foot. "I had a quiet day, so thought I'd come and pay you a visit."

She beamed at him. "It's great to see you."

He laughed. "You, too." He gazed at the front of the farmhouse. "You've done an excellent job. I can help you paint the higher bits, if you'd like."

"What, today?"

"Yes, right now. Shall we do it? Then it's done, and you can show me what other work you've completed since I've been away."

"Take that brush and tin," she said, delighted to think that the front of the building would be completed so soon. "I'll fetch another one."

He went to get a ladder and together they finished working on the front of the house. Gemma couldn't help singing. It made her heart soar to hear Tom's occasionally forgetting himself and singing along with her. She smiled to herself at how perfectly the day had turned out. It would also be a relief to have yet another task ticked off her To Do List.

They fell into silence as they painted, until Tom climbed

down his ladder to move it slightly, and asked, "How's it been, working here by yourself?"

"Not as bad as I thought," she admitted. "It was a little odd not having you here. It's done me good to spend time by myself though," she said. "I've worked through a few things that were troubling me." It felt strangely liberating sharing her insecurities with another person.

"Enforced peace can turn out to be very therapeutic," he said, climbing the ladder again and carrying on with the work. "Have you decided what you'd like to do next?"

She shook her head and mopped up a drop of paint with a damp cloth. "Not yet. But at least my lack of forward planning isn't worrying me quite so much now."

"That's good," he said. "If there's one thing I've learnt in my life, it's that worrying over your future can be a waste of energy."

"True," she agreed. "I don't know if I want to return to nursing, or if I do, where I'll move to next right now." Recalling her plans for the afternoon, she said, "I'm planning to walk to the village to see if Hotel du Nord still exists."

"It does," Tom said.

"That's amazing." She thought back to Alice's letter describing her time there with Ed and the others.

"Right, I've finished," Tom said, climbing back down the ladder and walking up the pathway. He turned to look at the wall checking he had covered everything. "Looks fine to me. What do you think?"

She went to stand next to him and studying their

handiwork, nodded. "Seems okay," she said, happy with what they had achieved, but still in a blissful daze to learn that the hotel still existed.

He put away the ladder while Gemma tidied up the paint tins and washed brushes. As she was drying them, Tom came into the kitchen and washed his hands.

"I've been reading more of Alice's letters and she and Ed met for afternoon tea at the Hotel du Nord," she explained, telling him about the first time the foursome had spent the day together. "I thought I would have afternoon tea there, if they still do it," she said hoping they did. "Would you like to come with me? It could be my way of thanking you for your hard work today."

Tom thought about it. "They'll probably do a French version," he said. "So, pastries, rather than sandwiches and cakes, but it would still be worth going to. I'm not dressed for it though. When were you thinking of going?"

"I was going to stroll into the town at about three-thirty."

"Okay, this isn't an invitation I get very often" he said grinning at her and drying his hands on the towel. "Or ever. I'll dash home now, freshen up and will meet you back here just after three. Is that okay?"

Gemma couldn't help smiling. "Perfect. I'll see you then."

She watched him leave thinking how happy he looked. She was relieved to have drummed up enough courage to ask him to accompany her. Tidying everything away, she ran upstairs and into her bathroom. Catching sight of herself in the mirror, Gemma gasped. "What the hell?"

Her makeup free face, puce from working in the heat,

was reflected back at her. Her hair curled at all angles making it look like she had been given a shock. The whole look was horrible.

"And I asked him out with me?" she groaned, splashing chilly water on her face to reduce the redness. He must have said yes out of sympathy, she decided, undressing and stepping into the shower. She stood under the cool water as her body temperature slowly decreased. Washing her hair, she thought she would have to make an exceptional effort to appear casually attractive enough to help erase the image he had experienced of her earlier.

By three o'clock, Gemma had dried her hair, curling several strands lightly. She could not help wondering why it took longer to get her makeup to look natural than it would if she was going out to a nightclub. Dressing in a cotton flowery dress and sandals she hoped to appear refreshed and vaguely sophisticated.

"Hi," she heard Tom say, as he knocked on the front door before entering.

She walked into the living room and noticing her he stopped and stared at her. "You look pretty."

Pretty? She was going for downright fabulous, but pretty would have to do.

"Thank you," she said, noticing that he was wearing chinos and a crisp white shirt. "You look very handsome, too" she said, thinking he looked sexy and very hot. "Shall we get going?"

"Ready when you are," he smiled, waiting at the door for her to grab her bag. She locked the front door and they walked down the pathway and out to the road together.

"Thanks for inviting me," he said. "It's been ages since I've worn anything in the day other than jeans and my work gear."

"Me, too," she admitted, aware suddenly that he had never seen her dressed up as much as she was today. "It makes a pleasant change to be going out somewhere nice, don't you think?"

"It does."

They walked in happy silence most of the way, Gemma relishing their comfortable silence interrupted only by their footsteps on the tarmac and the nearby birdsong. She asked him how his work was going at the other building project.

"Almost done," he said. "I should be back with you next week."

She beamed at him. "That's brilliant," she said, honestly. "Not that I'm in a hurry to finish the house too soon. I'm enjoying living there far too much now that it's home-lier."

"I noticed the other furniture you bought," he said. "It's made a huge difference to the feel of the place."

She was pleased to hear his enthusiasm for her choices. "I'll have to show you how the bedrooms look when we go back home." She replayed her words in her head. She had not meant it to come out like it had. "You know what I mean," she added trying to hide her embarrassment.

"I do," he said, smiling at her, thoughtfully.

She was relieved. She didn't want Tom to feel awkward

in her company simply because she had a bit of a crush on him. She also didn't mean to overstep the mark of their friendship.

"There it is," he said as they passed the market place and Marie's café before turning right down a road at the end of a row of shops. He pointed to Hotel du Nord and Gemma stopped to savour the view. It looked a little different to how she had imagined it, less like an imposing hotel and more like a large guest house.

"Not as you expected?"

She shook her head and began walking again. "It doesn't look as big as I'd imagined," she said. She thought back to the letters that were set in a war a hundred-years before. Life had changed drastically since that time and this was a country hotel not one in a major city.

He took her hand and gave it a light squeeze. "Come along. We've come this far, and you never know, they might still do an afternoon tea. If they don't then we'll think of something else to do instead."

She liked the sensation of his hand holding hers as they walked along the pavement to the hotel. Stopping outside she tried to imagine Alice and Ed meeting there with Mary and Peter. She doubted it looked much different. The frontage of the property looked as it probably had done when it was built and as they made their way up the stone front steps and Tom held the door open for her to enter, she looked at the wooden floors and plasterwork and doubted this had changed much at all.

She breathed in the scent of wood and beeswax polish

in the hallway. A gentleman came up to them and asked them if he could help.

She struggled to think what to say and after glancing at her to check she didn't mind, Tom chatted away to him and she assumed, by the odd word he said that she could make out, that he was asking about afternoon teas. More discussion ensued with hands waving and single-shoulder shrugs from the Frenchman. Eventually, Tom looked at her and nodded.

"We're to follow him," he said, doing just that.

They were led down the hallway to a dining room with a handful of people sitting at tables and talking quietly, over cups of tea and pastries. It was not exactly how Gemma had imagined, but it was quaint. After all, she had simply wanted to gain a sense of how it must have felt for the Alice to spend some time with her sweetheart in this very room. Realising that the couple must have walked along the same dark wood floorboards in the hallway and into this room, Gemma's heart pounded. It didn't matter after all whether the room was filled, or not, or whether the tea was English, or if they were served finger sandwiches with the crusts removed or French patisserie. Alice and Ed had spent time here, in this very room, doing exactly what she and Tom were about to do and she was excited to be walking in their footsteps.

"It's perfect," she whispered, sitting down in the seat that Tom was holding back for her.

He sat opposite and gave their order to the waiter.

Gemma noticed him giving her a strange look. "He thinks I'm a little dotty," she giggled, unsurprised. "I can see why."

"I shouldn't worry," Tom said smiling at her. "I'm sure he's seen all sorts here."

Relieved that Tom was unfazed by her distant behaviour, Gemma sat back and gazed at the room around her. She wondered where in the room Alice and Tom had sat. Had they looked at the pictures on the wall and through the windows at the garden behind the building, or had they been too much in love to care about their surroundings. She was sure they must have stared at each other the entire time they had been there, holding hands discretely under the table maybe?

She realised Tom was watching her. "You must think me very strange," she said, willing him to disagree.

He did not disappoint. "You're the most fascinating woman I've ever met," he said. "You've got courage and determination, as well as being incredibly pretty. What's not to like?"

She straightened the cutlery in front of her for something to do with her hands. Then gazing across the table at him once again, said, "I think you're ballsy, too," she said, wishing she had used a more eloquent term. "I mean, how you've not let your past experiences, hinder how you live your life now."

He frowned momentarily as he considered her words. "I don't really think it's like that, but when something happens to change your life, you have two choices."

"Which are?" she asked.

"Give up or adapt how you live to suit your new circumstances."

"Well, I think you're incredibly brave. To be honest though," she added. "I don't think I'd have ever noticed your leg if you hadn't told me about it."

"Really?" he looked surprised by her revelation.

"No. You do the same as everyone else. Let's face it, you climb ladders better than I ever could. You don't let it hold you back at all. Why would I have ever thought you had a prosthetic leg?"

He shook his head. "It never occurred to me that you wouldn't notice." He raised his eyebrows.

She thought about Alice's letters and how different life would have been at the beginning of the last century for men like Tom who had lost limbs.

"What are you thinking now?" he asked, his eyes twinkling in amusement.

She told him. "Life may be quicker now and more about technology and families living further away from each other, but at least we don't see the loss of a limb as the end of the world."

"Unless it happens to you," he said. "Initially, of course. When your limb heals, and you learn to walk with a prosthetic, life does seem more positive after that."

She took his hand in hers and smiled at him. "I wish I'd known you back then."

"I'm glad you didn't. I'm much happier that we've met after I've come to terms with all this and feel whole again."

"You are heroic to me, though," she admitted.

"Not at all," Tom argued, looking she was sad to note,

rather awkward and embarrassed. "It's not heroic when you have little choice in the matter."

She opened her mouth to retaliate when the waiter appeared with a plate of pastries and a pot of tea for two.

"Not quite a Cornish tea," Tom said, waiting for Gemma to take her pick of the mouth-watering pastries. "But it looks good to me."

"Me, too," she said.

They ate in relative silence, each lost in their own thoughts. Gemma wished she could take back what she had said about him being a hero. Sometimes she didn't think before she spoke and she just hoped she hadn't gone too far.

After waiting for the tea to stew a little, she poured some into each of their cups.

"This is delicious," she said taking a sip. "I wish I hadn't been so doubting in their ability to serve us a decent tea."

"You see?" He took a mouthful of his pastry and watched her as he chewed. "I can't believe I've lived here for several years and never thought to come to the hotel before."

"We'll have to do it again sometime," she said, adding. "If I haven't driven you mad by saying all the wrong things, that is?"

He shook his head. "You're honest, and in my book that's more important than saying what I want to hear. Do you know how rare it is to be with someone who says what they think, rather than what they think they should say?"

Gemma thought about what he had said. "Oh, yes. I see

what you mean. I agree. I'd rather hear the truth than some rubbish."

"Ready for your second pastry?" he asked, smiling as he waited for her to choose.

"No," she said, liking most of them on offer. "You first. I want to see what you like best. It might tell me more about you and how you think."

Tom threw his head back and laughed loudly. The other guests looked in their direction curious to work out what was so funny. He noticed and pulled an apologetic face at them.

"I'm not sure how you're going to psychoanalyse me over a pain au chocolat, but here goes."

She watched him take the pastry and wait for her to do the same. Then, when he was eating, her heart swelled with love for the brave, strong man in front of her. There did not appear to be any sides to him. He had stepped in to help her with barely any notice, and always seemed determined to do the best job possible. She knew that others could have at least tried to take advantage of an inexperienced woman trying to renovate a property in a foreign place without having a decent command of the language. But not Tom, he was too decent to do that sort of thing.

They ate the rest of their food and Tom, refusing to let her pay the bill, went to settle it while she freshened up in the Ladies. She stared in the mirror wondering if Alice had also come in here to wash her hands and brush her hair. Had she also been as happy as Gemma was now, she wondered?

Alice had spent an afternoon with a man she barely knew but was falling deeper in love with. Gemma thought Alice's feelings towards Ed probably reflected her own attraction to Tom. It made her feel closer to the woman who she wished she could have met and swap stories with. She had so many unanswered questions, not least what happened between her and Ed. Had they been able to enjoy their happy ever after? She hoped so.

She would just have to wait to discover what happened next in the rest of Alice's letters, she decided happily. She checked her reflection in the mirror and left the bathroom to find Tom. She saw him before he noticed her, and her pulse raced as she watched his handsome face deep in thought as he waited for her by the hotel entrance.

Chapter 21

Alice

July 1918

Alice turned a corner near one of the wards when she spotted a patient stopping to speak to one of the nurses. Thinking it was Ed, she took a breath to call out to him, her heart soaring. He waved at a friend and she realised he was a stranger. What was she thinking? Ed wasn't a patient any longer. He hadn't been for almost two years.

It had been two long months since she had last been held by him and she missed him terribly. She thought of the final kiss they'd shared and for a second Alice managed to recall the pressure of his firm lips on hers. Neither of them had wanted the moment to end. Knowing that he reciprocated her feelings went some way to sooth her.

"Is something troubling you?" Mary asked coming up behind her.

Alice sighed. "I was thinking about Ed."

"I thought you might be. What about him?" Mary linked

her arm through Alice's and pulled gently until they both began walking.

"I miss him," Alice admitted. "We exchange letters as often as possible, but we have to keep them bland, because he's supposed to be my cousin. He still writes about Stuart, my fictional nephew, sending his love and that helps a little." She sighed, miserably. "If only Matron didn't have to read our mail. There's so much we both want to say to each other."

"It's madness," Mary grimaced. "I write to Peter all the time and we don't have to worry quite the same as you and Ed."

Alice wished it could be the same for her. "It's a good thing Peter was never a patient, in more ways than one," she smiled.

Later that morning the postal van arrived. The women rushed with the others, hoping the orderly would allow them to take their letters before he delivered them to Matron's office.

"Now, now, ladies," he shook his head. "You know I can't break the rules for you. It would cause pandemonium if the other nurses were to find out. Off you go."

The others turned away, but Alice gave him a pleading look. "Not just this once?" she asked. "I promise I won't tell anyone."

He signed heavily. "I've always been partial to a pretty face," he said quietly. "Wait there while I have a quick look."

She checked that Matron wasn't about, or any of the others who might suspect what she was doing. "I can carry one of the bags for you to her office, if you like," she suggested, thinking it might divert attention if anyone did wonder what she was doing hanging around the postal van.

"Blimey, I've found one," he said, surreptitiously handing her an envelope. "Right, you'd better grab this bag and follow me."

She took it from his hand, her spirits soaring when she spotted Ed's untidy handwriting. She would have to wait for a lull in the ward before reading it, but slipping it into her uniform pocket, she was soothed by the knowledge that she had a letter from Ed to read later.

She waited for the orderly to pick up two other bags and followed him to Matron's office. "I'll leave it here," she said, putting the bag on the wooden boards outside the door. "And, thank you," she whispered.

It was almost an hour later when Alice had caught up with her duties. Deciding to make the most it, she took a chance that she wouldn't be missed and hurried around the back of the main ward. Withdrawing the envelope from her pocket, she noticed that the stamp was stuck on upside down this time. Intrigued, she gave up trying to decipher its meaning. She would have to ask him what it meant when she next saw him. Hearing Sister Brown's piercing voice nearby, she quickly opened her letter.

Dearest Alice,

I miss you and pray that you are keeping well. I think of you often and the long hours you work in the tightly-packed ward, wishing I could take you away somewhere serene where we could simply be.

I have written to Matron Bleasdale advising her that we have become close, I know we discussed doing this, and that I wish to request leave on your behalf. (My darling, I hope that I am not taking liberties with my timing by doing such a thing, please tell me if I am).

I have been granted leave for three days at the beginning of August, despite how things are, and hope to meet you at the farm, if possible. There is something I wish to ask you.

My fondest love, as always, dearest girl.
Your Ed x

Alice's heart pounded nervously at the thought of Matron's reaction to Ed's request. She knew well enough to expect to be summoned soon. No doubt Matron would question the status of their closeness and when their relationship progressed from that of nurse and patient. She did not care. She loved Ed. Whether this war carried on for another few years, or not, she was not going to waste her life worrying about what others thought of her.

They had both served their country long enough to earn the right to act as independent adults, hadn't they? Her parents would have to lessen their grip on her at some point, too. She was tired of living by everyone else's rules. Her mother would never be entirely satisfied with her choices, but Alice cared less and less whether or not she disappointed her. Life was short, everyone was only too well aware of that fact now, and she was determined to fight for what she wanted.

She folded the thin paper carefully and slipping it back into its envelope, pushed it deep into her skirt pocket to read again later, when she was alone and able to think further about what he had said.

The day passed slowly but with every sound of Matron's voice, Alice tensed, immediately expecting to be called into her office. The time finally came after her shift had ended and she was walking back towards her tent.

"Nurse Le Breton," Matron called, her voice more abrupt sounding than usual. "Step into my office."

She stood facing Matron, waiting for her to close the office door and take her seat. She did so rather more slowly than normal, Alice mused. Or maybe it just felt that way because she was willing Matron to have her say and get it over with.

Finally, Matron sighed wearily. "Nurse Le Breton," she said in her most disapproving tone. "I have today received a letter from Captain Woodhall, with whom you correspond." She waited for Alice to acknowledge the fact. "I am at a loss to understand how this has happened, since I have been vetting all mail."

Alice opened her mouth to explain.

"No, say nothing," Matron said, raising her hand. "I would rather you not implicate yourself. I believe we should leave the rest to my imagination."

Guilt coursed through Alice. She had never been underhand, always proud of her honesty and integrity.

"Nurse Le Breton," Matron said, raising her hand to stop her from speaking. "I would ordinarily press the need for regulations to be followed, however, I have given Captain Woodhall's letter and its contents my full consideration."

Alice clasped her hands together in front of her apron. "Yes, Matron?"

"In this instance, due to your unfailing dedication to your work and your consistent and thorough care of the patients, I have decided to overlook any," she hesitated, "inconsistencies with the truth. I shall grant permission for you to take leave for the three days in August, that has been requested."

Alice's mouth dropped open. She dared not speak until she had processed Matron's words. "Thank you, Matron," she said, slightly breathlessly.

"I'll write to the captain advising him that I have granted permission." Matron lifted the small watch attached to the front of her uniform. "I expect you to keep this matter to yourself. You'd better return to your duties now. I believe we are expecting a further admission of patients again later this evening."

Alice managed to retain her composure as she walked calmly out of the office. She was going to spend three precious days with her Ed, away from the hospital. The thought of being able to eat her meals with him, walk and talk for three entire days was almost impossible for her to take in.

She wrote to Ed immediately, aware that Matron would

see her reply and careful not to undermine her feelings in any way. Days later Ed replied.

Dearest Alice,

We are about to go over the top and so this letter will be brief, I'm afraid.

I am grateful indeed that you have been granted leave. I will meet you on 2nd of August outside the Hotel du Nord for afternoon tea. I have booked a room for you at Madam Gaston's bed and breakfast at her farm. I believe she is a kindly, respectable woman who offers rooms to females only. I hope that this arrangement will be acceptable to you and your matron.

I am thinking of you and look forward to being able to spend time with you.

Yours, Ed x

Alice winced at the thought of Ed having to leave the relative safety of his trench and climb out to cross the open spaces of No Man's Land. She said a silent prayer for his safety and read on. Yes, she decided, she was more than happy with his reservation. She believed Matron would be content to note that she would be sleeping at a women's only establishment for her time away from work, too.

One day, Alice dreamed, she and Ed would be able to spend their nights together going to sleep and waking up in each other's arms. That day could not come soon enough for her. She closed her eyes briefly picturing the scene. She had no assurance that the future they craved would be theirs, which is why, she reminded herself, she needed to make the most of any opportunity to be with Ed and relish his closeness.

She folded his letter careful not to crease it, before slipping it back into its envelope. "Dearest Ed," she whispered. "We will be together."

Now, all she had to do was focus on her work and keep as busy as possible to hope that the time between now and when she took her leave would pass as quickly as possible. As if on cue, the emergency siren sounded and the thunder of wheels on hard ground rumbled closer. She checked that her cap was straight and her apron smooth and hurried to join the other nurses to await the arrival of these new batch of injured men. She stood looking out towards the gates as Matron arrived, hands clasped in front of her apron, waiting in silence. The ambulances arrived, and the usual appointment of nurses and volunteers began. Grateful to be kept busy, but her heart aching at the sight and sounds of these traumatised and damaged men, Alice set to work.

As she accompanied an injured man on his blood-soaked stretcher to the surgical ward, she tried to gauge how many men she had helped look after since her arrival. It must be hundreds now. Alice thanked the orderlies as they lifted the patient who looked barely eighteen onto a freshly made up bed.

"We'll soon make you comfortable," she assured him, aware that it would take more than a wash and a change of clothes to help this poor boy. The bandages around his arms and one leg were caked in blood and his face was contorted in pain. She wondered how long he had been in these dressings, and spotting Doctor Sullivan, waved at him.

"Please, doctor," she said quietly, trying not to alert the patient to her concern. "Can you look at this soldier? I believe he may need to be operated on sooner rather than later."

"I think I should be the judge of that, Nurse Le Breton," he said. Alice was shocked by his tone and glanced up at him, catching him giving her a stare that was most disconcerting. She could not imagine what she had done to cause him disapproval. She hoped he hadn't changed his mind about reporting seeing her the day she'd met Ed for tea. What if he did and matron rescinded her permission for her leave. Her stomach contracted in fear. "Doctor Sullivan," she said trying not to panic.

He shook his head. "Not right now, Nurse. I must look at what needs to be done for this patient."

Aware that she would have to wait, she said, "Would you like me to begin removing the dressings?"

"Bring that trolley over here and we can both do it," he said. "I need to be in surgery in a few minutes and can't waste any time."

She pulled the trolley over, noticing that by the time she had picked up scissors to pass them to him, he had already removed one of the soldier's bandages on his left arm.

"This needs cleaning and re-dressing, but other than that it's fine." He took the scissors and cutting through the bandage on the soldier's leg, studied the wound in silence.

"Your instincts were right, nurse. This wound needs urgent attention. Put a temporary dressing on it and arrange for him to be brought through to be operated on." He walked away without looking at her to the other side of the bed and checked the patient's other arm. "Fine." He finally looked up at her. "Do the same with this arm, as the other and I'll call for two orderlies. By the time they get here, you should be finished." He stared at her silently for a moment, before adding, "Well done, Nurse Le Breton."

She watched him walk away, his broad shoulders drooping slightly and wondered if maybe the strain of his work was beginning to get the better of him. She could not help thinking that he was a good man, and hoped she was right. It was sometimes hard to tell.

"What are you day-dreaming about, Nurse Le Breton?" Sister Brown bellowed, glancing at Doctor Sullivan before shooting a disapproving glare at Alice. "Concentrate on what you're supposed to be doing. If you find yourself at a loss for something to do after that, I'll direct you towards urgent work that necessitates your attention."

The older woman glowered at her. Alice could not understand the cause of her distain, she was not aware she had ever done anything that could rankle her in any way. She could see that Sister was waiting for her to do or say something. Alice turned her attention to cleaning and redressing the soldier's arms.

"He's fine to go now," she said to the two orderlies who had arrived. She watched them carefully transfer the boy onto a stretcher. The grey pallor of the young man was worrying, and she hoped she would see him again. After being so brave, didn't he deserve to survive?

Noticing Sister Brown watching her from across the ward, Alice itched to find the doctor to plead with him not to speak to matron. What if he had already done so. She took a deep breath to steady her nerves and set to stripping the bed and bundling up the filthy discarded bandages. She tried not to let the woman's silent observation of her put her off what she was doing, but it was a little disconcerting. Refusing to give in to the passive bullying, she focused on the task in hand.

Alice looked away, peeking out of the corner of her eyes to check the ghastly woman had indeed left and gone to bother some other poor nurse.

"She's a right old cow, that one," whispered a young soldier with a bandage covering half his face. "She's always picking on you younger ones and creepin' up to the doctors. Can't stand 'er, myself. We think she fancies that surgeon bloke, Doctor Sullivan."

So, was that it? Alice wondered Did Sister Brown think Alice was closer to the doctor than she actually was? As amused as Alice was by the patient's attempted words of comfort, she bent to puff his pillow and straighten his bedclothes. "I couldn't possibly agree, or disagree with you," she said smiling at him, enjoying his cheerful mood and the distraction from her concerns. "Do you need me to fetch anything for you?"

"No, thank you," he said, smiling up at her. "You get on with what you need to do before the old bag comes back."

He glanced at the doorway and then back at Alice. "She will, you know. Mark my words. I know 'er type. I 'ad a Captain like her before this 'appened," he said pointing to his bandaged head. 'Was always appearin' and tryin' to catch us out. Nasty bugger."

"He sounds vile," Alice agreed. "Right, if you're happy, then I'll get on."

She knew she should not encourage him to say such things, but at that moment it helped her feel better about what had happened. Encouraged by the thought that it was not her actions behind Sister's nastiness, Alice moved on the next patient.

Eventually, it was time for her break and she hurried towards the theatre, hoping to find the doctor. If Sister Brown liked him then that was her issue. Alice needed to speak to him and sort things out. Nothing was going to get in the way of her spending time with Ed, not if she could help it. She paced back and forth for a few minutes, before the doctor marched outside, undoing his bloodied apron. He spotted Alice.

"Are you waiting to speak to me, nurse?" he asked finally ridding himself of the apron.

She held her hand out. "I'll take that from you, if you like."

He narrowed his eyes and passed it to her. "Nurse Le Breton, do you wish to speak to me? I have five minutes' break, so if you do, then you'll need to accompany me to the canteen. I'm parched."

Nodding gratefully, Alice ran to keep up with his fast

pace. "I wanted to know if you'd changed your mind about reporting me to matron?"

He stopped and swung round, glaring at her. "Why would I do that?"

She hadn't expected him to look hurt by her question. "I'm sorry, I didn't mean to offend you."

"Then why ask?" He walked on, shaking his head. "For your information Nurse, I have other more pressing matters to focus on. So, to answer your question, no, I haven't changed my mind." They reached the canteen and he stopped, facing her. "Nor will I." He stared at her for a moment, his disappointment in her obvious. "Good day, nurse."

She had been dismissed. Realising that her leave was safe, she focused on the fact that it would not be long until she saw Ed again. The thought lifted her mood, despite her being unable to forget the look in the doctor's eyes. Aware that her break was at an end, she returned to the ward to carry on with her shift.

Chapter 22

Gemma

July 2018

Gemma leant as far forward as she could without toppling onto the grassy bank. She was determined to reach the sunshine yellow marigolds. Hopping down onto the pathway near the field, she strolled back to the house as swallows swooped above her before diving in formation over the field. She doubted she had ever experienced a more blissful day. She expected Tom back today. Their venture out had been fun, and she had enjoyed seeing another side to the reserved handsome man.

She spotted the letter on the doormat when she walked into the living room. Why did she never hear the postman when he came to the house? She stepped over it and grabbing the vase from the windowsill took her yellow flowers into the kitchen. Pouring water into the vase, Gemma suspected she knew who the letter was from. She popped most of the flowers into the water, and then picking up a

303

small glass, did the same with the rest. They would brighten up her bedroom, she mused putting the larger vase back on the living room windowsill before carrying the glass up the stairs and placing it on her bedside table.

Gemma stood back to study the effect and then, unable to put off the inevitable a moment longer, returned to the living room and picked up the letter. Checking the frank mark, she could see it was from the trauma clinic. The time had come to make her decision, she thought, sadly.

Gemma tore open the envelope. Unfolding the single piece of paper inside she read it twice.

Dear Miss Kingston,

Despite our attempts to contact you on three separate occasions, we are yet to receive a reply. As I am sure you are aware, your position at the centre requires filling. Unless you confirm within the next seven days from the date of this letter whether or not you will be returning to your position, we will assume that you are serving your three months' notice from the above date and will look for a permanent replacement with immediate effect.

She checked the date of the letter. It had taken two days to reach her, which meant she needed to reply in the next day or so if she was to ensure the letter reached the Trauma Clinic by the deadline.

Gemma stood at the open front door and folding her arms stared out across the small front lawn, listening to the birdsong. How could she leave this place now? It had become her home, her sanctuary. What was calling her back to England? Nothing much.

Sighing, she sat down on the doorstep. She had very little in the way of savings, but she did have her flat. She could sell that, but where would she live? It couldn't be the farmhouse, she was supposed to help sell this place, not keep it for herself.

No, she had little choice. It was time to be sensible. Tom would carry on with his life, she thought miserably, and she should focus on returning to hers. Standing up, she took the letter and placed it on the table. She would reply later. First, she was going to enjoy her day. After all, how many other days like this was she going to experience?

She stared at the batches of Alice's letters on the table. She only had one more to read from the first batch. She had initially suspected Alice of having two sweethearts, but now knew that Peter was covering for her and Ed. Her mood dipped when she realised that she would have to leave Alice's letters behind.

Someone rapped on the door, disturbing her thoughts and Gemma looked up to see Tom silhouetted in the doorway, the sun bright behind his back. For a split second she pictured Alice sitting where she was looking up at Ed in the same way.

"Hey, what's up?" Ed asked rushing over to her, hugging her from behind. "Did you read something sad in one of Alice's letters?"

She shook her head. Pulling a tissue from her shorts pocket, Gemma blew her nose. "No," she said taking a deep breath to give her the energy to say the words that needed to be spoken. "I've received a letter from work. I need to let them know today or tomorrow whether or not I'm going back, or they'll fill my position." She felt Tom's arms stiffen slightly.

"And, if you don't?" he asked eventually.

Gemma turned to face him, causing him to have to move back from her. She hated to see the look of disappointment on his face. She knew exactly how he felt.

"I have very little choice, really don't I?" There, she had said it. This was the real world.

"You always have a choice," he said, a sadness of his own creeping through.

"Not realistically. I don't have any other skills, for a start," she said, thinking about the desperation of the patient Alice had mentioned in her notes on the back of the most recent letter that she had read. "And I need money to live on." She raised her hands in despair. "I could sell my flat but then I'd need to use that money to buy somewhere else to live." She cleared her throat.

For the next few seconds the only sound in the room was the birdsong coming from the garden. "I don't want you to leave," Tom said eventually.

Delighted to hear his admission, she said, "And I'm not ready to go. I don't know if I ever will be."

"Come here," Tom said, opening his arms.

Gemma stepped into them without a seconds' hesitation. She closed her eyes as he held her tightly against his chest. If she was honest with herself, loving the house was only part of her problem, she also loved Tom. She didn't want to leave him. She took a shuddering breath. He had said he didn't want her to leave, but did he feel as deeply about her as she did him? Enough for them to make it work if she did stay?

"You say you've got time before having to give them your answer?"

She nodded, breathing in the fresh laundered smell of his white tee-shirt. "Yes, but only for a day or two," she replied, unsure why she should delay the inevitable. "I may as well get it over with."

"Don't reply just yet," he said. "Take what time you have left to consider all your options."

She knew he was right. However, she was too used to dealing with issues by making a considered but quick decision and living with the consequences. Gemma could not bear uncertainty, it unnerved her. She was sure this was partly why she had felt unable to cope towards the end at the trauma unit. She puffed out her cheeks. There was nothing stopping her from doing as he suggested, only her own fear.

"Fine, I'll give it until tomorrow," she said after a moment's hesitation. There, she thought, I've done it again. Made another snap decision.

"One of the things you do need to consider," Tom said letting go of her. "Is, who'll complete this work and show prospective buyers around if you do return to your job?"

"I suppose Dad can pay you to finish the work, if you're free," she said, wishing Tom wouldn't scowl at her like that.

"As far as the selling goes, I'd have to secure an estate agent before I leave." Her thoughts began gathering momentum. It was doable, she decided, feeling a little more confident. "They could hold a set of keys. That way they wouldn't need to worry about timings for showing the farm to prospective buyers."

"So, there's no reason for you to stay, you mean?" He asked, pushing his hands into his jeans' pockets.

Practically, Gemma realised that there was no reason at all. It was a little alarming.

"Emotionally I want to stay here, of course I do," she said, relieved when he seemed to cheer up a bit. "I'm not ready to go. I have letters to read," she looked down at the remaining batch.

"And?"

She tried but could not voice her thoughts. What if he didn't feel the same way? Locking eyes with him, she wanted to admit what he meant to her. But the thought of being humiliated again, even in this room with no witnesses, held her back.

He stared at her. She could tell he wanted her to say something. But dare she?

Chapter 23

Alice

August 1918

Alice walked hand-in-hand with Ed up to the small farmhouse. She wished she had brought a lighter coat to wear. It was far too hot for so many layers and she was beginning to perspire. He lifted the rusty latch on the wrought iron gate and pushed it open, waiting for Alice to walk through before closing it behind them. Alice could see that someone was trying to keep the place as well as possible under the difficult circumstances where everything from paint to food was scarce. The sight of the peeling paint on the front aspect of the house saddened her. Was the husband away at war? Before she could contemplate other scenarios for the rundown appearance of the place the front door opened.

"Bonjour," a tiny world-weary woman greeted them as she dried her hands on her immaculate apron. "Vienez ici."

Ed spoke to the woman in broken French as she

welcomed them into her home. Ed placed his hand in the crook of Alice's back to guide her inside.

Alice smiled at her temporary landlady. She was overwhelmed by an overriding sense of sadness about the place and was unsure if she wanted to stay here. After a few seconds, the woman, who she now knew was a Madam Gaston, indicated for Ed to take a seat at the scrubbed pine table. She then picked up Alice's small case and motioned for Alice to follow her.

They walked up the creaking wooden stairs, and Alice could see the place was immaculate inside, despite the peeling paint outside. She wanted to see where she was expected to sleep for the next two nights and argued with herself that anything would be better than her camp bed in her shared bell tent, especially if it meant spending precious time alone with Ed.

Madam Gaston pushed back a door on the left-hand side on the landing and waited for Alice to go inside. As Alice walked in, the sunlight pouring into the room almost blinded her. She stepped back away from the glaring light and noticed the utter peace in the room. The window was wide open, and a cow mooed somewhere nearby and birds chirped cheerfully in the trees surrounding the property.

Alice opened her mouth trying to work out how to express her delight, when the ground shuddered as bombs exploded several miles away. The women looked at each other. For the first time, Alice saw the furrows on her brow and wondered how old this woman might be. It was difficult to tell, but Alice suspected that Madam Gaston was much younger than she appeared. She had seen enough people age drastically after experiencing pain. Maybe, she thought the cause of Madam Gaston's premature aging was due to the strains of running a farm alone. She suspected though that it was due to loss – enduring a life without a loved one seemed to age people so much more than anything else.

She realised the woman was waiting for her to show her approval of the bedroom. Not wishing to cause any further anxiety, Alice nodded. "Trés bien," she said nodding. "Trés belle."

Madam Gaston's expression changed. Her face lit up, as she showed her relief that Alice liked the room. Alice wondered how she must have looked when she was younger and before life took its toll on her.

Alice realised that her approval of the room and Ed's payment for her to stay here would probably be the difference between the woman eating or not over the next few days. How difficult it must be to run this place without any help. She wondered if the woman had any sons living at home with her.

"Vous vivez seule, ici?" Alice asked, assuming she must live alone because there was only one other bedroom by the looks of things.

"Oui," the woman answered lifting a corner of her apron to dab at her eyes. "Mes fils et maris sont morts."

Sons, and her husband, all dead? What, all of them? She daren't ask. Alice could have bitten her tongue to have been

311

so stupid and insensitive to ask if she lived alone. She should have known better. Too busy trying to fill a silence, that was her problem. Horrified, she rested a hand on the woman's right shoulder. "Pardon, Madam," she said apologetically. "Je suis vraiment désolé."

The woman shook her head, "Non, non," she said, forcing a smile, before leaving the room and returning downstairs. Alice stayed behind to give the woman space to collect herself. Walking up to the window she stared out, breathing in the scent of nearby pine trees, mixed with a vague hint of the distant smoke rising behind them from the bombardment. If she used her imagination, she could almost forget there was a war on nearby. She would certainly try over the next few days. Alice heard Madam Gaston talking to Ed and offering him coffee.

She sat on the side of the bed. It was comfortable and she looked forward to falling asleep in here. She checked her appearance in the small wall mirror and went to join the others in the living room.

"Happy?" Ed asked, nervously.

"Very," Alice said, relieved to be able to say so honestly.

They drank the thick dark coffee and thanked Madam Gaston as they went outside.

"Come along," Ed said. "She told me I must take you to see the poppy field."

Alice adored poppies, especially more so now that Ed had picked one for her. It always felt like summer had truly arrived when the poppies were out. They held hands and followed the pathway around to the side of the house and then up a slight incline to a five-bar gate. Arriving at the gate they stopped.

Alice gasped. "It's a sea of scarlet," she said, breathless with awe at the glorious sight stretching ahead of them; the blood red petals swaying slightly in the light breeze. "I've never seen anything quite so enchanting."

"I have," Ed said, kissing her. "I thought you'd like this view," he opened the gate. "I discovered it when I came here with Peter. He was asked to deliver mail to Madam Gaston and she told us about the poppy field."

Happier than she could ever recall being, Alice let him lead her into the middle of the field. "I wish I could stay here forever," she said. "It's magical."

"I thought so when I found the farm. I wanted somewhere for us to be alone, if only for a couple of days. We need to spend time getting to know each other away from other people."

Alice agreed. "This is perfect," she said, pulling Ed's hand until he bent his head so that she could kiss him. "Let's sit down," she said, when they came up for air.

"I have a gift for you," he said, seeming a little shy.

Alice wondered what he could have found for her. She waited as he carefully withdrew a box from his lapel pocket. He placed it in the palm of her hand. "I hope you like it," he said. "When I spotted it on leave after being discharged. It reminded me of our first kiss and I had to buy it for you."

She smiled up at him aware she would treasure whatever he had chosen for her. Pressing the little brass clip, she lifted the lid, and gasped. "Oh, Ed, it's exquisite." She took the scarlet enamelled brooch from its cushion and held it closer to take in its shining beauty. "I love it. Here," she said, holding it against her blouse. "Help me fasten it, will you?"

He did as she asked.

Alice leant forward and taking his face in both her hands kissed him. "Thank you, my darling. I'll treasure this, always."

They sat, and Ed draped his arm around her shoulders, hugging her to him. Content to be in his arms, especially in such a beautiful place, Alice rested her head against his chest.

"I love you," Ed said breaking the silence between them.

Her heart swelling with joy, Alice stared at the pretty scarlet flowerheads all around them, trying to etch the moment in her mind forever. "I love you, too," she said wishing the moment would last forever. "Thank you for arranging this for us."

"I'm grateful you agreed to come here with me." He moved so that they were facing each other as he went on one knee.

Alice's brain could not process what was happening, but she instinctively knew that what happened next was going to change the course of her life. She held her breath.

"Alice, my beautiful darling sweetheart, will you do me the honour of agreeing to become my wife?"

She covered her mouth with her left hand.

Ed's smile slipped slightly. "Alice?"

She could see he was worried she might turn him down, so forced herself to reply. "Yes, I'd love to marry you, Ed," she said, leaning forwards and almost losing her balance. He caught her, and they fell back onto the hard earth, her landing softened by falling onto him. "Mr and Mrs Woodhall," she said dreamily, delirious at the image in her head of the two of them dressed in their finery at her parish church.

"You're picturing us at our wedding, aren't you?" he teased after a few seconds.

How did he know? She giggled. "Yes, I am," she admitted, shyly.

Ed held her tightly. Then lifting her slightly by the shoulders, he kissed her. Alice returned his kiss and instantly they were lost in their own world. She vaguely heard an explosion. For a split-second Alice tensed at the reminder that her beloved man would soon be back at the Front risking his life for his country.

"Don't think about it," he soothed, pulling her into another kiss.

She forced the thought aside and immersed herself in the sensations she was experiencing.

They spent the rest of the day lying in the field in each other's arms each swapping dreams for their future together.

"How many babies do you want?" Alice asked him.

"As many as you like," he whispered. "I think we should at least try for a pigeon pair."

"A what?"

He kissed her. "A boy and a girl."

Alice loved the idea. She pictured her with their baby in her arms, a toddler running around the living room, while Ed sat in his favourite armchair proudly watching his family.

"We're going to have a magical life together," she murmured, certain that as soon as this war was over, the rest of their lives would be theirs to live as they chose. "Where will we live?"

He hugged her to him and closed his eyes. "I have a cottage in Scotland, near to my family estate," he said.

Alice had never heard of this estate before and certainly did not know about a cottage. "Tell me what it's like, so that I can imagine it."

"It's stone. It's painted white and the garden in front of the cottage leads to a lake," his Scottish lilt soothed and delighted her. She closed her eyes in contentment as she listened to him. "There are mountains behind," he continued, his words interspersed with silence as he thought of what else to add. "In the depths of winter, we can be cut off, but I love that time best. Then again, I also enjoy the long summer nights. I sometimes spend the night in my boat on the lake fishing, or simply relishing the peace and quiet." He hesitated and hugged her tightly. "I'm going to love it even more now that I'll have you there to share everything with."

Alice sighed. She had never been so happy.

"We don't have to live there, if you'd rather not. We can always keep the cottage for our holidays in the summer."

"Why wouldn't I want to?" Alice asked, rising and resting on her right elbow.

"You might wish to return to Jersey, set up home there."

It dawned on Alice that he had misunderstood her sigh. "No," she said kissing him. "I love Jersey, you know I do, but I want to live with you, in your cottage."

"Our cottage," he corrected.

Thrilled to hear him say such a thing, she smiled. "Thank you. Our family cottage."

He beamed at her. "I love you, the future Mrs Woodhall," he said, pulling her down and kissing her, hard.

Moments later when they stopped, Alice said, "I can't wait to marry you, Ed," she said. "How long do you think we should wait?"

He shrugged. "How long would you like to wait?"

No time at all, she thought, but resisted voicing aloud. "I don't know."

Ed smiled at her. "We could see how soon we can be married. On my next leave, maybe? Or should we wait to be back at home when our families can celebrate the occasion with us?"

Much as Alice liked the idea of having a big family wedding with all their friends coming together to celebrate their day with them, she did not like the notion of having to wait. "We don't know how long this war is going to last," she said, thoughtfully. "Or, how soon you and I will be sent home at the end of it."

Ed nodded. "I agree. We could always hold a reception later. Our loved ones can meet each other then and have a special day with us."

Alice liked that idea, very much. "We should get married sooner, rather than later then."

"Yes, I think we ought to do that," he said pulling her into his arms and kissing her.

The sun was slowly setting behind the trees. They sat in each other's arms watching nature at its best, both ignoring the distant roar of explosions. Ed said, "I'm going to have to leave soon."

"I didn't ask where you were staying?" Alice said. "I hope it's somewhere nearby."

"I've rented a room at a house in the village. It's only a five-minute walk."

Alice was not ready to end their perfect day yet. "Can't you stay just a little longer?"

He kissed the top of her head. "Five minutes. Madame Gaston has been paid to give you a meal tonight and she'll be serving it any time now."

Alice felt like a petulant child. She didn't need to eat anything. "I don't want to waste the time I have with you," she argued. "Couldn't we walk into the village and have a meal together?"

He shook his head. "Your Matron gave me strict instructions about where you had to stay and that you could only be seen with me in the village during daylight hours." He put his finger tips under her chin and lifted it slightly. "Anyway, Madam Gaston needs the money and I've paid her for the meal. We don't want to insult her by you not eating it."

"No, of course not."

"We can make up for it tomorrow. I'll buy food for a picnic, if there is any, and we can spend the afternoon by the river."

She shook her head. "No, let's bring our picnic here. There's something about this place that makes me want to stay here with you for as long as I can."

"Then that's what we'll do," he said. "Our own private paradise."

They strolled back to the farmhouse where Ed thanked the landlady and wished them both a good evening before leaving.

Alice watched him go, wishing things were different and that they were already married. No one could tell her to stay here without him then, she mused. She sat down on the chair Madam Gaston indicated and a delicious plate of stew was served to her. Alice could tell by the amount of vegetables and lack of meat that the woman was struggling to pay for food and was grateful to Ed for reminding her that her stay here was also helping Madam Gaston.

"Délicieux," she said. "Merci."

They ate their meal, communicating by using the few words each knew from the others' language and a lot of gesticulation. Despite the lack of understanding, Alice enjoyed a surprisingly pleasant evening with the woman. She discovered that her husband had died at the beginning of the war and her three sons killed over the following four years. It was heartbreaking to watch the grief still etched on the older woman's face. She told Alice that she wanted to return to her family in Brittany after the war but did not think she could afford to.

Alice hoped she found a way to achieve her ambitions. She could only imagine how sad it must be to spend your life alone living with ghosts. She hoped Madam Gaston found a way to move on.

The following morning, Ed arrived just after they finished their breakfast of porridge and honey. Alice rarely ate the oat breakfast but did not wish to offend her hostess by refusing the food she placed in front of her.

"Bonjour," Ed said standing at the open front door, a hessian bag in his hand. "How are you this morning?"

Relieved to have a distraction from her sadness learning about Madam Gaston's bereavements, Alice thanked her and left the table to join him. She waved goodbye to the lady, who seemed more confident and less haunted this morning. Alice hoped their chat the previous evening had helped in some way. She always felt better sharing her worries with Mary.

Alice winced as several explosions went off nearby. "I'd love to come here after the war," she said. "When the area around the Somme has returned to how it once was, and the peace isn't constantly interrupted by reminders of what's really going on."

"Me, too," Ed said, glancing at the house before kissing her.

If someone had told her before this day that she would happily spend two days sitting in a poppy field day-dreaming and staring into space, Alice was certain she would not believe them. This, however was bliss. She realised Ed was speaking.

"You weren't listening, were you?" he asked, his eyes twinkling with amusement.

Alice ran her right hand over a poppy, her skin barely touching the scarlet petals. "I was thinking how perfect my weekend with you has been."

He kissed her shoulder. "It has been even more incredible than I could have ever imagined." An explosion interrupted his next words. "Even with that crescendo going on. We'll return here after the war and spend longer than two days. We can sit here. Nothing will interrupt our peace."

"Promise?"

"Yes." He pulled her down on top of him and soon they were kissing again. "I love you so much," he murmured. "I can't until we're married, and we can make love freely."

Alice faltered and sat up slightly. Her mind briefly considered what she was about to suggest, but reason and forethought were not things she cared about at that moment, only her adoration of her future husband. "Why can't we do it now?"

His eyes widened, and his mouth fell open.

Aware that she was acting out of character, but desperate not to waste the precious time they had together, she blushed. "What's the matter? We're going to be married soon. What difference will it make?" She waited for him to mull over her words, then added, "Will we ever find a more romantic, or private place to love each other than here?"

He stared at her. She could see he was unsure. For a

moment she wondered if she had gone too far. She had obviously shocked him. She had shocked herself.

Ed rested his right hand on her cheek. "I don't know what to say," he admitted. "I love you and want you more than anything, but I'm not sure." He studied her face. "Are you truly certain this is what you want?"

She had never been surer of anything. She knew it was out of character, but this place seemed enchanted, as if it was not part of the real world. She smiled, covering his hand with her own. "I am."

He took her in his arms and kissed her with more passion than she could have imagined.

Later, they lay in each other's arms staring silently up at the azure blue cloudless sky waiting for their heart rates to return to normal. Alice had imagined what it would be like to be made love to. She closed her eyes and could still feel how it was to be so utterly as one. The experience had been enlightening and far more enjoyable than she had ever dreamt.

Alice knew she would remember this day forever. Here, in the most idyllic field, surrounded by poppies and in the arms of the man she was soon to marry, nothing could mar her happiness. Nothing.

Chapter 24

Gemma

August 2018

Gemma opened her eyes confused for a moment. Why was it still dark? Reaching for her watch on the bedside table, she rubbed her eyes trying to focus.

"Six fifteen," she groaned, before putting the watch back and closing her eyes. She could tell it was going to be a warm day by the heat in her bedroom, despite the open window. She realised she hadn't experienced the sight of a sunrise at the farmhouse before and decided she wasn't going to miss the opportunity.

She got up and showered, standing for several minutes under the cascade of cool water waiting for it to bring her round. Dressed in her shorts, a clean tee-shirt and her trainers, Gemma hurriedly brushed her short curly blonde hair. By time she stepped out of the front door the sun was ready to rise.

She ran along the path towards the poppy field, standing

in awe just inside the gate at the vision that greeted her. The gold, orange and yellow sunrays spread like wildfire across the scarlet heads through the early morning mist. Gazing at the sea of poppy heads dancing in the gentle summer breeze, Gemma thought it was the most glorious thing she had ever seen. She pictured Alice and Ed standing where she stood one hundred years earlier experiencing the same vision.

"Beautiful," Tom said quietly at her shoulder.

Surprised to hear his voice, she smiled, delighted he was there to share such a magical moment. Without averting her gaze, she said, "Why are you here so early?"

"It dawned on me last night that if you were leaving, then I needed to come here to see the sunrise, just in case it was as spectacular as I had hoped. Who knows when I would get another opportunity to do so."

"And, is it?"

"Oh, yes."

She could feel his warm breath on her cool skin and shivered.

"Do you want me to fetch you a jacket?" he asked quietly.

"No, thanks," she said, unsure why they were keeping their voices so low. "We're not going to wake anyone by talking, you know?"

Tom laughed. "I know that, but somehow it seems disrespectful to be noisy at a time like this." He put his arm around her shoulder. "Do you mind?"

"No," she said, relishing the heat from his body as they

both stared at the sunrise. "If I leave, I'll never be able to see this again," she said almost to herself. The thought upset her. Even more since the decision to leave was hers alone.

"You know what I think," he said.

She didn't, not fully. She wanted more than anything to stay here, at this special place, with him. "But what would I do for money?"

He didn't reply. She felt him tense very slightly. "Can't you take a chance and see what happens?"

She was unsure whether she would have the courage to do such a thing. Then again, she was not ready to return to nursing. Gemma felt her emotions getting the better of her and cleared her throat. "I'll make a decision today, one way or another."

Tom turned her to face him. Placing his hands either side of her cheeks he moved closer to her, kissing her. After, he smiled. "Why don't you hold a party for the people you know here and the neighbours who you haven't met yet?"

Flustered by his kiss and surprised by the change of topic, Gemma frowned. "What's the point? It's not as if I don't still have a lot to do before I leave. Not to mention the letters in the second batch that I still haven't read."

"You've finished the first batch then?" He smiled at her. "And?"

"I'm completely absorbed by their love affair," she said. "I know it happened a century ago, but it affects me as if it was happening right now. I can sense them here together," she said hoping he didn't think she was being ridiculous. "It's as if I can go into the next room and find Alice. Or maybe come out here and see her and Ed laughing together. I'm disappointed each time I realise it's not going to happen."

"I haven't read much of the letters," he said. "But I get a sense of them here, too. I'd love to know how their future together panned out."

"Me, too." She thought of the date stamps on the last letter of the first batch and the first one of the second. "There's a large gap in the dates between each batch," she said. "I didn't notice until I reached the end of the first one. I haven't discovered yet why Alice stopped writing to Ed. I hope they didn't fall out or something worse happened to him."

"Most lovers argue at some point." Tom said. "Maybe he was sent somewhere far away, and his letters took longer to reach her."

Gemma liked that she wasn't the only one enthralled by Alice and Ed's story. It occurred to her that her relationship with Tom had vague connotations with their romance. Both women were nurses, though at very different times with many different problems and medical experiences. They each loved men who they couldn't keep close as much as they'd wish to. She thought about how unalike the men's experiences of war had been, although both had been injured. Ed had fully recovered, while Tom needed to find a way to alter his life to fit the changes to his body.

She noticed he was waiting for her to reply. "Maybe, I'm not sure."

"So, the party?" Tom asked. "Do you want to go ahead with it?"

"Do you really think there's a point?" she asked, honestly.

"I do. It'll be fun for you to meet people you don't already know from around here. If you do decide to leave, then they'll have seen how incredible this place looks now. They might know someone who could want to buy it. If you stay, then you've made new friends. Win, win."

He did have a point. She also wouldn't mind seeing how this place looked with a group of people enjoying themselves. "I suppose it would be a way to say goodbye to the people I have met, like Marie and Marcel."

Tom beamed at her. "If you're sure, then I can go and invite people, while you plan what food and drink we need."

Concerned about his intended timing of the party, Gemma frowned. "This is for when, exactly?"

"This afternoon," he said, winking at her. "Two-thirty suit you?"

She could see the mischief in his eyes and his enthusiasm for his idea. Gemma pondered the pros and cons for a few seconds, then inspired by his idea, said. "Go on, then. Why not?"

He was right. It would be a fun way to spend a Sunday and gave her the impetus to clean out the barn area. They were going to need it for shade from the heat of the day.

Gemma watched Tom drive away, happy that he had

come up with such a fun suggestion. Checking her watch, Gemma realised that if she was going to hold a party in the barn area, she would need to get a move on and clean it. An hour later, despite it still being early, Tom drove into the yard with two trestle tables and various chairs in the back of his pick-up.

"You've been busy," he said, staring at the freshly swept and washed barn floor. "I've brought some lights to hang from the rafters, too" he said. "My mum uses them whenever she entertains outside." He lifted them from the back of the vehicle and carried the long string of tiny lights to her. Let's put them up quickly and see what you think?"

They took a few minutes to link them over the roof rafters. Tom had also brought an external extension lead which he hoisted over the yard with two ladders and plugged into the kitchen through the window.

"Okay," he shouted. "Try switching them on now."

She did. "They look gorgeous," she cheered, knowing they would be even better in the dark.

They set up the tables and set the chairs around them. Gemma was relieved to find a box full of plates, cutlery and glasses inside Tom's pick-up.

"You really have thought of everything, haven't you?" she said following him into the kitchen as he carried the box inside.

"Hopefully," he said. "It was me who pushed the idea on to you," he said, giving her a quick peck on her nose. "I thought it was the least I could do. There should also be a box of old jam jars with candles in them for the tables and dotting around the seating area."

He placed a box carefully onto the table in the kitchen. "When we go to the village to buy the food and booze, we can pop by people's homes and invite them."

"Good idea," Gemma said, taking everything out of the box and setting it up neatly. "I'm looking forward to meeting neighbours," she said, unsure how many there would be. Gemma was excited about the idea now that Tom had brought so much for the party. "Music," she said, as the thought came into her head. "We can't have a party without a little music."

"Leave it with me," he said.

Gemma grinned. "Is that your mum's as well?"

He turned and tickled her. "No, that's mine."

Once she was happy that they had done all they could, they went in Tom's pick-up to the village, stopping off on the way at each of her neighbours' homes. By the time they had visited Marcel's hardware store and left Marie's café Gemma was relieved she had agreed with Tom's idea.

"I can't believe fourteen people have accepted," she said thinking about the differences in ages of some of their guests. "Do you realise we have people ranging from grandfather to teenager. It's going to be great fun."

"I told you it would be," he laughed. "Oh, yea of little faith."

"Well, we'll have to see how I feel after they've all left, to be certain you were right," she teased as they entered the boulangerie. "I think I'll do platters of meat, cheeses and then we can have crackers and baguettes to eat. I can do a few salads and we can have strawberries and ice-cream for pudding. What do you think?"

"Sounds just right," he said grabbing a trolley. "The wine is at the far end of the shop. You find the food you want, and I'll go and pick up some wine."

Back at the farmhouse, they unpacked the shopping and set everything out in the kitchen. She was happy with what they had bought. Tom assured her, too, that the neighbours would bring plates of food to share at the party and bottles of drink.

Gemma checked her watch and grimaced. "I'm going to run upstairs and change," she said. "I'll prepare the food when I get down." She didn't have a clue what she would wear. She knew Tom thought it was fine for her to stay in her shorts and tee-shirt, but she wanted to dress up a little. She opened her almost empty wardrobe and took out her solitary dress. She hung it up on the outside of the door and smiled. She always felt good in the daisy patterned spaghetti-strapped cotton dress.

Showered and changed, Gemma put on a little mascara and lip gloss. They probably wouldn't last very long, she mused, but she could at least try to make a good impression on her guests.

"You see?" she said, entering the kitchen. "I didn't take very long."

Tom looked up from preparing the salad. It was the third bowl he had made. "The meat is in the oven, I hope that's alright."

"Yes, of course," she said, thrilled he was being so helpful. Cooking wasn't her forte and she never minded help in the kitchen.

"You look very pretty," he said, continuing to chop a spring onion. "That dress suits you."

Gemma smiled. At least she had made a good impression to the most important person. "Thank you," she said.

"I thought we could leave the bread whole and let people take what they want."

"Very rustic," she said. "I like it."

She washed and cored the strawberries, putting them in a bowl and then into the small fridge. "It's not much cooler than outside, but it's better than nothing," she joked.

"Right, that's as much as we can do, I think," Tom said. "How about we open one of the bottles of red wine and take a glass each up to the poppy field?"

"I love that idea," she said realising how much she wanted to make the most of the peace before their guests descended.

Glasses of wine in their hands, they ambled up the slope to the field.

"You do know I'm hoping you change your mind about leaving, don't you?" he said his fingers grazing hers as he passed her his glass, so he could open the gate.

The skin on her hand tingled where he'd touched it. She walked in to the field and waited for him to close it behind them, smiling at him. "I'm glad. I would hate to think you were counting the days until I left."

He took his glass back from her and together they

walked to the small area just into the sea of poppies and sat down. "Do you really think there's nothing you could do here?"

She shrugged. "I'd like to think there is, but what? It's not just earning a living, it's finding somewhere to live."

"Aren't you just making excuses because you're frightened to commit to something new?" He drank some of his wine and stared out across the field thoughtfully.

Gemma didn't like what he had just said, but he had a point. "I have a feeling you know me better than I imagined," she said, aware that he was not only the kindest but the sexiest man she had ever known. She could feel her mind changing. "Fine. I'll do what I can," she said before allowing herself to think anything through.

He narrowed his eyes. "What? About staying?"

"Yes, I hate that I've missed out on so much fun by being too self-contained and keeping to myself. I'm going to try and find a way to stay here, if possible."

He smiled at her. "Good for you. You can always stay at mine, if you like." He stared at his glass. She gave his suggestion some thought.

"Like it?" he asked, confusing her.

"Sorry, what?" She hoped she hadn't said anything out loud.

"The wine," he said. "You sighed. I presumed it was because you liked it."

Relieved, she nodded. "Yes, it's an excellent choice," she said taking another sip. "Well done." Hearing voices she sat up straighter. "What was that?"

"Damn, I think some of the guests have arrived," he said, standing and taking her hand to help her. "We'd better get a move on, otherwise they'll think the party is over."

"If I have my way," she said. "It's only just begun."

Chapter 25

Alice

10 November 1918

Alice ran outside as soon as she heard the familiar rumbling sound of the postal vehicle arriving. She waited with the others, each of them desperate for news from their loved ones. It was three days since receiving her last letter from Ed. Surely, he hadn't been injured again, she thought, dreading the thought of him being sent elsewhere if he had been.

"Sorry love," the postman said. "I don't think there's anything in the post bag for you today. Not that I noticed anyway. I did look, like you asked me to. Maybe I've missed it and Matron will pass it on to you later."

"I hope so," Alice said. "Thanks for looking for me."

"No worries. The mail might be 'eld up somewhere?"

"I'll just have to wait and see," Alice said, hoping that the man was right. As much as she would miss him, she knew she would rather he be relaxing in his beloved cottage in Scotland and far away from noise and danger.

There had been talk of a ceasefire for days. She could not imagine being back home again with everything back to how it used to be. Alice began walking back to her tent. The nausea she had suffered during the past week hitting her once again. She had missed her monthlies for the third time now. She was unsure whether to tell Ed after the second month and knew he would hate her to keep news of their baby from him. If only he would respond to her letter.

A second's doubt smacked her in the chest. It hit her so hard that she had to stop walking and rest against the rear wall of the supply hut. No, Ed would never leave her. Especially not now. Pushing away the hateful thoughts, she straightened up and took a deep breath. They would be married, just as they had planned. Hopefully no one would notice their baby was born a little earlier than expected.

Both had experienced and witnessed too much death for the joy of a baby to upset them. Alice continued her way down the muddy pathway to her tent. She shivered in the cold drizzle. Leaving this place could not come soon enough. Any satisfaction she once had from working here had long since vanished. Alice was desperate for a nights' sleep in a comfortable bed. Sharing that bed with Ed by her side was something she dreamt of constantly.

She smiled, picturing his perfect mouth pulling back in a smile as he read her letter telling him about the pregnancy. It was early days yet but working until the end of the war would keep her busy, just so long as it ended soon.

Alice hadn't expected pregnancy to tire her so badly. By the end of each day, she ached to her very bones. It was emotional tiredness, as well as physical. She wondered how long she could bear to tend to men while they struggled to breathe day after day. She was beginning to think that maybe she should begin planning to return home to Jersey. She shook off the thought before it had barely registered. No, she was going to wait here for Ed. At least her being in France meant that she was closer to him, just in case he managed to get leave and spend a little time with her.

"Nurse," one of the patients called out to her, his voice hoarse from the damage to his throat.

Alice looked up from carrying in several clean bed pans, to see a young private waving for her. "I'll be right over," she said, placing them out of the way. The last thing she needed was Sister Brown walking into an untidy ward.

She went to him and saw he was distressed. "What do you need me to do?" she asked, hating to see his face still disfigured with yellow blisters.

"I can't breathe very well," he whispered. "I'm sure I'm worse today."

She thought so too, but she didn't say so. "Don't worry," she said, giving him a reassuring smile. "Doctor Sullivan will be carrying out his rounds very soon. I'll tell him how you're feeling."

"Thank you, Nurse."

She straightened his bed clothes and was about to take the trolley back to the supply hut to re-stock it, when Mary hurried into the ward.

"Matron wants to see you," she said quietly. "Have you done something you shouldn't?" she teased. "Again?"

Alice shook her head, nervously. "I've no idea."

"You have to go straight away," Mary said. "I'm to accompany you."

She asked one of the other volunteers to speak to Dr Sullivan about the private in case she hadn't returned before his rounds. Then left the ward for Matron's hut.

They arrived at the door and glanced at each other before Mary knocked.

"Enter."

They walked in. A wave of nausea washed over Alice. She swallowed a few times and took small breaths to try to quell the sensation.

"Sit down," Matron said, her face expressionless.

Alice noticed two chairs, instead of one. A sickening feeling began creeping through her mind. She forced it away and saw Matron's clasped hands trembling slightly.

Matron cleared her throat. "I'm afraid I have some bad news, Nurse Le Breton."

Alice instinctively knew that her worst fears were being realised. "No."

Matron pushed an envelope across her desk towards Alice. "I thought it best to ask Nurse Jones to be here with you. I hope that was the right thing to do. If not, please say."

Alice stared at the envelope on the edge of the desk. Everything around her slowed. She knew what it would say. She could hear Matron's voice, but it was muffled, as if she was under water. Taking a deep breath, Alice concentrated on remaining calm. If she left the envelope sealed, she would never have to read the words inside. She watched as Mary's hand picked up the envelope and placed it into hers.

"You must read it," Mary said, a catch in her voice.

"I can't," Alice whispered, staring down at her shaking hands, aware that this letter was going to shatter her future happiness.

"Sometimes we have to face our worst fears," Matron said.

Alice looked across the desk at her and noticed the haunted look of someone who had suffered. Hands shaking, Alice opened the envelope and slowly withdrew the telegram.

Deeply regret to inform you that Captain E D Woodhall was killed in action 7th November. Lord Kitchener expresses his sympathy.

Secretary War Office

Alice stared at the words as they swam in front of her eyes. He could not be dead. They were going to be married. Had he learnt about their baby before being killed, she wondered?

She could not move.

"Alice?" Mary said, resting a hand on her shoulder.

"Nurse Le Breton," she heard Matron speak, but could not force her eyes away from the life-changing words in front of her.

Needing air, Alice stood up. "I have to go," she said,

desperate to get away from their sympathetic faces. She would never be held in his arms again. She reached for the door. As her hand touched the handle Alice felt her legs give way. It was a relief to give in to nothingness.

She didn't know what was worse, the initial reading of the telegram, or regaining consciousness and realising all over again that she would never see Ed. Alice opened her eyes. She was alone in a side ward. Tears began rolling down her cheeks. Somewhere nearby an animal howled. Seconds later it dawned on her that the sound had come from her.

Fear and blind panic clenched at her throat. How was she going to live without him? How was she going to have this baby by herself? She curled into a foetal position and cried great gulping sobs, terrified at the thought of facing the rest of her life without him.

A cool hand placed a damp cloth on her forehead. "Here," Doctor Sullivan said, his deep voice comforting, as he handed her a handkerchief.

Taking it from the doctor, she wiped her eyes and blew her nose. "I—"

Before she could say anything else, grief washed over her. She gave in to it, unable to help herself. What was she going to do without him?

He took the cloth from her head and smoothed her hair back from her face. "I'll leave you be," he said, quietly. "but I'm only next door if you need me."

At some point later, she had no idea how long, Alice woke. For a split second she was confused to find herself fully clothed in a hospital bed. Then she remembered what had happened to her and her loss overwhelmed her again.

Doctor Sullivan entered the room and stood at the end of her bed, watching her, sadness etched on his face. Alice looked at him through swollen eyes. "I'm very sorry to hear about Captain Woodhall," he said. "I want you to know that if there is anything I can do, you only need ask."

"Thank you."

"If you want privacy, you're welcome to sleep here tonight. I don't need the bed for a patient."

She opened her mouth to reply, but he cut her short with a shake of his head. "No need to answer. Would you like me to bring you a drink? Tea? Water, maybe, of if you'd prefer, I have brandy."

Alice shook her head, tears once again streaming down her face.

"I'll go now," he said walking out of the door before she could manage an answer.

She closed her eyes. Her mind tormented with snapshots of the last time she and Ed lay in each other's arms in the poppy field. They would never be able to return there now.

The following morning, Matron visited Alice. She patted Alice's hand. "I've decided you should return to Jersey. You should be with your family at a time like this."

Alice's instinct was to argue, but she didn't have any fight left in her. "Whatever you say, Matron."

"Arrangements have been made," Matron continued, her voice gentle. "Nurse Jones will assist you to pack up your belongings." She hesitated. Alice could see Matron wanted confirmation that she was happy to leave, so she nodded. "An ambulance will take you to the dock. You can take the boat back to the mainland and then on to Jersey from there." She took Alice's right hand in hers. "I didn't approve of your relationship with the captain, as you are aware, but I am sorry to hear of his loss. We will miss you, Nurse Le Breton."

Alice blew her nose. "Thank you, Matron. You've been very kind."

Matron left. Alice realised that now her return home had been decided, she was looking forward to being with her family. At least in Jersey there were no shared memories with Ed to taunt her.

The thought that she had lost the chance to introduce him to her family and her island brought on fresh tears. How was she going to live without him in her life?

Chapter 26

Gemma

August 2018

Gemma sat at the head of the table with Tom to her right. She had to concentrate on what the old man was saying to her from the opposite end of the table. She really was going to have to improve her French, she thought. She was relieved her food had received her guests' approval and was grateful for the bowls of couscous and three quiches that a couple of the guests had brought with them.

She was fascinated when one of her older neighbours talked about the citadel in the village and how Doullens was situated between places she recognised from reading historical novels, Arras to the north-east, Amiens to the south.

"Did you know," she said to Tom as they went to the kitchen to fetch more wine. "There was a meeting at the town hall here during the Great War, where representatives from the allied forces agreed to Marshall Foch being appointed as supreme commander of the French military forces? Isn't that exciting? Maybe Alice was staying here when it happened?"

"It's possible, I suppose. I had heard something about it," he said. "I believe that's why coloured banners are hanging outside the town hall."

She had so much to learn about this pretty place. The thought that it had played its part in the First World War fascinated her. It gave her more of a background to Alice's letters.

The heat of the day eased with the setting sun. Later, Gemma sat back in her chair and took a sip from the glass of wine in her hand, watching her new friends chatting and laughing with each other, under the twinkling lights Tom had erected earlier. The air was filled with the scent of jasmine and lavender and Gemma couldn't ever imagine being happier than she was right now.

"Having fun?" Tom asked leaning closer to her.

"Yes," she said. "I'm surprised how many of their stories I've understood despite my appalling French. Hand signals have helped."

Tom laughed. "Conversation, however stilted, is the most effective way to learn. You've probably picked up more than you realised since being here."

"I must have," she said, taking his hand under the table discretely and giving it a gentle squeeze. "I'm glad you persuaded me to do this today. I feel like I've known some of these people for ages, even though I can't understand everything they're saying." She looked from one guest to the other. "They're so welcoming."

Tom refilled her glass. "That's because they like you and what you're doing to the farmhouse. I heard one of them say how he's been hoping someone would give this place a new lease of life."

"It's certainly had that today," she said.

The song on the iPod changed. A couple got up and began jiving in the courtyard. Gemma wished she could do the same with Tom, but not wanting to put him in a position where he would have to refuse, she kept quiet, humming along to the music and tapping her feet.

Tom stood up and took hold of her hand, taking her glass and putting it down next to her seat. "Come along. Let's give it our best shot," he said, pulling her to her feet. "Though don't expect me to do what they're doing."

Gemma beamed at him and immediately began dancing. Tom seemed unfazed by his lack of skill. She had to admit he was a great host, waving for the others to get up and join them. His enthusiasm made her forget her inhibitions and lose herself in the music.

After several dances, Tom pulled her into his arms and hugged her, smiling. "I'm going to have to sit down for a bit."

"That's a relief," Gemma laughed. "I wondered when you were going to take a breather." They sat down, and she quenched some of her thirst with her wine. "You've got far too much stamina."

He threw his head back and laughed loudly. "You've had fun though?"

"Oh, the best," she said, smiling at him. She stared at him as he studied her, relieved she had chosen to give France a try. The concern she felt about how she was supposed to support herself crept into her mind for a moment. No, she thought, refusing to let it dampen her enjoyment of the evening. She pushed her worries away. There would be time enough for that tomorrow morning.

Later, with the last of the stragglers gone, Gemma stood with Tom and waved them goodbye.

"Don't worry about the mess out there," he said. "I'll help you tidy everything away in the morning."

"Thank you," she said grateful for the offer. She stifled a yawn, not wishing Tom to leave just yet.

He gave her a kiss on her cheek. "I think you should get some sleep, it's been a long day."

She had enjoyed her evening with him, chatting, watching him interact with everyone in his relaxed, charming manner. "I don't want you to go," she said, not caring if he was shocked.

Tom's eyes widened. He stared at her silently for a few seconds. "Are you sure, Gemma?"

She nodded. "Perfectly."

"We've been drinking," he said after a moment. "I wouldn't want you to wake up and regret anything. I think we should wait?"

She didn't want to wait. What if she was unable to stay in France, as she hoped to do? How many opportunities would they get to be alone, like this one? As far as she was concerned they had waited long enough.

"I haven't had much really," she said. "Anyway, what should we wait for? We've spent more time together than most people who've dated for months." It occurred to her that maybe he'd been trying to let her down gently. "But, if you don't want to stay the night, then that's fine." He went to say something, but Gemma shook her head. "I'll understand," she fibbed, aware she'd be mortified if he turned her down.

Tom crossed the room, taking her in his arms and kissed her. "You don't have to persuade me," he said eventually, his voice soft. "I want this, too. I just needed to be sure you're certain."

"I am." She took him by the hand and led him upstairs to her bedroom.

The following morning, Gemma woke to hear gentle breathing beside her in the bed. She lay still recalling all that had happened the night before between her and Tom, and smiled. How could she leave now, knowing she would not spend time with him like she was able to do here? She turned slowly, careful not to wake him. Facing him, she rested her elbow on her pillow, her cheek against her palm, staring at his perfect mouth, wanting to kiss it again.

His brown hair sun-kissed from working outside, stuck up at various angles. Despite his bed hair and need for a shave, he was still the most beautiful man she had ever seen. Gemma watched his muscular chest rise and fall. He was sexy even in a deep sleep. She reached out to touch his chest, stopping before her skin met his. She didn't want to wake him. Not yet. Let him sleep, she thought. It had been a long day preparing for the party and it felt good simply having him here.

She slid quietly out of the bed. Pulling on her shorts and tee-shirt, Gemma grabbed her trainers and walked quietly downstairs.

Opening the tin, Gemma took the first letter from the second batch. Maybe now she'd discover why Alice had kept the letters in separate batches, she mused, walking outside. The day was already warm, and pollen floated in the sunshine. Gemma walked up to the field and stared across the low mist. Turning to face the freshly painted farmhouse, she sighed, gazing at its white walls shining brightly in the morning sunlight.

Was this how Alice felt living here when she stayed at the farm that first weekend here with Ed? Gemma sat down on the damp grass and began reading Alice's next letter. Within seconds, her heart was pounding in shock. Surely not, she thought, breathlessly. She re-read it, hoping she had misunderstood what was inside.

"No," she cried, covering her mouth with her hand, before reading it a third time. Ed couldn't be dead. There must be a mistake, she thought angrily. This can't be how Alice and Ed's love story ended? It would be too cruel.

"Bloody war," she shouted, forgetting Tom was asleep inside the house with the windows wide open.

Stunned, Gemma pictured Alice's distraught reaction. Her notes on the back of the letter adding snippets about her devastation. She thought of Doctor Sullivan and how he had shown his true friendship by taking care of her until she was able to leave the hospital. Ed and Alice never did return here, she thought, miserably. She wiped her eyes with the bottom of her tee shirt, trying to come to terms with the notion that the couple didn't spend the rest of their lives happily bringing up their brood of beautiful babies at the farmhouse.

Damn the war. Damn all wars, separating families and loved ones, causing men and women's lives to change beyond all recognition. It was all so wrong.

She felt a gentle hand on her right shoulder. "Hey, what's all this?" Tom asked, sitting down next to her a little awkwardly. "If it's about last night—"

"No, it isn't," she said. She grabbed his forearm with her free hand. "Last night was, well it was amazing." She handed him the letter. "It's nothing to do with us. It was reading this that upset me," she said. "It's the first letter from the second batch."

She sat silently while Tom read, frowning as he did so. "But this is horrible."

"I know," she swallowed. "It seems that the letters are in two batches because the second batch were written after his death."

"But why would Alice write to Ed if she couldn't send them anywhere?"

Gemma shrugged, taking back Alice's letter and reading it for a fourth time.

He put his arm around her shoulders. "Was it her way of keeping him alive, do you think?"

Gemma hadn't thought of that. She liked the idea and could imagine Alice's motives behind it. "Yes, I suppose it must have been," Gemma wiped her eyes with the backs of her hands. "Something like that."

They sat in silence for a while.

"I think I should stay here," she said breaking their silence.

Tom didn't speak for a while. The silence disturbed by several starlings on the branch of a nearby tree and bees buzzing on the few cornflowers next to her feet.

"You mean in the field now, or at the farmhouse?"

She could tell he was surprised, and hoped he was happy with her decision. It had been an unexpected one. Thinking about Alice's life and how it had suddenly changed, Gemma knew that she, too, had no way of knowing what would happen in her own future.

"We think we have all the time in the world," she said thoughtfully. "I've seen enough tragedy at the trauma unit to know we might not be that lucky. You know that only too well."

"I do."

"Reading Alice's letter has made me think." She took hold of his left hand in hers. "I don't want to waste any time I have with you," she said. "However long this thing we're sharing lasts, I want to enjoy it. I'm not going to end it by choice."

Tom pulled her towards him and kissed her, hard. "Good," he said eventually. "I'm relieved. What will you do about the farm?"

She thought for a moment. "I'm not sure. The first thing I need to do is speak to my dad and try to persuade him not to sell. Though why he'd agree to that, I can't imagine."

"The most important thing for now," Tom said. "Is that you've made a decision." He kissed her on the nose. "The right decision."

She was relieved to hear him being so enthusiastic about her decision to stay in France. She stood up and held out a hand for him to take it.

"I think the first thing I need to do though, is tidy everything up from the party and then give my dad a call. Get it over with."

"Good plan," Tom said, picking her up and swinging her round. "It was a good party though, wasn't it?"

Gemma pushed Alice's letter carefully into her shorts pocket. "It was," she said, as he put her down. They strolled to the barn and Gemma couldn't help wishing Alice had been able to enjoy family parties with Ed at this place, too. What a tragic shame, Gemma thought, miserable for the couple.

Tom placed his fingertips under her chin, lifting her head slightly. "Just remember one thing," he said quietly. "The only person stopping you from realising your dreams, is you."

She considered his words. They made sense. "You're right. I know you are. It's only today though, that I can envisage a new dream to replace my previous career-led one."

"And?"

She stared into his beautiful eyes and kissed him quickly

Chapter 27

Alice

January 1919

Alice folded away Doctor Sullivan's letter. It still felt odd thinking of him as Jack, but since he had begun corresponding with her soon after her return to Jersey, he had become one of her closest confidantes. She was grateful for his friendship. Now that Mary was so happy and recently married, it had been a relief to have him to write to.

"Alice, we're going to be late."

The last thing Alice felt like doing was going out for afternoon tea with her mother's friends. Being back in Jersey had been comforting for the first few weeks. She had her own room and could sob in peace when she locked the door. Now, though, she was expected to be sociable. Making small talk and answering endless questions about her time working at the casualty clearing station was agony. The constant mention of the place where she had met and learnt that she had lost Ed was something she wasn't ready to discuss, with anyone.

She stared at her reflection in the cheval mirror, her hand lightly encircling her rounded belly. Recalling Jack's care of the nurse who had terminated her own pregnancy in France, she was certain he would not judge her predicament like most people. He was a good man. She thought of how he had operated on Ed and it was comforting to know someone who remembered Ed, however tentative their relationship.

She stared at her swollen belly. Ed would have made a perfect father, she thought, picturing him gazing at their baby as he held it in his arms.

Hearing her mother's footsteps coming up the stairs, Alice quickly grabbed her coat. She couldn't hide her pregnancy for much longer, she knew that, but until she could find a way to break the reputation shattering news to her mother, she was going to have to keep concealing her condition.

Alice was fastening the last button when her mother entered her room.

"Darling girl, I know you don't wish to join me today," she said, patting her immaculately coiffed hair needlessly. "But I believe it's time for you to meet people and find your place back in island society."

Alice understood her mother's need for her to meet someone and marry. No one would ever match up to Ed though, she knew that and would rather remain a spinster than settle for a loveless marriage. Her conscience pricked at her. Could she really let this baby grow up illegitimate? She would do what no doubt thousands of other girls in her situation did and pretend to be widowed.

"What I need, Mother," Alice said, trying to keep her voice gentle. "Is to find a position somewhere."

Her mother looked aghast at the suggestion. "You do not need to work," she said, picking up Alice's handbag and passing it to her. "The war is over now. There is no need for you to volunteer for anything else."

"Can't you see how lost I am having nothing to keep my mind occupied?"

Her mother smiled. "I understand how you feel," she said holding open the bedroom door, waiting for Alice to pass. "Which is exactly why I've insisted you accompany me today. It will take you out of yourself. You've spent far too much time wallowing up here in your bedroom. It isn't seemly."

Alice didn't have the energy to argue. She stepped forward to leave the room. The baby kicked several times and, forgetting she was in company, let her hand automatically go to her stomach. Realising what she had done, she glanced at her mother's face. She was staring at Alice's stomach, her eyes wide with unsuppressed shock.

Horrified, Alice forced her legs to work. Hoping to divert her mother, she walked out to the hallway. "Come along, or we're going to be late," she said breaking the silence.

Her mother didn't move. Bracing herself, Alice turned. Her mother was still motionless, her mouth open as she tried and failed to speak.

"Mother?" she asked, willing her to pretend she had misunderstood what had passed between them.

Jeanette hummed as she walked between the dining room and kitchen, and Alice's mother moved instantly stepping forward and grabbing her by the arm. She pulled Alice back into her room, quietly closing the door. Alice's heart hammered against her ribcage. It was time to face up to her family.

Her mother reached out a trembling hand, hesitating before resting it lightly on Alice's stomach. She gasped feeling the roundness of it, all colour vanishing from her face.

"You're with child?" she asked, shaking her head as if to dispel the inconceivable notion. "Unmarried, and too far to find a husband to marry." She sat down heavily on the side of the bed.

"Mother," Alice said, desperate to calm her. "Ed and I were to be married. Before, well before he died."

"Never mind what you had planned, you naïve, irresponsible girl," she said through gritted teeth. "What were you thinking? Having," she considered her words, before adding. "Intimate relations?" She closed her eyes. "I have no idea what to say to you."

Alice winced. She could feel her mother's crushing disappointment. "I'm fully aware of my predicament," she whispered, taking her mother's hand in hers, only for it to be snatched away. "Don't you think I've wished a thousand, or more times that Ed was here with me now?"

"Why didn't you wait to be married, Alice?" Her mother

looked close to tears. "You've ruined your reputation and your entire life. And what about ours? How can you remain living on the island?"

"You're telling me to leave? Now?" Alice replied in shock.

Her mother stood up and clasped her hands in front of her waist. "I have no choice."

"You do," Alice argued. "Please, Mother."

She shook her head. "No. My mind is made up."

Alice could see her mother's face harden. She hesitated before going over to the window and staring silently out. "It will break my heart to send you away, truly it will. However, you've left me with little choice."

Alice knew in her heart that her mother was right. What she had done by bringing her shame home was appalling.

"I understand," Alice admitted. "Where shall I go? I have no one else."

Her mother turned to face her, her face ashen. "You have the legacy your grandfather put in place for you," she said, obviously working things through in her own mind. "You must have made friends while volunteering in France? You mentioned Mary several times."

Alice thought of Mary currently on honeymoon with Peter in Cornwall. "No," she said, unable to help feelings of envy towards her dearest friend. "She's away right now."

"Then I have no idea." She took a deep breath. "I'll keep your secret for you," her mother said. "There's no need to upset your father."

The baby kicked again. Alice understood her mother's reasoning but knew that whatever happened to this child of hers and Ed's she'd never turn her back on it, for any reason.

"Whatever you wish, Mother."

"I'll leave you to pack and go and take tea with my friends alone," her mother said, finally. "I'll make your apologies, tell them you've fallen ill with a headache. "We'll speak later, when I return. Maybe by then you'll have come up with a solution about where you could live."

Alice watched her leave the room, closing the door quietly behind her. She had never felt truly alone before now. Bracing herself, she pulled her case down from above her wardrobe and placing it on the bed, opened it. Her sluggish brain seemed incapable of forming a cohesive plan. Unable to find a solution about where she could go, Alice focused on deciding what to pack. She would not be coming back, of that she was certain.

She decided that clothes could be replaced, but photos and her favourite books could not. Alice packed up her letters and Ed's personal belongings, relieved that he had given instructions for them to be sent to her after his death. She took the black tin box she'd found for keeping his letters, watch and wallet and placed it inside her case. It took up two thirds of the case, but she didn't mind; she could not bear to leave behind.

"Oh, Ed," she cried, brushing the tears from her cheeks with the backs of her hands. She had to be practical. This wasn't a time for self-pity. She was going to be a mother and needed to think of somewhere safe where she could go to have her baby. But where?

She spotted her poppy brooch lying on her bedside table. Recalling the evening Ed had surprised her with the precious memento, from their weekend at the farm, it dawned on Alice where she would go.

That evening, her mother came to her room. Spotting the packed case at the end of Alice's bed, with her handbag, and a smaller case next to it. "Have you decided?"

"I have," Alice said, her guilt assuaged slightly by her mother's obvious relief. "I'm returning to France."

"Whatever for?"

"There's a small farmhouse on the outskirts of Doullens. I stayed there one weekend."

"With him?" her mother scowled.

"No, Mother. It was all very proper," she insisted, not admitting that she must have fallen pregnant during her stay in a poppy field. "I stayed with the landlady. Ed stayed elsewhere."

"You have a plan, that's good to know." Her mother shook her head. "However, I have to say, I honestly don't know what's become of young girls since this war began. Standards seem to have been ignored or forgotten. Many rushed marriages with families pretending they don't know the reasoning behind them, and now this." She stared at Alice's stomach. "Oh, Alice, what were you thinking?"

Alice stepped forward to hug her mother goodbye. She moved away, as if Alice's touch would taint her.

Her mother raised her hands. "I'll help arrange your passage to the continent. I'll also ensure you have access to your grandfather's money, but that is all I'm willing to do." She gave a shuddering sigh, as if her world was ending. "I never thought you capable of something like this."

"Neither did I," Alice answered, honestly. It seemed as if her mother had shrunk in stature during the afternoon. "I'm deeply sorry, Mother," she said. "I hate that I've disappointed you so terribly."

"As do I, Alice."

They stood in silence.

"I'll go to the docks first thing," Alice said, desperate to move on, now that she knew she must. "I'll take the first boat to St Malo. I'll leave a letter for father," she added. "I'll write that I've been asked to return to work in a hospital in France for some time. Will that suffice?"

"It will have to." Her mother stared at her for a moment. "Write to me when you're settled. I'd like to know where you are and that you are well."

"I promise, I will," Alice said, aware that her mother had not mentioned the baby, but relieved not to have all contact severed.

"I'll wish you a good night then," her mother said stiffly. Alice noticed tears threatening to fall and turned away, saving her the humiliation. "Good night, Mother," she said. "I'll leave before you rise for breakfast."

"Very well."

She waited for her mother to go. Hearing the door close before she turned, Alice longed to be back at the farm already. She wasn't sure how it would feel to be there without Ed, but it was the one place in the world that still existed where they had shared memories.

She hoped Madam Gaston still lived at the farm and would allow her to rent a room when she learnt of her condition. Alice's mind whirled. Her life in Jersey was at an end.

Grief washed across her. It was all well and good to try and make plans, but she wasn't ready to let go of the ones she and Ed had made. Not yet. Slumping down on her eiderdown, Alice sobbed. Frightened and alone, she was determined to make the baby the focus of her life now. She took a deep breath and blew her nose. She had much to do. Now though, she needed to be brave.

Days later, on a frosty afternoon, Alice arrived at the farm. Her feet ached where her shoes pinched. She prayed that Madam Gaston still lived here. If she didn't, Alice had no idea where to go next. Hand trembling, she pushed open the front gate and stared at the house. It still had the green moss discolouring the front wall, but there were fresh flowers on one of the living room window sills. Relieved, to find the place occupied, she walked up to the door. She put down her cases and knocked on the door, inadvertently displacing tiny flecks of paint.

Hearing footprints, Alice held her breath, willing them to be Madam Gaston's. The door opened and there she was. She peered at Alice, frowning as if trying to place her. Then she smiled.

"Mademoiselle Le Breton," she stepped back enthusiastically waving Alice inside.

"Je m'appelle, Alice," she said picking up her cases and

going into the familiar living room. She accepted the offer of coffee and sat down at the table. It was a relief to take the weight off her swollen feet. Should they already be this big? She wished some of her nursing training had prepared her for the arrival of her baby. Her thoughts were interrupted by the sight of cases and two tea chests in the corner of the room.

Madame Gaston returned carrying a tray.

"You are leaving? Partir?" Alice asked, concerned.

The older woman nodded. "Oui." She handed Alice a cup of dark coffee and pointed to herself. "Odette."

She sat opposite Alice and took a sip of her drink. Her eyes drifted to Alice's stomach. "Bebe?"

Alice swallowed her mouthful of coffee, wincing as the hot liquid flowed down her throat. She had not expected such a direct question from someone she barely knew. There was no point in trying to cover up the obvious, so she nodded.

"You wish, er, sleep 'ere?"

"Yes, I mean, oui."

"Papa? C'est mort?"

Alice nodded, unable to speak for a moment. Clearing her throat, she took a deep breath. "He died, last year."

Odette shook her head, her eyes glistening with unshed tears. "Mon fils," she said holding up three fingers to show that she had lost three sons. "Et mon mari, aussi."

Alice recalled that she had lost her husband and sons. "When will you go?"

Odette gave a slow shrug. "Two, maybe three?"

"Days?" Alice asked horrified

Odette shook her head. "Non, er." She couldn't find the word.

"Weeks?" Alice suggested.

Odette nodded.

"But this house? Who comes to live here?" She was unsure how well her attempt at making Odette understand her was going to come across.

Again, Odette shrugged.

She didn't know? A ray of hope pierced Alice's bruised heart. Surely, she wouldn't be lucky enough to be able to buy this place? Could she?

"Madame, I mean, Odette. Will you sell the farm to me?" She made gestures to show the exchange of money.

Odette lowered her cup onto her slightly chipped saucer and placed a hand on her chest. "Oui?"

Alice laughed. It looked like she was finally in the right place and at the best time. "Oui. I would love to achete votre maison."

Odette burst into tears. Sobbing loudly. Taken aback for a second, Alice was unsure what to do. Then, remembering that she was not at home with her mother and her strict codes of conduct, circled the table and hugged Odette from behind. "Shush, please don't cry."

After an hour of stilted conversation and notes on scrap paper, they agreed a price. Alice could tell that Odette was as delighted with the exchange as her. She was even more relieved that Odette had agreed to postpone her departure for several months until the baby was born.

Finally, she had something to look forward to. If only she could share her news with Ed. She decided that if she couldn't speak to him, then she would write to him. That night, ensconced in the farmhouse spare room, resting in the same bed she had inhabited during her weekend there several months before, she penned her first letter to Ed since learning of his death.

> *My darling Ed,*
> *You will never believe what I am about to tell you. I have come back to where we were happiest, and I believe I have found a way to cope. I am to live here at our farm with our baby. It is not what we planned, but it is the best I can do after all that's happened.*

She continued writing into the early hours, aware that there was no point posting the letter. She would have to find somewhere to hide it for now. Alice recalled standing on a squeaky floorboard on her last visit and moving from the bed walked quietly on the floor until she located it. Bending down, as best she could, she took her metal nail file and managed to work the short piece of board until it lifted.

She sat back. This was where she would keep her treasures, until she needed a bigger space. She would enjoy searching the farm and its outbuildings to find an alternative hidey hole when the time came for her to discover one, but for now this would do. She felt like she had come home.

Three months' later, Alice thanked the postman as he hand-delivered the mail. Only one letter. She stared at the handwriting. It was vaguely familiar, but she couldn't recall where she remembered it from. She slowly lowered her heavy bulk onto one of the wooden chairs and shouted to Odette that there was only the one piece of mail.

Opening the envelope, she withdrew the single sheet of paper and unfolded it. Curious, Alice began reading, her mouth dropping open in surprised when she realised who had written to her.

Dear Alice,

I want to write 'Nurse Le Breton' but then I remind myself that the war is now over. Thankfully. I hope you don't mind me corresponding with you in this way. I contacted your mother and explained how we knew each other and she very kindly gave me your address.

I hope this letter finds you well. I must admit that I was surprised to learn that you had returned to France. I am working for the next few months at a hospital near Amiens, which is not far from where we were all stationed until last year. If you are happy for me to do so, I would very much like to call on you and maybe I can take you for tea at the Hotel du Nord.

Please do not feel pressurised to accept this entreaty, but should you be happy to accept, then I look forward

to hearing from you with regard to a convenient date
when I may call upon you.
   With sincerest wishes,
   Jack Sullivan (Dr)

The baby kicked. Alice wondered how enthused the doctor would be to take her out if he saw her bulging stomach. She stroked her belly to sooth the lively baby. Should she accept his invitation? Although she wrote weekly to Mary, it had been months since she'd spoken to a connection to her life at the casualty clearing station. Odette was kind, but she had taken on a motherly role to Alice. Should she write to him, she wondered? Would it be fair to allow him to come here and discover her condition?

Alice reasoned that Jack Sullivan would not have too far to travel, therefore inviting him to the farm would not put him out too much. And, she mused, if they were to be friends, he needed to know that she was having a baby out of wedlock. She had no intention of hiding her child from anyone. Her decision made, Alice wrote back.

Dear Jack,
   Thank you for your letter, which was most welcome.
   I would very much like to meet with you. However,
I will only be able to consider your invitation on the
proviso that you visit me at this address first. You will
understand my reasoning when we meet.

I apologise for the subterfuge and look forward to hearing from you.
Kindest regards,
Alice

There, she thought, folding the letter and writing her address on to an envelope. Once they had met and he had seen for himself how things stood with her, he could make up his mind about going out for tea.

She was more nervous than she had expected to be hearing Jack's rapping on the front door. Alice hoped the griping pains she had been experiencing for the previous day or so, weren't contractions. They didn't seem to be increasing in strength, so she assumed not. She remained in her bedroom, waiting for Odette to welcome him in. It surprised her how much she wanted him to accept her situation. He had always shown himself to be an honourable man during the time they worked together, but she couldn't be friends with someone who had an issue with her pregnancy.

Hearing his deep voice speaking fluent French to Odette and their laughter, gave Alice a pang to her stomach. What if she had been wrong to test him this way? Maybe she should have simply written and told him that she wasn't interested in making his acquaintance once again.

"Alice," Odette called from downstairs. It was time for her to face him.

Alice checked her reflection once again in the mirror. The dress only just fitted, but it looked passable now that

Odette had worked her sewing magic on it. Alice went downstairs to join them, taking a deep breath before entering the living room.

"Hello, Doctor Sullivan," she said, studying him as he looked over at her, the smile on his face faltering only minutely.

He opened his mouth to speak, but no sound emerged for several seconds. "Nurse, I mean, Miss Le Breton," he said, as they crossed the room to shake hands. "You are looking very well."

Alice smiled. She could see he was trying his best not to look shocked. It was all that she could expect from him. "How lovely to see you again, Doctor."

"Please," he said, shaking her hand. "We're past any formalities now, thankfully. I'd rather you call me Jack. May I call you Alice?"

She nodded, happy. "I'd like that," she said. "Can you understand my odd reply to you now?"

"I can." He stood, his hands behind his back. "Will you accept my invitation?"

"Yes," she said. "I'd like that very much."

Odette clasped her hands together and took Alice's coat from the coat stand. She held it for Alice to slip her arm into, just as a contraction took hold. Grimacing, Alice held her stomach.

"Are you all right?" Jack asked, going over to her.

"I'm not sure," she said panting.

"You should sit down," he said, pulling out a chair and helping her to it. "Have you had many pains today?"

"A few." She let him take her pulse just as another contraction took hold. "I think we'll have to delay our afternoon out," she said through gritted teeth.

"You seem to have far more pressing matters to deal with today."

Alice groaned. "I think you could be right."

He spoke to Odette in French and then taking Alice by the arm, helped her up. "You need to get upstairs, young lady," he said in his strict tone that she recognised. This time, Alice thought, he didn't seem at all scary.

"Will you stay with me?" she asked, suddenly terrified to give birth.

"I will," he said. "I'm a doctor, aren't I?"

Chapter 28

Gemma

August 2018

Gemma helped Tom load the trestle tables onto the back of his pick-up, together with the chairs and everything else his mother had lent him for the party.

"I'll come with you to see her in the next day or so," Gemma said. "I'd like to take her a bottle of something and some flowers as a thank you."

"I'm sure she'd like that," he said, getting into the pick-up. "It was a shame she couldn't make it to the party. Maybe next time?"

"Yes, she'd like that."

She watched him go, relieved that the barn had finally been reinstated to its former tidy self and looked forward to meeting the woman responsible for bringing up this man who had unknowingly taught her to trust her instincts and be bold.

She went back into the house to read more of Alice's letters.

Now that she was planning on staying she would need to work out how and where to live. But before she arranged anything definite, she needed to finish reading Alice's letters. She still found it painful to come to terms with the knowledge that Ed had died. Whichever way she fantasised about their future, him dying had not ever been a part of it.

Gemma still longed to know what had happened to Alice after Ed's death, so taking the last batch of letters, she grabbed the rug from her armchair and took them outside. Wanting to make the most of each area at the farm, she lay the rug on the grass under the large oak tree and settled down to read.

She slid the single sheet of paper out of the yellowing envelope and unfolded it. She stared at the letter thinking about Alice's reason for returning to the farm and why there were no letters from Ed replying to the ones she wrote to him. How many women had needed to find a way to continue with their lives once they had lost husbands or sons? The First World War, Gemma thought. Wasn't it supposed to be the war to end all wars? What a shame that had not been the case. She pictured Tom, until recently fighting in an army, the uniform and weapons different, but lives still changed permanently by the injuries sustained. At least now men without limbs has useful prosthetics to help them continue their lives, unlike those having to accept basic replacements that Gemma assumed were barely useful.

She studied the peaceful, lush space around the farmhouse and listened. Nothing but birdsong and bees disturbing her. How had Alice and Ed managed to spend time in the poppy field, making love and planning their future with explosions echoing through their day? So much had changed, Gemma thought, yet so little when it came to matters of the heart.

Tom. He was the first person who had ever believed in her or shown an interest in her life. Her mother had been disinterested in her nursing career and her father too emotionally exhausted from giving her mother all the attention and reassurance she needed to then have the energy to spend time on Gemma. For the first time in her life she felt confident enough to step off her planned route and follow her heart. Tom, the bravest man she knew, had shown her that it was never too late to be exactly what you wanted to be.

Wishing to bring happiness to a place that had been a home to her and Alice, Gemma knew she had to find a way to persuade her father to let her buy the house. It was early in her relationship with Tom, but she was tired of being timid. She knew he had strong feelings for her, hadn't he said so? Maybe the two of them could make a home for themselves here?

She thought back to Odette losing her husband and sons in the war, then Alice returning to live here without Ed. And Gemma's great-uncle had lived here alone for years, the house falling into disrepair around him. It was about time this farm witnessed some happiness. She and Tom would enjoy a future here even though Alice and Ed had been denied theirs.

That was her new dream.

She went inside and found her mobile phone. Turning it on, she sent a quick text to her father.

Did you find out about your cousin and if his mother's name was Alice?

He must have had his phone right next to him, because he immediately replied. *Yes, sorry. I meant to let you know. His mother was an Alice Le Breton. She was my mother's much older sister.*

Impatient to speak to him, Gemma called her father. He answered immediately.

"So, the farm has come full circle then." She liked the idea, very much.

"I suppose so," he said.

She could hear he was somewhere echoey. "Where are you, Dad?"

"Airport. I'm accompanying your mother to Scotland. She's the key note speaker for a legal conference. I thought I'd make the most of some sight-seeing."

"Sounds good," she said, hearing his impatience at having to speak to her. Thinking of Tom and how he believed in her, she took a deep breath. "Dad, I want you to sell the farm to me." She held her breath waiting for his reaction. When there was none, she added. "Dad? Did you hear what I said?"

"Yes," he said quietly. "You were only supposed to be there temporarily. Until you got over whatever it was that had upset you at work. I'm not sure I understand."

She hadn't expected him to. "I know you asked me to

renovate the farmhouse to get me away from moping in Jersey and you were right to do that," she said. "But I've fallen in love with this place," she said. "I'm going to put my flat on the market and I want you to agree to sell this place to me, as soon as I've got the funds to buy it off you. What do you think?"

"Well, I don't see why you can't be the purchaser?"

She could hear him mumbling to himself and wondered if he was actually conversing with her mother.

"Tell her she'll have to pay the going rate," she heard her mother say in the background.

Alice shook her head. It would have been nice for her mother not to see her as someone to guard herself against, but Gemma knew that would never change. Why would her mother change her behaviour when she didn't see that the way she acted was unusual?

"I'd expect to," Alice said. "So, Dad, what do you say? I'll contact an agent, get them to come out and do a valuation and then make you both an offer for the farm." Encouraged by the excitement of forging ahead with her plan, she added, "Naturally, I'll expect a significant discount for all the work I've done here."

"Yes, of course," her father said and Gemma could sense that he was smiling. "I'm very proud of you, Gemma," he said quietly, just as she was about to disconnect the phone.

Stunned by this affirmation, Gemma said, "Thanks Dad, that means a lot." She ended the call and stared at the screensaver of the Brighton Pier. "We'll soon change this photo," she said, striding outside and up to the poppy field.

She raised her camera, breathing in the warm air and took a test photo. Checking it to ensure she'd captured as much of the scarlet covered field, she lowered it slightly and took several more. "Perfect," she said, smiling, already planning to make the photo her new screensaver.

"I thought so," Tom said, behind her.

Gemma spun round to face him, laughing. "What?"

"That the scene in front of me is perfect."

Gemma turned to look out over the poppies. "I can't imagine anywhere else I'd rather be."

Tom came up behind her, slipped his arms around her waist and said, "Not the poppies," he whispered, sending shivers down her neck. "The exquisite woman taking a photo of them."

Gemma smiled. Today was turning out to be exceptionally good.

They stared at the view. Gemma closed her eyes, savouring being held in his arms. This was the future she wanted, enjoying Tom's company and living here. She was glad she finally had the nerve to fight for it.

"I spoke to Dad and told him I want to buy the farm," she said.

"Good for you," Tom said, kissing her neck and making her tingle all over. "And?"

"He agreed."

"I'm so pleased for you, Gemma."

She turned to face him, slipping her arms around his neck. "Is that all?"

Tom raised an eyebrow. "Inside I'm dancing," he said. "I'm just doing my best to act cool."

Gemma giggled. "You, Tom Holloway, are the coolest man I know."

"You think?" He asked, and she nodded. "Would you still think I was cool, if I told you that I loved you?"

Gemma bit her lower lip. "You do?"

"Yes," he said, kissing her. "Well?"

"I love you, too," she said, breathless from excitement.

"I meant do you still think I'm cool," he said, eyes twinkling mischievously.

Gemma gasped. "That's so mean," she said, lowering her hands and tickling his sides. "I thought you were asking if I loved you, too."

"Stop it," he laughed, making a grab for her wrists to hold them away. "I hate being tickled."

"Then behave yourself," she said, trying her best to keep a serious face.

Tom pulled her wrists around his waist. "I like them there," he said, letting go and taking her face in his hands. "And I like this." He kissed her. And kissed her again.

Gemma sighed, losing herself in the sensation of his firm lips on hers.

Finally, Gemma said, "Would you like to come and live here with me?"

Tom stared at her for a moment. "I can't think of anything I'd like more."

Chapter 29

Alice

August 1919

Alice sat cross-legged in the poppy field, her baby snoring gently in her lap. Resting her hands on the cool earth behind her she closed her eyes finding it hard to believe that it was already one year since she and Ed had conceived their baby in this very place. As the heat of the sun warmed her face, she sensed his presence. It was a relief to know she had done the right thing returning to live at the farmhouse.

She was grateful to Odette for agreeing to stay with her until the baby was born and she treasured their friendship. But now it was time for Odette to move on with her own life. At least now Alice had someone else to write to and more importantly, Odette would write back. She still missed Ed horribly, but living here alone with baby Stuart and her memories, helped. She wanted to share her peaceful day, so decided to write to Ed again this evening, when the baby had been put to bed.

It was easier to cope, now that she had resumed her letter writing to him. The release of her thoughts on paper as she shared the small events in her new life went some way to alleviating the loneliness of living their future by herself.

Alice glanced at the basket containing the dead poppy heads she'd collected earlier. She would store these in the cool pantry, she thought. Then, when they were dried, she would bring the baby out to the field and scatter them as a memorial to Ed. The thought boosted her.

The baby moved his legs before settling once again. Alice pulled the muslin sheet draped from her right shoulder that was shading him. He was a happy little boy, so like his papa, she mused. Her mood dipped briefly as she remembered how Ed would never hold this little cherub in his arms. She was going to be the one to teach him to swim and ride a bicycle. She took a shuddering breath and wiped her eyes with a corner of the muslin. She was determined to do all the things for baby Stuart that she knew Ed would want to do.

She pulled the telegram she had received from Jack Sullivan the previous afternoon from her pocket to read.

Arriving in Doullen. Looking forward to spending time with my god-son. Hope all is well. Jack

"Alice."

Thinking she could hear her name being called, she tilted her head. Surely Jack couldn't be here already?

"Alice?" a deep voice called out.

It was him. Alice grinned. She went to stand up, carefully

380

cradling her baby, she peered towards the house and saw him walking towards her waving.

"Jack," she called. "I didn't expect you to arrive until later. Wait there," she said, not wishing him to disturb any more of the poppies than she had already done by walking into the field. "I'll come to you."

He did as she asked, smiling as he waited for her. His eyes connected with the bundle she was carrying. "Stuart is sleeping soundly, I see," he said as she reached him. "I can't believe he's so big already!"

Neither could she. "He's such a contented baby," Alice said. "I'm so lucky." She pushed away the pang of pain reminding her that she wasn't as lucky as she had hoped. "The sun is very strong out here, I think we should go."

His eyes went to the basket of poppies. "Shall I carry those for you?"

"Yes, please." She waited while he fetched the basket. "It's a sweltering day. We're making the most of the poppies."

He stared at the view ahead. "They do make a spectacular display," he said, before continuing, "It occurred to me that I never conveyed to you how very sorry I was when Captain Woodhall was killed," he said matter-of-factly. "He was a good man and fought hard to survive."

Alice cleared her throat. "You did tell me once," she said. "Unfortunately, he was one of many who died too soon."

Jack stopped walking. "He was. But he was the one you loved, and for that reason, I was especially saddened by his death."

Alice's step faltered. What a strange thing to say, she

thought, determined not to let her grief for Ed come to the surface today. "Come inside, it's cooler in there. I can pour us fresh lemonade. I made it yesterday."

She indicated a seat at the table for him to take and carried the baby up to her bedroom, laying him gently into his cot. She pulled the cotton curtains closed in front of the open window, to take the brightness out of the room.

Returning to the living room, Alice smiled. "Sorry, I didn't hear your reply. Lemonade?"

He nodded. "That sounds perfect."

She served the drinks and sat opposite him as they exchanged pleasantries.

He glanced down at his hands, holding the cool glass for a few seconds. Then, looking back at her across the table, he said. "I found myself unable to get you from my mind, Alice."

She was unsure if she had misunderstood him. "You mustn't worry about me, I'm fine here with Stuart. We're pretty organised now with our routine. I'll admit it was a little strange when Odette first left, but I now find that I'm enjoying the solitude."

She noticed a sadness about him. "Is there something wrong? You can always confide in me, we're friends, aren't we?" Alice thought of her relief that Jack had been there to assist with Stuart's birth and their growing closeness since then.

"I worried about you losing the captain. It seemed even more tragic as he had fallen so near to the signing of the amnesty."

Alice took a sip of her lemonade to shift the lump in her throat. She couldn't understand why he was talking about Ed so much.

"You don't mind me being so forthright?"

She was unsure but shook her head. "No, please continue."

He took a deep breath. "My experiences of the war have made me somewhat reckless, so I'll simply say my piece."

"Go on," she said, intrigued, wishing he didn't look so troubled.

"Alice, I've always had feelings for you."

"I beg your pardon?"

He pushed the glass aside. "I'm aware that you probably still love the captain. I see you with his child and had meant to be satisfied at simply being your friend." He leant forward slightly, raking his hands through his hair. "I never want to jeopardise our relationship," he said. "But I feel compelled to ask if you," he hesitated. "If at some point in the future, your feelings might change towards me?"

"Romantically?" She stood up, shocked.

"Yes." He rested his hands on the table. "Alice, I've loved you from the first moment you entered my ward. My dearest wish is to have a future with you. And with Stuart." He took a deep breath. "There, I've said it."

"And if not?" she asked, trying to take in what he'd said.

"If that is not possible, then I'll be content to be your friend as now."

Stunned, she stared at the dark-haired man she had admired for so long. Hadn't he dedicated the last four years of his life to saving others? Now she thought of it, hadn't he also been there for her when she most needed someone? He was handsome with looks that any woman would find attractive. And she liked him.

Alice considered the experiences they had shared and his true friendship of her since Stuart's birth and it dawned on her that she cared for him rather more than she had imagined. He wasn't Ed. He never would be, but couldn't she have two loves in the course of her lifetime?

"I didn't come here to distress you," he said, taking her silence for upset. "Please, don't concern yourself with what I've said." He stood and walked over to the front door. "I should not have been so direct. It was wrong of me. I apologise."

Alice followed him. "No, Jack. It's fine." She said, grabbing his arm to stop him. "A little startling, I'll admit." She stared at him, hating the thought that her reaction had humiliated him. "We shared four years where time was a valuable commodity, so I don't take offence in you being forthright. I appreciate it."

"That's very generous." He took her hand lightly in his. "May I call on you again, in a few days, when you've had time to consider what I've said?"

She realised she did want to see him again. "Please, sit down," she said. "I just need to have a think. I'll be right back."

She walked up to the poppy field, lost in her own thoughts. She had enjoyed Jack's company ever since he'd come to France and had ended up assisting with her baby's delivery. Each time he visited he brought flowers for her, or little treats for the baby and it occurred to her that she missed him when he wasn't at the farm and had begun confiding in him about the difficulties she experienced, or the latest thing Stuart had learnt to do.

Alice gasped. Her feelings towards Jack had grown so slowly that she hadn't noticed. Maybe it was spending her waking hours focusing on her son. Alice thought how Jack made her laugh and how he doted on baby Stuart.

She laughed quietly, covering her mouth in surprise. She did have feelings for him. The realisation surprised her. Ed wouldn't want her to grieve forever, she was certain of that. And as she stood in the field where they had once declared their love for each other, she could almost feel Ed now, giving her his blessing to move on with her life. He'd loved her enough to want her and Stuart to be happy, cherished and loved. Just as Jack did.

With a joy in her heart Alice ran back to the house to see Jack.

Standing at the doorway, breathless from excitement and exertion, she smiled at him.

"You're not scowling," he said staring at her. "So, will you? Marry me?" he asked taking her a little by surprise.

"Oh Jack. I've so enjoyed spending time with you these past months," she said, honestly. "I think I am even beginning to love you a little, but—"

"Don't say 'but'," he said, putting his finger up to her lips. "I know I'll never be Ed. I saw for myself how much you loved him and how his death almost destroyed you. I can't and won't try to be like him. I am my own man and now I want you for my wife."

Was she ready to move on, she wondered? He was good and kind and, if she was honest, she did suspect that she was already falling in love with him. Was it a betrayal of what she and Ed had shared to love another man now?"

"Stuart deserves a family," he added. "You deserve a future. I love you enough for both of us."

"I'm not sure if I'm ready for marriage, but I do love you, Jack," she admitted.

His eyes widened. "You do?"

Alice's heart swelled to see how delighted this news meant to him. "Yes. How could I not love you? You're handsome, clever, brave and the dearest friend to me."

He took her hand in his. "You don't need to give me an answer to my proposal yet," he said. "Think about it though, will you?"

"Yes," she said, standing on tiptoes and kissing him on his cheek. "And thank you, Jack."

"What for?"

"There are many men who wouldn't consider marrying a woman with someone else's child. If I agree to marry you, it's because I want a future with you, not because I feel the need to be married. You must understand that. I've survived perfectly well by myself and will continue to do so, married or not."

He shook his head. "I'm fully aware of your independence," he said, the love in his eyes obvious. "And I love you more for it. I don't think you need to be married, but I hope that you want to be, to me. I'd be proud to call you my wife and would love nothing more than to have a future with you and Stuart."

That night, Alice sat on her bed, her baby snoring peacefully next to her. She knew as soon as Jack proposed to her that she would accept. In her heart she knew she loved him, too. But she couldn't deceive him, not even with Ed. It was time to move on.

Taking her poppy brooch from her bedside drawer, she pinned it on to her nightdress and stood in front of the mirror. This would be the last time she wore it. She undid the clasp and took it off, then lifting the loose floorboard near the foot of her bed, carefully placed the brooch into the small cavity and replaced the floorboard. It would be near her always, as would her love for Ed.

The following morning, she fed Stuart and led him up to the poppy field. Then taking a piece of paper and pen, she sat down to write one final letter.

My darling Ed,

I am sitting watching our son laughing and playing with the poppies in our field. He's a happy little boy and soon he will be running through this beautiful place without a care in the world. It shocks me on occasion how similar his milk chocolate-coloured eyes are to yours and I tell him constantly about his brave Papa and how he would have loved him. We each have a picture of you in a silver frame by our bedsides.

Earlier today, Stuart and I scattered more poppy seeds from the dried flowers I picked last autumn. This year there are blue cornflowers dotted throughout the scarlet poppy heads, too. At first, I was unsure whether I liked them, but now I see how pretty they are and that their contrasting colour does not detract from the beauty of our poppies.

My precious love, I'm writing this letter to tell you that I am to be married. You will always be my first love, and the father of our boy. It is important for me to let you know that.

You remember Doctor Sullivan, the serious but kind doctor who saved so many lives? Most importantly to me, he saved yours and gave us the chance of happiness together, however short-lived it ended up being.

He helped bring our baby into the world and we became close. He is aware of my love for you but has asked me to marry him. I have to be honest and tell you that I find myself falling in love with him, too. I know you would want me to be happy.

Therefore, my love, I am going to attempt to stop writing these letters to you. It's unfair to Jack. I will keep them always, but I will attempt to hide them somewhere only I can ever find them.

I love you. I will always love you and will never completely recover from losing you. I am, though, determined to make the best of my future with our son and now Jack. So, my darling, I must say goodbye, at least for now. I will hold you in my heart always, but it is time to let you go and rest in peace.

Until I am with you again,

My love, always,

Alice X

Acknowledgements

Heartfelt thanks to everyone at HarperCollins and the fantastic team at HarperImpulse, especially Charlotte Ledger for giving me this opportunity and for your structural edits and generous guidance, it's been a wonderful experience working with you. Also, thanks to Emily Ruston for your excellent line edits and Laura Bevis for proofreading this book.

To my writer friends, especially Christina Jones and my fellow Blonde Plotters, Kelly Clayton and Gwyn GB for your encouragement; also, my non-writer friends for your support and for continuing to read and review my books, thank you.

To my family who have always encouraged me to follow my dreams – publication of The Poppy Field is the realisation of a very, very big dream, as you all know.

HELP US SHARE
THE LOVE!

If you love this wonderful book as much as we do
then please share your reviews online.

Leaving reviews makes a huge difference and
helps our books reach even more readers.

So get reviewing and sharing,
we want to hear what you think!

Love, HarperImpulse x

Please leave your reviews online!

amazon.co.uk   **kobo**   goodreads   L♥ve**reading**   iBooks

And on social!

f/**HarperImpulse**   🐦@**harperimpulse**
📷@**HarperImpulse**

LOVE BOOKS?

So do we! And we love nothing more than chatting about our books with you lovely readers.

If you'd like to find out about our latest titles, as well as exclusive competitions, author interviews, offers and lots more, join us on our Facebook page! Why not leave a note on our wall to tell us what you thought of this book or what you'd like to see us publish more of?

f/HarperImpulse

You can also tweet us ✈@harperimpulse and see exclusively behind the scenes on our Instagram page www.instagram.com/harperimpulse

To be the first to know about upcoming books and events, sign up to our newsletter at: http://www.harperimpulseromance.com/